On Eagles' Wings

THE WYLDHAVEN SERIES
by Lynnette Bonner

Not a Sparrow Falls - BOOK ONE

On Eagles' Wings - BOOK TWO

Beauty from Ashes - BOOK THREE
Coming soon.

Consider the Lilies - BOOK FOUR
Coming soon.

On Eagles' Wings

Wyldhaven 2

Lynnette BONNER

Serene Lake Publishing

On Eagles' Wings
WYLDHAVEN, Book 2

Published by Serene Lake Publishing

Cover design by Lynnette Bonner of Indie Cover Design, images ©
    www.bigstock.com, File: # 178105501
    www.depositphotos.com, File: # 34346217
    www.depositphotos.com, File: # 87443482

ISBN: 978-1-942982-08-1

To All who are Hurting:

People fail. They wound with words or actions that cut
deep and leave scars.
But know this...
There is One who never fails.
He loves you more than any other.
So much so, that He even knows the number of hairs
on your head at any given moment.
He is constantly good and loving.
He notices when sparrows fall, yet loves you more.
He is worthy of your heart.
Worthy of your service.
He created you because He wanted to deeply and
intimately, as a closest friend, fellowship with you.
Do you know Him?

If not, but you would like to know more
please visit:
www.peacewithgod.net

ISAIAH 40: 30-31

Even youths grow tired and weary,
and young men stumble and fall;
but those who hope in the Lord will renew their strength.
They will soar on wings like eagles;
they will run and not grow weary,
they will walk and not be faint.

Chapter One

ixie Pottinger rinsed the last of the soap suds from the sink and wrung out her rag good and tight. She glanced around the kitchen. Satisfied to see that everything was cleaned and put away as it should be for the night, she pressed both hands into the curve of her aching back.

Thankfully, they had no guests in the boardinghouse tonight, so the dinner crowd had been light, and now she could go up to check on Ma.

Even though Ma had taken to her bed for the past two days, she'd still been coughing something fierce, and Dixie feared she hadn't been sleeping much. She hoped rest had not eluded her this evening.

She'd really missed Ma's help for the past couple days. The work of cooking and cleaning for the boardinghouse was much harder on her own, but Dixie hadn't minded. She was just glad Ma had finally agreed to try and rest.

She tugged a tea tray from the cupboard. Opening the warming drawer on the oven, she withdrew the bowl of chicken broth and the biscuit she'd set aside earlier. Adding the pot of tea that had been steeping while she cleaned, a slice of lemon, and the jar of honey that Washington Nolan had come around selling last week, she hefted the tray and headed upstairs.

She could hear Ma's hacking cough even before she reached

the door to their rooms. Carefully balancing the tray, she twisted the door handle and pushed inside. The main room was just large enough for a settee and a rocking chair. Ma's chamber lay to the right, and Dixie's own small room to the left. The only other room in their little suite was the small lavatory that sat between the two bedrooms, a luxury Dixie was even more thankful for now that Ma had grown so sick.

She nudged Ma's door open and stepped into her room, then set the tray on her dresser and approached the side of her bed. "How are you feeling tonight? I've just finished with the cleanup and brought you some soup. Does that sound good?"

The only response she got was a low moan and another round of rasping coughs. That sent her pulse skyrocketing. Ma had always been a hardy soul. Dixie never remembered seeing her this sick before.

She laid a hand to Ma's forehead and her alarm rose even more.

Burning with fever!

That did it. Whether Ma would be upset or not, she needed to fetch Flynn.

Just the thought of seeing him eased some of her concern.

Dixie gritted her teeth at her impropriety. Had he worked his way so far into her affections that she was thinking of him as a comforter now? She must banish that propensity, post haste!

She lifted two handfuls of her skirts and hurried down the stairs and out the front. An icy wind whipped along the street, making her glad she only needed to step next door. She folded her arms and huddled into her shoulders. Clouds, a telling color of pasty blue-gray that indicated snow, hung low and menacing above the evergreens that surrounded Wyldhaven. Dixie was thankful to escape the chill as she pushed into McGinty's.

The alehouse was always quite busy at this time of day. Several men played cards at a table in the corner, a bottle of rotgut making the rounds and liberally shared by all. Several others lounged at the bar chatting with Ewan McGinty, the proprietor.

Dixie hung back by the door until she caught Ewan's eye.

As usual, his gaze lit up and then drifted a lazy sweep down the length of her.

It made her stomach curl. Mostly because a look like that might have at one time turned her head. In fact, *had* at one time turned her head, and look where that had brought her.

Ewan aimed a stream of tobacco toward the spittoon he kept behind the bar. "Dixie darlin', what can I do for you?"

Dixie fiddled with the brooch pinned at the base of her throat. "Is Doc in? Ma's powerful sick."

"Doc!"

Dixie jolted. She should be used to the fact that Ewan never went up the stairs to get Doc from the room he rented, but simply hollered at the top of his voice. Yet she never seemed to be prepared when he did.

Flynn, dark hair disheveled and a liberal growth of scruff shadowing his angled jaw, appeared on the landing at the head of the staircase a few moments later, doctor bag in hand. He was still shrugging one shoulder into his coat. His red rimmed eyes and a huge yawn proved Ewan's call had woken him.

Dixie felt sorry to have disturbed his sleep. The poor man always snatched bits of slumber at odd times of the day due to the long hours he put in caring for the sick.

He finger-combed his curls as he descended the stairs rapidly, searching the room for whoever might be in need of his services.

His steps slowed for just a moment when he saw her by the

door, but he quickly recovered and hurried to her side. "What is it?" A furrow of worry grooved his forehead and darkened the hazel-blue of his eyes.

Dixie felt a tremor course through her, and to her surprise, tears stung. She blinked hard. She shouldn't be so unaccountably relieved to see him. "It's Ma. I need you to come check on her. She's been sick for a few days. But her fever…" The words choked off and she couldn't seem to say more.

Flynn quickly shucked off his coat and swept it around her shoulders. Then he held a hand toward the door and stretched the other, holding his bag, behind her to urge her forward. "Lead the way. I'm glad you came for me."

She really ought to refuse his coat, but she didn't have the energy for that battle at the moment. Dixie swiped at the tears, which had now spilled over. Her fingers, which barely protruded from the ends of the coat's sleeves, trembled.

Doc walked beside her, his worried gaze fixed on her face.

She huffed. "I'm sorry. I just… If I lose her…"

"Hey." Flynn settled his hand in the middle of her back, directing her around an ice-crusted puddle in the street. "I'm going to do my very best not to let that happen. Don't borrow trouble and all that, aye?"

Dixie nodded. "Yes, you're right. I'm sorry." He opened the door of the boardinghouse for her, and she nodded her thanks as she stepped through. "I just got a little flustered. I don't like to see her this way." She lifted her skirts and took the stairs ahead of him.

Ma was coughing when they stepped into the warmth of the apartment. Thankful that she'd paid Kin Davis to fill her wood box earlier today, Dixie shrugged out of Flynn's coat. She laid it across the settee and hurried to add more wood to the stove. Cold as it was outside, she dared not let it go out.

It only took her a moment and then she led Flynn into Ma's bedchamber. She went around to the far side of the bed. "Ma, I'm here. I've brought Dr. Griffin."

Flynn took charge the moment he stepped into the room. He set his bag on the bedside table and leaned over Ma so she could easily see his face without having to turn her head. He smiled in that special way he had with the infirm.

"Hello, Rose. It's me, Doc. I'm just going to listen to your lungs and do a little poking and prodding, alright? Don't mind me." He rested the back of his fingers against her forehead, then lifted Ma's wrist in one hand, his pocket watch in the other.

Dixie's fingers plucked nervously at the pin on her blouse. There wasn't much space, but that didn't stop her from pacing, first one direction and then the next. She kept her study focused on Flynn's expression, wanting to see if there would be any hint of despair or sorrow, but for now his face remained frustratingly impassive.

From his bag he pulled a device that looked like a clamp of some sort with a bell on one end. He put the two prongs of the clamp into his ears and then bent over Ma and placed the bell-shaped end against her chest. He listened, first in one area, then moved the device to another area and listened again, then again, and again.

Dixie was practically holding her breath by the time he straightened and tugged the tubes from his ears. She studied his face, willing him to look at her. But his gaze was still trained on his patient.

Finally, after a long moment, his shoulders slumped and he lifted his gaze.

Her heart threatened to stop. She'd seen that look in his eyes before. She'd seen it on the day that Hiram Wakefield's son had been crushed by the logging wagon and died only moments after arriving in town. She'd seen it the day that the Kings' newborn had come into the world, still, blue, and lifeless.

She shook with denial, feeling the tears stacking up against her lids like thunderclouds on the horizon.

Flynn tilted his head and reached a hand to grip the back of his neck, so much pain reflected in his eyes that they appeared more brown than blue. With a jut of his chin, he indicated they should talk in the other room.

All she seemed capable of, though, was covering her mouth with one hand. Her feet felt rooted to the floor.

Flynn stepped to the foot of the bed and stretched an arm toward her, compassion and regret filling his expression as he motioned for her to join him.

There was something in the look that lent her strength, and she angled past him and out into the sitting room of their chambers.

She heard him come to a stop just behind her. With a sigh, he set his doctor bag on the floor near his feet, then stepped around to look her in the face. "I believe she has pneumonia."

Dixie pulled in a breath. "That's bad, isn't it?"

Flynn sighed and folded his hands. "It's not good. We'll have to keep her as cool as possible for the next few days to make sure her fever doesn't get any higher, while at the same time keeping the room warm. We'll also have to keep fluids down her so she doesn't dehydrate. And we'll need more pillows to prop her up. Some medical journals I've read say there are better survival rates when patients are made to sit up in their beds. Steaming the room is also said to help. So we'll need to keep hot water going round the clock."

Relief eased some of her tension. "When I saw your expression, I thought..." She was unable to finish the sentence.

Flynn settled his hands on his hips. "Listen, I don't want to give you false hope. The mortality rate for pneumonia is one in four. But I will be here every moment that I can and will do my very best to bring her through this."

Her relief was so great that Dixie threw her arms around his neck. She felt him stiffen, but then he chuckled and returned her embrace. Dixie lurched back, face flaming. "I'm sorry. I don't know what came over me. I just—she means so much to me, and..."

Flynn folded his arms and tilted her a lazy smile. "Far as I'm concerned, you can throw yourself into my arms any time you want. But I think you know that already."

Dixie felt her mortification rise and clapped both hands to her cheeks. This secret of hers had carried on long enough. Especially where Flynn was concerned. "Dr. Griffin...I'm terribly sorry that I've never told you sooner. But the truth is...I'm a married woman."

Flynn's eyes widened. He stepped back and propped his hands on his hips. "You're what?!"

Chapter Two

lynn noted Dixie's fingers curled tightly into the material of her skirt. Anger surged through him. How could she have left such a vital piece of information a secret? He'd been pining over her for months! And her, a married woman! The thought made him a little sick—though he wasn't able to pin down if it was because he'd been harboring feelings for a married woman, or over the fact that her marriage had obviously been so painful she'd felt the need to flee it. The thought of anyone hurting her clamped his teeth so tight the hinge of his jaw hurt.

He scrubbed one hand around the back of his neck and paced away from her.

He heard her take a little breath. "Yes. You heard me right. I'm married. At least I think I am."

His jaw ached, and he took another step away from her. Without facing her he asked, "How can you *think* and not *know*." His voice rose a notch with each word he spoke, and he deliberately unclenched his hands. Forced himself not to storm from the room.

When she remained silent, he turned to face her, needing to read her expression now that he'd had a moment to digest the news. She plucked at her bottom lip, as though searching for words to give him.

But he wasn't willing to wait a moment longer. "I'd like an answer." The demand emerged louder than he'd intended it to.

Dixie held a finger to her lips, giving a little nod to her mother's door. "I'll run down and fetch some hot water now."

Oh no. She wasn't going to get away with that. "Dixie!" His hand shot out and settled around her forearm.

She spun back to face him, eyes wide.

He gentled his grip and took a calming breath. "What do you mean you *think* you are married?"

She pulled away from him and rubbed her hands in a nervous little gesture. "I mean that I'm not sure if my husband is still alive. The last time I saw him he was lying on the floor of our home bleeding profusely from...a b-bullet wound."

With that she turned and fled, and Flynn was too shocked by the news to do anything other than stand there and stare at the empty space she'd just vacated.

He roughed one hand through his hair and gave himself a little shake. Her explanation had raised more questions than it had answered, but right now he had a patient to attend to. He stepped back into Rose's room and pulled the vial of acetylsalicylic acid from within his bag. Carefully, he poured a half cup of tea and added a drizzle of honey. Then he measured acetylsalicylic acid into the cup and stirred. He pulled a chair from the corner of the room over near Rose's bedside and sank into it. Placing one hand behind her head, he urged her to rise up a little. "I have some medicine I need you to take, Rose. Just a few sips, hmmm? You'll be feeling better in no time."

She sipped weakly at the rim of the cup, and he felt his anxiety climb. Dixie should have called for him days ago. *Father, please, mercy for this daughter of yours. Healing, I ask.* "Good, Rose. Well done. Rest now." For the time being, he let her lay back down, but he needed to get her propped up as soon as possible. He also needed to fetch basins for hot water and a large cloth so they could tent her bed and keep steam close to her lungs where it could do its work.

He returned the vial to his bag and then headed over to McGinty's to fetch his tenting sheets and some string. When he got back he was pleased to see that Dixie had already brought in two large basins of hot water and set them on the floor near the head of Rose's bed. Steam wisped throughout the little room. She'd also brought in several more pillows and Rose now reclined with her head elevated to a satisfactory level.

He gave Dixie a nod of thanks and set to tying off the strings of the tent.

All these months...married. Tension was giving him a headache. His jaw ached, and he purposely stretched his neck from side to side to relax the muscles.

"I have two more basins heating downstairs." Her voice was so soft he barely heard her.

"Good thinking." The words emerged clipped and gruff.

He gritted his teeth. He shouldn't be so hard on her. It wasn't like she'd ever invited any of his attentions. In fact, quite to the contrary, she'd rebuffed his every advance. Why, just a couple months ago he'd bid for the pleasure of enjoying her company at the town's boxed supper which had been organized to raise funds for building a schoolhouse and church. Instead of thanking him, she'd taken him aside and told him she would be happy to share her basket dinner with him but that he must never again press his suit. Then she'd promptly invited Sheriff Callahan and Miss Brindle to join them for the meal. He'd been puzzled by her resistance. Because there had been times when he'd felt that Miss Pottinger—Mrs., he silently corrected himself—had feelings for him as well.

With a quick glance in her direction, he forced his thoughts back to the present. "If you could help me by tying this string to the foot of the bed?" He held out one end of the string to her like a white flag of surrender. After all, it was good that he now knew where he stood with her. At least they might be friends.

She took the string hesitantly, her large brown eyes searching his.

He gave her a nod of reassurance, accompanied by a gentle smile that he hoped offered a guarantee of his friendship. "Stretch it nice and tight."

Was her sigh one of relief, or regret? He couldn't quite tell. Nevertheless, she did as he'd asked, and it was only a moment before he had the sheets draped over the string frame and the steaming basins of water tucked beneath the hems that hung all the way to the floor.

He stepped back and assessed. They'd done all that they could do. Now the waiting would begin.

It would be up to the good Lord, and to Rose, whether she lived or not.

When Dr. Griffin turned to the door, Dixie called his name softly. "I know I've hurt you by withholding my story from you. I'd like to explain a little, if you have the time?"

He eyed the door as though he might regret not having made his escape, but then settled into his heels and nodded for her to continue.

Now that she was on the verge of telling him her story—a story she'd almost spilled to him more times than she could remember—she felt anxious to get it over with. Still, she had to make sure he was ready to hear it. "This might take a while. Are you sure you have time?"

He nodded. "I've no other patients pressing for my attention at the moment."

"Very well." She swept a gesture into the sitting room toward the settee. "Please, let's sit."

He took the settee and she took the chair. She ran a trembling hand over her skirt, searching for the best footing to begin on. Finally, she lifted her gaze to his. "I believe you know I was from South Carolina originally?"

Flynn shifted. "I knew you were from the east, somewhere."

"Yes. Well...I left home at the age of seventeen"—Flynn's brow furrowed, but he held his silence, so she pressed on—"and moved to the town of Birch Run, South Carolina. I was young and naïve the first time I met Steven Pottinger, my husband, at a city fundraiser. Rose was—is—Steven's mother." She tipped her head toward the bedroom where Ma lay resting and waited for his certain reaction. It wasn't long in coming.

He jolted forward. "Wait. Rose isn't even your own mother?"

Dixie shook her head. "I think all will be clear when I'm done with the telling."

He leaned back into the seat and folded his arms, giving a stiff nod for her to continue.

She winced, recognizing that she had hurt him more than she first realized with her deceptions. But there was nothing for it but to press ahead now. "Rose had asked me to help run the auction portion of the night. The benefit was to raise funds for a new clinic in town. Steven, the newly-elected town mayor, was handsome and charming. For several months he wooed me with flowers, and dinners, and gifts, and then he asked me to marry him. I had just fled from a father who was more often drunk than sober since the death of my mother two years before. I didn't see myself ever going back to a man who resented the work of providing for me, so I agreed to Steven's proposal."

Flynn's fists clenched until they were white around the knuckles.

Dixie pressed on, determined to get the telling over with. "It wasn't until after we returned from our wedding trip that things took a turn for the worse. Rose, who had been widowed years earlier, lived in her own apartment at the back of Steven's house. As you know, she is a quiet woman, and I found it difficult to connect with her. Those first days at home alone with Rose while Steven went to his office resonated with awkward silences and stilted conversations. But slowly Rose and I built a tentative connection. Rose appreciated having me in the house during the long lonely days, and I was thankful for a mother-in-law who seemed to want to be a friend more than a competitor."

Flynn's gaze bored steadily into her own, one of his fists pressed to his lips.

Dixie's hands trembled fiercely now, for this was to be the difficult part. She laced her fingers together tightly in her lap. "I noticed the scar on Rose's forearm as we did the lunch dishes one day. Rose had rolled up her sleeves, and it was when she had pulled her hands out of the soapy water that I saw a ghastly round mark. I reached for the wound, asking if she was injured and what had happened. But Rose quickly pulled back and brushed away my concern. She said it was nothing. That she'd bumped it on the stove."

Flynn snorted. "I hear similar stories so often."

Dixie nodded. He'd shared his concerns over women from the logging camps with her on several occasions. "Anyhow, I didn't press her. I'd never seen a stove-burn quite in that shape before but figured perhaps there was something inside the door that might have caused it. Rose seemed fine, so I set aside my concern. It was two days later that I experienced Steven's carefully hidden anger for the first time."

Flynn's eyes dropped closed, and he shifted on the settee.

Dixie pressed ahead. "We had attended a town council meeting. The council members wanted to raise funds to bring Birch Run its own doctor. Steven disagreed. He said the traveling doctor who came through once every three weeks was sufficient. When I spoke up on the side of the council, I saw that I'd upset him. But I had no idea what was coming..."

As though he could no longer be bound to stillness, Flynn lurched to his feet and paced to the window that overlooked the street below.

Dixie alternately smoothed and disturbed one of the lace tiers in her skirt. "Steven maintained his calm demeanor until we walked into our home. The moment the door closed, he... he...knocked me to the ground."

Hands clasped behind his back, Flynn tensed. His gaze remained fastened out the window.

"I tried to fight him. But I was so shocked. And then..." Her fingers trembled to the point of uselessness as she fought the buttons at her cuff.

Flynn turned to look at her, and there was so much pain in his gaze that Dixie couldn't meet his eyes.

She tugged her sleeve up and held out her arm, revealing her shame to another for the first time.

Flynn ground out a sound that fell somewhere between a grunt of shock and a groan of despair.

The marks on her arm were of course healed over now, but she would never be able to forget the anticipation in Steven's eyes as he'd pinned her arm to the floor and very deliberately pulled a cigar from the inner pocket of his suit jacket.

"He lit a cigar and...I again tried to fight him, but...he planted his boot into my chest and pinned me to the ground. Each of his movements were slow and purposeful, calculated to elicit the most terror possible, I'm certain. All the while, he never took his eyes off of me." Dixie's throat felt so tight she thought her voice might fail her, but she forced herself to continue. "With his foot still pressed against me, he folded his arms over his knee and inhaled slowly on his cigar and then blew the smoke into my face. 'Don't. You. Ever. Disagree like that. With me. In public. Again.' He gritted every word between clenched teeth. I was unable to respond for lack of air."

Flynn dropped to one knee before her and gently tugged her sleeve down to cover the scars. Carefully and ever so gently, he smoothed the material and then fastened the buttons at her wrist. He curled both hands around hers and met her gaze. Moisture shimmered in his eyes, but his voice was steady when he urged, "Go on. Tell me everything."

Enveloped by Flynn's tenderness, Dixie fought her own tears. If only she'd met Flynn years ago. "That first time, he kept me pinned to the floor, easing up his foot just enough to allow me to snatch a quick breath every once in a while. Periodically, he tapped the hot ashes off above my face. When the cigar was down to a nub, he straddled me and pinned my arm to the ground. And...and..." Unable to meet Flynn's sorrowful gaze for a moment longer she looked away.

"Shhhh. I understand. I'm so sorry." Flynn pressed a kiss against the back of each of her hands.

"I lived every moment in terror after that day. I never knew what was going to set him off. It was on the day that he took a baseball bat to me that Rose shot him."

Flynn released her hands but remained on one knee before her. He rubbed his fingers across his forehead, and Dixie could tell that it was taking him a moment to process the fact that

Rose had shot her own son. Or perhaps it was anger at the base of his agitated movements, for his jaw bunched repeatedly.

The bone-deep weariness that Dixie seemed to have carried with her for years had sapped so much of her strength she could only be glad she was already seated. But the telling was almost finished now. "One moment he had me pinned to the wall and was ramming the end of the bat into my stomach, and the next a shot rang out and he slumped to the floor. I remember that smoke still spiraled from Rose's gun when I looked over. Rose wanted to go immediately to the sheriff and turn herself in. But I had personal experience with the attitude of Birch Run's sheriff. I'd gone to him many times. Showed him my scars and burns and tried to get him to help me, but he always scoffed and said I must be concocting stories—one time he actually accused me of injuring myself. Because of that, I talked Rose into running. We left Steven bleeding where he lay, and ran with only the clothes on our backs. So you see, that's why I don't know if I'm a widow, or not. Because, Lord forgive me, I left him there. And...I can only hope that he did indeed die." She sighed. "But I'm so tired, Flynn. So tired of constantly thinking about a man I wish I could never think about again. But every day there's so much hate inside me. And now I've hurt you. I couldn't bear it if—"

With a quick tug, Flynn brought one of her hands close, curled his thumb around hers, and dropped a fervent kiss on her knuckles. He didn't offer any words, but when he met her gaze there was a world of forgiveness shining in his eyes.

A sigh of relief slipped from her. The terrible task of telling all was done. And Flynn would still be her friend. For now, that was all that she could ask for.

Chapter Three

Charlotte Brindle sat at her desk and studied the children spread out at the various tables around Dixie's dining-room-cum-schoolhouse. All of them were studiously writing the essay she had assigned about what Christmas meant to them.

All of them except Washington Nolan and Kincaid Davis. Washington was staring across the room at Zoe Kastain. And nothing she'd tried since the school year began seemed to keep Kincaid engaged for more than fifteen minutes. The boy was probably the smartest one in the room.

Charlotte cleared her throat softly.

Washington jolted a little and looked at her.

She pinched her lips together and arched a disapproving brow.

His face flushed till it nearly matched the berries on the clusters of holly they'd strung about the room just yesterday, and he returned his focus to his lessons.

When she narrowed her gaze on Kincaid, he only held up two sheets of paper for her to see that he was already done. The boy was too smart for his own good. They'd discussed this in the past, however. Even if he finished early, she expected him to search the paper over and neatly erase and make any corrections he felt might improve the clarity of his words. After a moment more of her meeting him, challenging gaze for challenging gaze, he finally picked up his pencil and turned his focus to the paper on his desk.

Satisfied that he was, at least for the moment, back to his lessons, Charlotte turned her attention to the clock. Only two minutes closer to half past three than it had been the last time she checked. She groaned mentally and then suppressed a chuckle. In all honesty, she could hardly keep her lips from spilling her secret to the children. She had forced herself to wait till the end of today's lessons, but the clock seemed to be ticking slower with each passing second.

Just another week and then school would let out for the Christmas season. Several weeks back, she had wired her father and mother asking them if they would be willing to collect some donations of toys for the children of Wyldhaven and ship them out on the train from Boston. And just today when she'd stepped over to the post office on her lunch break to see if she had any letters, Mr. Ben King had handed her a telegram from Father. A thrill of anticipation had zipped through her when she read that he would be shipping the toys on next week's train. That meant the toys would arrive well in time for Christmas.

She nearly clapped her hands in glee even now as she thought about it. Perhaps she shouldn't tell the children though? What if something happened to the shipment and it didn't arrive in time? But no... She really couldn't help herself, and this was almost the twentieth century. Nothing was going to happen to the train. In all the months she'd been here the train had arrived in Snohomish on its regular schedule like clockwork. The Wyldhaven coach then took on any supplies destined for Wyldhaven and arrived promptly each Saturday—a recent change from Thursdays, which used to be the day it arrived. Dixie's food order for the boardinghouse came on it, and had never been a day late. So...

Washington's focus had wandered to Zoe again.

Charlotte cleared her throat. This time he didn't look up at her, but merely jerked his attention back to his desk. His ears did turn pink, however.

Charlotte returned her gaze to the papers she should be grading at her desk, but she was having a hard time concentrating. She picked up the other letter she'd received when she went to the post office and fiddled with one corner of the envelope. She didn't need to read it again. The contents had been indelibly seared on her memory the first time.

The truth was, she felt a little put out with the species known as men in general, lately. It had been more than two months since Sheriff Callahan had kissed her at her shooting lesson, yet the man had hardly said two words to her since then. She saw him about town, and at his mother's place where she boarded, of course. But whenever she appeared, he seemed to have sudden urgent business that called him to another part of town. She could read unspoken messages as well as anyone. And the message the sheriff was sending was that their kiss had been a mistake of the gravest proportions. A mistake that he did not wish to repeat.

Thus the second letter she'd received from Mr. Zebulon Heath, Wyldhaven's founder, really ought to be a relief. Yet somehow she hadn't been able to talk her way around to seeing it that way. Sheriff Callahan, on the other hand, would likely be elated.

So stop thinking about him, then, and move on with life.

Finally, the minute hand pointed at half past three. She gave the little bell on her desk a ring. "Class, you may put away your papers and pencils. We'll work on your essays again tomorrow. For now, I have a surprise to share with you."

Murmurs of anticipation traversed the room as the students stored their supplies and then turned their focus on her.

Realizing she still held Mr. Heath's letter, Charlotte set it down and folded her hands on the desk. "As you all know, Christmas is just a few weeks away."

A chorus of excited yelps and "hoorays" greeted her.

"After this Friday, I'm going to give you three weeks off to enjoy the Christmas season, and we'll resume school again after the first of the year." The tail end of her sentence had to be practically shouted overtop the choruses of cheers that were resonating through the room. She held up her hands for silence. "And I just wanted you all to know that I need each of you to finish out these last few days of school with hard work and good attitudes."

This sentiment was greeted with a round of subtle grumbles.

"Because... I'm going to have a surprise for each of you. And it's all the way from Boston!"

"Oh my lands! Something direct from Boston!" Zoe Kastain leapt out of her chair, raised her newly cast-free arm above her head and spun in a quick circle. Several others jumped up and down or danced little jigs by their desks. Washington Nolan wore a slight smile, but he and his brothers were much more stoic than the rest of their younger classmates. And at the back of the room, Belle Kastain, Zoe's sister, had a gleam of satisfaction in her eyes, if not a smile on her face. Kincaid Davis watched her with curiosity in his eyes, but Charlotte suddenly realized she couldn't recall ever seeing the young man smile.

Charlotte set aside her worry over the boy and returned her attention to the rowdy bunch dancing by their desks. She couldn't help but grin at the students' exuberance. "Sit down, everyone, please."

The students complied, even if it was with a great deal of clamor.

"My surprise will be put on the train next week, so should be arriving in Snohomish before we know it! I'll give it to you at the town's Christmas festival—"

"Festival?" This again from Zoe. "But we ain't never had a festival before."

Charlotte was so shocked by the statement that she forgot to correct the girl's grammar.

"Yeah!" chimed in the youngest Nolan brother, Grant. "Our pa says there's no time for celebrating during the month when the ground is frozen good and hard."

No Christmas Festival? Charlotte put one hand to her throat. "What does the ground being frozen solid have to do with not celebrating Christmas?" Even to her own ears she could hear the breathy disappointment in her question.

Most of the students looked back and forth at each other with expressions that indicated they couldn't believe she didn't already know the answer.

Washington came to her rescue. "Hauling logs is heavy work. Any kind of mud, and the wagon wheels sink right down into it and make for some miserable slow days of fighting with stuck wagons. But when the ground is frozen, well, that's good log-hauling time."

"I see." Charlotte tugged at the lace of her cuffs. "But surely... taking off for one day can't hurt too much? To celebrate the birth of our Lord?"

Washington merely lifted his hands as though silently saying, "I'm just telling you the way of it."

Charlotte pulled in a breath. Wyldhaven would have Christmas this year if she had anything to say about it. "Well, I'll just have to see what I can do. For now, you are all dismissed. Remember to button up your coats, everyone. It sure is cold out there!"

Today of all days, Charlotte would miss being able to just stay in the warmth of the building to dart up the back stairs to her room. Since she'd been staying at Mrs. Callahan's place, she would have to button up just like the rest of the students. She didn't envy those who had several miles to walk in this weather. The two blocks to Mrs. Callahan's place was going to be cold enough. The weather had turned decidedly menacing. This morning she had woken up to blustery wind blasts accompanied by icicles dangling from her window frame. And all day long low hanging, blue-gray clouds had hung eerily quiet above Wyldhaven.

She slipped on her coat and gathered up her books and the reports that a few of the children had finished. She would need to correct them tonight. Taking her scarf from the rack in the corner, she wrapped it snugly about her neck and lower face and made her way out into the elements.

Thankfully, this cold weather had transformed the mud that normally sucked at her boots into a hard ungiving surface. Still, she really needed to talk to the town council about getting some boardwalks built in town. The wind whipped up her hems and blasted chill gusts around her ankles. Clutching her books tightly to her chest, she hunched her shoulders against the weather and tucked her face as far into her scarf as she could get it to go. Half a block down, one and a half blocks to go. She dashed around the corner between the sheriff's office and McGinty's Alehouse and smacked into a person coming the other way.

"Whoa!"

"Sheriff!" Her heart hammered even as her books and papers clattered out of her hands and tumbled before the wind.

"Oh no!" She started after them.

But Sheriff Callahan gripped her shoulders. "You stay here

in the alley where there's less wind. I'll grab your papers."
Clapping his hat to his head with one hand, the sheriff chased
some students' reports down the street. He caught one,
then two. And then gathered a few more that had plastered
themselves against the side of the watering trough.

Charlotte picked up the heavier books that had fallen at
her feet.

The sheriff had caught all but one final report now, and he
hurried after it. Each time he got close, a wind gust picked the
paper up again and scuttled it a few feet farther. Holding the
reports that he had gathered in one hand—which also kept his
hat atop his head—and scuttling low as he tried to catch the
last report, the sheriff looked rather like a crab skittering down
the main street of Wyldhaven.

Charlotte couldn't help a giggle.

Even from here she heard his grumble of disgust as he bent
to retrieve the paper and yet again the wind skipped it out
of his reach. Charlotte's laugh was a bit malicious this time.
Served the man right for ignoring her for all these weeks!

He finally caught up to the last report and returned with
them to the alley. "Got them all. Sorry about that."

She took the papers and then lifted one side of her skirts
and gave him a deep curtsy, still clutching her books in one
arm. "Much obliged, Sheriff." She let the icy feeling that
encapsulated her heart seep into the tone of her words.

He blinked, opened his mouth as though to say something,
but then snapped it shut again. Tugging on the brim of his hat,
he made to step around her and hasten on his way.

She couldn't let him go because she really needed to tell him
about Mr. Heath's letter, even if the sheriff already seemed
determined to cut off their courtship. Courtship? Was that
what they'd had? Could one call a single kiss a courtship?

The sheriff had taken a couple steps away by this time.

"Might I talk you into a piece of pie, Sheriff?" Despite the chill wind whipping past the end of the alley, Charlotte felt her face heat. The man likely thought her rather forward. Well, there was nothing for it now that the invitation was offered but to press on. She glanced down and doodled her toe against the frosty side of a rock. "I was just headed home to your mother's place. I'm sure she probably has some pie left over from last night's dinner?" She hurried on to add, "My way of repaying you for the kindness of chasing down my papers, you understand."

Reagan stepped back into the wind-break offered by the alley. He tugged at the leather gloves encasing his fingers, his gaze drilling into hers the entire time. After a long moment he scrubbed his chin against the shoulder of his coat and transferred his focus to the ground. "Miss Brindle, perhaps there is something we need to discuss—"

Charlotte held up one hand to keep him from going on. She was piqued enough with the man without allowing him to exacerbate her feelings by apologizing for the kiss. "Sheriff Callahan, I can assure you that there is no need for a discussion. I have clearly received the message you've been sending the past few weeks, and I merely wanted you to know that I agree. I received a letter from Mr. Heath just today." Reagan's gaze darted to hers, but she pressed on before he could interrupt. "And after... well... after our last shooting lesson, despite the distance that has come between us since then, I figured it would be best for me to discuss its contents with you. In the letter Mr. Heath lays out a list of rules that he had forgotten to include when he hired me. And amongst the rules is one that says..." By the amount of warmth in her face, her cheeks were probably as rosy as Zoe Kastain's looked when Washington

Nolan twitted her about one thing or another in the classroom. She cleared her throat. "It says that I'm not free to, ah, socialize with gentlemen. So you see...you've nothing to fear from me. I think our feelings are actually quite aligned on the matter."

He stepped closer. "Actually, I'm not convinced they are."

Charlotte felt her eyes widen. Now whatever could he mean by that? But in his typical silent manner, he didn't elaborate. The alleyway suddenly felt like very close quarters with him looking at her as softly as he was.

She licked her lips and stepped back, hugging her books and papers before her like a shield. "Anyhow, you see, since we live in such a small town and ought to be on friendly terms, I thought...a slice of the pie I made yestereve might suffice as an offering of friendship?"

"Forgive me, Miss Brindle, for assuming. You see, I received a telegram from Mr. Heath several weeks ago. He informed me in no uncertain terms that as sheriff it was my duty to make sure the laws of the town were upheld. He sent me an abbreviated list of the rules for the new schoolteacher, and..." Puzzlement furrowed his brow. "Ben King informed me that you had also picked up a telegram. I assumed yours was the same as mine."

Charlotte felt a shiver that had very little to do with the gusting wind shake her shoulders. "I see." So he had known about Mr. Heath's rules for weeks?

"You are telling me that you only just today received his list of rules?"

She nodded. "The telegram I received a few weeks back was to inform me that my cousin and her husband had been blessed with a new daughter."

If possible, Reagan's face softened even more. "Then I

sincerely apologize for what must have seemed to you my rather callous and cavalier behavior."

Her throat was so tight she barely managed to breathe out, "Have no fear, Sheriff. All is forgiven."

Reagan rubbed the back of one gloved hand against his chin. "His list, and perhaps that last run-in with Waddell, did get me to thinking about my own job. It carries a great deal of risk. Not a job for a family man."

Charlotte felt her brow furrow slightly. So... He was telling her that even if it wasn't for Mr. Heath's list he wouldn't want to come calling on her.

Before she could gather her thoughts enough to question him on it, he said, "As for your invitation... Did *you* make this pie?"

Charlotte blinked, scrambling to catch back up with his return to the earlier topic. "Indeed, I did."

"Well then...I'm afraid I have pressing business on the other side of town."

Her jaw dropped, despite all the harping Miss Gidden, her former finishing school mistress, had leveled her way for that particularly unladylike habit, but then she took note of the twinkle in Reagan's eyes.

He laughed outright and offered her the aid of his elbow. "If we are to be friends, you'd best get used to a little teasing now and again, Miss Brindle."

Charlotte tucked one hand into the crook of his arm, relieved to have the awkward discussion behind them. Now to move them on to a different topic. She glanced up at him. "I'm actually glad I ran into you. I was just talking with my students and they have informed me that there is no formal Christmas celebration in town. I would like to remedy that."

Reagan gave her a look that could have almost been

interpreted as a grimace. "I'm afraid that's not going to be an easy battle to take on. As you know, logging is a serious business 'round these parts. And with this storm whipping up, the ground is setting in to freeze good and hard any day now. There will be lots of log hauling that begins the moment that happens. The men don't get paid unless those logs make it to the mill. As soon as the road between the logging camp and the creek freezes up, none of them will be wanting to take any time off, even to celebrate Christmas."

"Well, that's just positively barbaric!"

Reagan helped her up the stairs to his mother's porch and then opened the door for her. They swept inside, and Charlotte set her books down on the side table and allowed him to help her off with her wraps.

"There's nothing barbaric about wanting to get paid so you can provide for your family."

Charlotte scrunched up her nose. "No. I suppose not. Still... It seems such a shame to allow the celebration of the Lord's birth to pass the town by without so much as even a hint of celebration. I'll put my mind to coming up with something."

Reagan sighed. "I'm sure you will."

She spun toward him. "And what does that mean?"

He lifted his palms. "Only that you have a singular mind for accomplishing whatever you set your heart to, and I wouldn't expect anything less in this situation."

His face held innocence, even if there was a bit of a devilish gleam in his eyes.

"Very well, Sheriff. I suppose I shall let your potentially reprobate comments slide, just this once."

"Reprobate? You must have me confused with someone else!" He winked at her.

She held aloft one finger. "But only if you agree to take me into Snohomish in three weeks to collect some boxes that my father will ship to me."

Reagan frowned. "Can't you just let them arrive on the coach in the normal fashion the next week?"

Charlotte shrugged. "I suppose I could. But that would only give me two days to get the presents all sorted and wrapped. This is a special shipment of Christmas toys I had Father put together for the children, and I know I shan't rest until the whole load of them are safely in my own hands."

Reagan hung his head, obviously doing his best to look put-upon. "Very well. I believe I could manage to suffer through a trip all the way to Snohomish snuggled beneath a bearskin with you."

Charlotte pinched her lips together and narrowed her eyes at him, doing her best not to respond to his flirting. "Very kind of you, I'm sure."

The sheriff pressed one hand to his chest and offered her a deep bow.

Charlotte couldn't help the laugh that burst forth. So much for not responding. "Oh do get on with you."

"What? Without my slice of pie? Not on your life, little lady."

Charlotte gave him a roll of her eyes. "Very well. I suppose a girl can't go back on her word." She turned and led him toward the kitchen where his mother would no doubt be sitting by the lamp at the dining table putting the finishing touches to some of the darning projects she took in each week.

Reagan's boots clumped down the corridor after her. "No indeed, Miss Brindle. No indeed."

Chapter Four

Jacinda Callahan listened with a bit of trepidation to the conversation taking place between her son and Miss Brindle in the entryway. There seemed to be a bit of reservation crackling in the air between them. That was good, she supposed. They had grown close much too quickly when Charlotte first came to town. Not because she objected to the girl. Not at all. Quite the contrary, it was her love for the girl that made her not want their relationship to work out.

She had been waiting for a long time for her son to discover the love of his life, and she had a feeling she was finally seeing that dream come to fruition before her very eyes. And yet she couldn't feel easy about it. Not when she knew full well the dangers of Reagan's job.

The young people bustled into the dining room and she tucked her head over her mending and pretended great interest in darning the hole in the sock she was working on.

Charlotte inhaled appreciatively. "Dinner smells delicious. I hope you don't mind that I invited this drifter I found loitering about town to share the meal with us?" There was a note of levity in her words.

Jacinda smiled fondly at her son. "I don't mind in the least. It's good to see you, son. How were things about town today?"

Reagan pulled out a chair and hooked his Stetson over the

back of it as he sank down and folded his hands atop the table. "Rather quiet today, which is just fine with me. The cold weather is keeping people indoors, I suppose."

"I'll set the table." Charlotte squeezed Jacinda's shoulders, a sweet gesture the girl offered each day when she arrived home.

A gesture she would dearly miss if the girl ever decided to go back home to her people in Boston. A feeling of despair settled into the region of Jacinda's heart as she watched her son's gaze follow Charlotte into the kitchen. His blue eyes were soft and full of an emotion Jacinda never recalled seeing there before.

She pulled her thread taut, but kept her focus on her son's face when she said quietly, "She's a nice girl."

Reagan seemed to start at the realization that she was still in the room. He fidgeted in his chair like he'd done as a boy when she'd caught him stealing cookies from the jar. One of his fingers traced over the darker wood of the knot in the center of the table. "Yes'm. Right nice."

"A very nice girl who deserves a man who will come home to her every evening and not leave her widowed at twenty-nine."

Reagan's jaw bunched, and he rubbed it with the pads of his fingers. "Yes, ma'am. Zeb sent me a telegram that got me thinking on that."

"Thinking on it with the intention of doing something about it? Or just thinking on it?"

Reagan gave her a sharp look. "You know Zeb. He won't brook any of his employees bucking his rules."

"Well, that's true enough." She sighed. How many times had she asked him to give up working for the law? Not that she wanted him to switch sides. Just that she wanted him to do something safe like farming or cattle ranching. But Callahan men were nothing if not stubborn.

Still... She released a breath. "I'm sorry. I've broken my word. I told you I would endeavor not to bring it up again, and now I have."

Reagan's expression softened. "I know you worry about me, Ma, but I just—"

A knock sounded at the front door. Jacinda frowned. Whoever would be out and about in this kind of cold weather? She stashed her needle into the sock and tucked the project back into her sewing basket. "See who's at the door, would you dear? I'll help Charlotte put the finishing touches on our dinner." Their conversation would be over for now. Until the next time her worry got the best of her and she miss-stepped and brought it up again. Whyever couldn't she learn to live without worry like the birds of the air and the lilies of the field as the good book said?

Reagan returned a moment later as she and Charlotte were setting the cornbread and stew on the table. "Got room for one more, Ma?" he asked. He gestured to a man at his side. "This fella here is new in town. McGinty saw me headed this way and walked him over here to chat with me a bit about any land that might be available hereabouts."

"Of course."

Behind her, she heard Charlotte step back into the kitchen. She would be fetching another place setting. The girl was thoughtful like that.

Jacinda offered the newcomer a smile as she moved around the table. "Welcome."

"Ma'am." The man doffed his Stetson, and heaven help her if he didn't have the comeliest blue eyes, lined with lashes long enough to give any woman envy. The laugh lines about his mouth put him at about her own age. She wondered if a wife and family were nearby.

She swiped her hands on her apron, then held one out. "Like I said, welcome, Mister…"

"Holloway," Reagan offered quickly. "And this is my mother, Jacinda Callahan."

The newcomer took her offered hand. "Zane Holloway, ma'am." The reach of his arm opened up his long leather coat enough for her to catch a glimpse of the Colt—butt-forward, tied down, and wooden-handled—slung at his hip.

Her lips pressed together at that. There weren't many good reasons for a man to tie down his gun.

In spite of that, she couldn't help but notice he had a firm grip and a well-groomed appearance, even if his hair was long around his collar. "Is your family nearby, Mr. Holloway? There's plenty here." She swept a gesture to the table, indicating that his family, too, would be welcome. It was a neat trick that let her quickly extract her hand from his.

Mr. Holloway twisted his brown leather hat through his fingers, but there was a twinkle in his eyes that led her to believe that perhaps she wasn't quite as good of a thespian as she'd hoped. "No family, ma'am. Just me…for now." A devilish gleam lit his expression, and he winked so quickly that in the next moment she had to wonder if it had indeed been a wink at all.

She took in a little breath of indignation and narrowed her eyes at him.

But now complete innocence wreathed his features.

The man's eyes brought to mind the chill waters of the Wyldhaven Creek during spring melt, and when connected with hers as they were now, had about as much impact as jumping into said waters on a warm day. His dark wavy locks were sprinkled with the scantest touches of silver at his temples, and long as they were, gave him a roguish air. The broad shoulders that stretched the long leather duster to maximum capacity, and the several days' worth of dark beard that coated his angular jaw only added to that perception.

His upper lip quirked up at one corner with a tug of humor. She blinked and gave herself a mental shake.

The man cleared his throat. "As said, no family. But I do have a horse. However, I assure you he is wholly comfortable down at the livery. Besides that, I doubt he'd care for the taste of stew, no matter that it smells as fine as it does." He dipped a little bow over those last words.

Jacinda didn't miss the conspiratorial look that passed between her son and Miss Brindle as they then in turn bounced looks between her and this brash newcomer.

Irritation that the younger generation obviously thought she was smitten with the man shot a ramrod up her spine. "Yes. Well... Horses would not be welcome at the table anyhow, Mr. Holloway."

His face turned immediately serious, and he searched her face as though to see if she had taken offense.

Now why had she gone and said something like that? The man had obviously only been teasing her. She softened her words with a belated smile, and it was as though someone had just popped the tension in the room with a straight pin. There was a collective release of breath and smiles all around.

She needed to regain control of this situation. "Please, everyone, let's be seated." She glided as gracefully as she could to her seat at the head of the table, and Reagan scrambled to pull her chair out for her.

Reagan also held Charlotte's chair, after which he took the seat on the far side of the table, which left Mr. Holloway in the seat directly to Jacinda's right. The man stripped off his coat and hung it carefully over the back of his chair, hooked his hat on one corner just as Reagan always did, and then sat quietly.

Jacinda straightened the silverware by her place setting, even though it was quite straight already. "Reagan, say grace, if you would."

Reagan did, and upon the conclusion she served everyone's plates. Mr. Holloway at least appeared to have table manners. He even waited to begin eating until she had served the stew to everyone and taken the first bite herself.

It had been a long time—a very long time indeed—since a man had intrigued her so. She'd obviously been spending overmuch time ruminating about love and such lately, because her fascination was ridiculous. She certainly didn't want to get involved with the likes of a man who felt it necessary to tie down his guns. Determined to put the man from her mind, she focused on her stew.

Reagan introduced Charlotte to the man, and for a few moments pleasantries were exchanged. But it wasn't long before Reagan ventured, "So what brings you to Wyldhaven, Mr. Holloway? Ewan mentioned something about land?"

Mr. Holloway carefully spread a thin layer of butter over his cornbread before he set his knife just-so across the top of his plate. "Well now, I'm not rightly certain what gave Ewan that impression. He must have misunderstood something. What I said to him was that I'd come to town because an investor had told me there might be something here that I've been looking for. I suppose he took that to mean I was here to invest in land."

"But it's not the reason you've come?" Charlotte asked. She sipped daintily from her spoon, yet kept her curious gaze fixed on the man across the table.

Mr. Holloway shook his head. "No, miss. You see"—he dug into the front pocket of his shirt and pulled out something that he set on the table before his plate, clearly visible for them all to see—"I'm a federal marshal, and I'm here hunting a couple of murderers."

Jacinda's spoon clattered quite loudly against her bowl, and Charlotte gasped, "Murderers?!"

"I'm afraid so, miss."

Jacinda's gaze fell to the metal badge.

A lawman. Of course he was a lawman. Oughtn't she to recognize that bold, bigger-than-life air that seemed to accompany lawmen wherever they went?

Wasn't it that very confidence that had led to her attraction to Wade? The same confidence that had gotten him shot in the gunfight he'd had with the outlaw he'd been hunting for months. No matter that he'd killed the outlaw outright while that man's bullet had missed Wade's spine by less than an inch. The festering infection had gotten him in the end, anyhow. Her one consolation was that both she and Reagan had gotten to say their goodbyes.

At least she knew right upfront to avoid any attachments. That was more than she could say for Wade. Wade hadn't decided to pursue the law until after they'd been married.

Thankfully, Mr. Holloway, as a marshal, would only be traveling through. Marshals never stayed in one place for long.

"Surely there is a better time to be hunting murderers than during the Christmas season, Marshal Holloway?" She didn't even care that there was an unprovoked bite in her tone.

"I'm afraid tracking down murderers waits for no season, ma'am. Though I can honestly say I wouldn't mind spending Christmas in a cozy little town like Wyldhaven, especially if all the meals are to be as pleasant and delicious as this one." His gaze landed on her, bold as a peacock in full feather.

Jacinda calmly drizzled honey on her cornbread. "Actually,

I think you'll find our town rather dull during the holiday. It tends to be seen as a regular work day around these parts."

"But I intend to change that this year," Charlotte piped up as she dabbed at her mouth with her serviette.

"Here we go," Reagan groused good-naturedly.

Nevertheless, Charlotte pinned him with a glower.

"What's this?" Jacinda prodded.

Charlotte's enthusiasm didn't wane. "I'm hoping to encourage the men to take Christmas day off this year. I've just had a wire from Father, and he's loading the toys I asked him to send onto next week's train. That means the gifts will be here well in time for Christmas, and I want to have a festival one evening in McGinty's to celebrate our Lord's birth as a community, and so I can hand out presents to all of the children."

Jacinda turned her gaze on her son. Clearly, he needed to do something about this. The men were not going to be pleased if Charlotte put a bug in their wives' ears about them needing to take time off in addition to the Lord's Day, which some of them already grumbled about during any freezes.

Reagan very subtly lifted his palms as if to tell her there wasn't much he could do about it now that Charlotte had gotten the idea in her head.

He was right, of course. The men certainly wouldn't be happy about it. But Charlotte was one determined woman once she got a bee in her bonnet.

And Charlotte was correct as well. Every child deserved to have a bit of happiness and something to look forward to. Especially on Christmas. "I'm sure Charlotte will be able to come up with some sort of compromise that keeps both parties happy."

Reagan's twisted lips and the tilt of his head said he believed otherwise, but like the smart man she had raised him to be, he didn't object.

"I'm going to do my best," Charlotte concurred. "And perhaps we could do something along with the festival to raise some more funds for the building of the church, come spring?"

"If the men are wanting to get their logs to the mill, and the women are wanting a festival, why not do something to combine the two?" Zane leaned back until only two legs of his chair rested on the floor.

If he broke the legs of her chair... Jacinda pressed her lips together. Perhaps the man wasn't as well-mannered as she had thought. It really wasn't like her to get riled up so easily, but something about his cocksure attitude got under her skin and hung there like an itch that couldn't quite be dispatched. She resisted the notion to kick out one foot and give one of the front legs of the chair a lift to send him over backwards as her father had done anytime she had acted so ill-mannered.

"Oh! That's a brilliant idea!" Charlotte exclaimed. "Back in Boston we'd do hay rides in the summers. I organized one to help raise funds for a surgery our neighbor's child required. We had three fiddlers who rode on the front of the wagon, and then we drove it about town and anyone who wanted a ride paid two bits for rides of a quarter hour. We could do something similar with the wagons here." She held up one hand to stop the protest Reagan was leaning forward to voice.

At the irritated look on Reagan's face, Jacinda had to bite back a grin. How she wished she could be pleased for her son to have found a woman who seemed such a perfect match for him. How she wished Reagan felt free to give her his heart. But wishes were a little bit like frost upon a window pane. Pretty to look upon and ponder, but of little substance, and easily vanquished with the first warm rays of the sun which brought reality blazing back to the fore.

Charlotte had barely paused to take a breath. "Of course we

couldn't ride *on* the logging wagons, but what if we added a couple extra wagons? From what I've seen, the men load up all the wagons with the logs during the day and then drive them down to the creek to unload them into the water, correct?"

Reagan wore a look of resignation when he nodded.

"Well then, that's perfect! Women and children who want to contribute to the fundraiser could ride on wagons from the logging camp. We could start out at the camp and all ride to the creek and the festival could take place after that. Oh, I need to make a list!" Charlotte stood and dashed into the entryway, still muttering to herself. "We could hang lanterns in the field across from McGinty's. And maybe Dixie would help me put up a tree and string garland about." She was back now, with a nub of a pencil and a tablet of paper in her hands. A worried look suddenly crossed her face. "If we managed to combine a full day's work with the festival surely the men couldn't object too strenuously, could they?"

Reagan sighed. "If anyone can convince them it's a grand idea, I'm sure it is you, Charlotte."

"Do you think?" Her face lit with pleasure. "Well good. We can go and talk to the camp foreman on Saturday. Can you take me? Please say you will take me, Sheriff?" She put one hand on his arm and Jacinda saw Reagan swallow.

"Saturday. Of course. I'll plan on it."

"Oh, you are a dear. That's wonderful. But now, if you will excuse me, I have several papers I have to grade tonight. So I think I will retire to my room while you all have dessert. Jacinda, I'll return to help you with the dishes in a while." With that, she whirled out of the room without so much as a backward glance.

Reagan swept his hands over his face and shook his head. "I do believe the good Lord forgot to install the brakes on that one."

The admiration in his tone made Jacinda's heart pinch. She wanted nothing but his happiness, but she knew all too well the heartache of carrying on alone after the death of a husband with a dangerous job.

Jacinda stood and hefted the soup tureen. "I'll fetch dessert. Why don't you two take your business into the parlor?" She tipped Marshal Holloway a nod. "It was a pleasure to meet you, Marshal."

"Ma'am." He stood quickly to his feet and touched his forehead in a quick salute.

She felt his gaze boring into her all the way to the kitchen.

Chapter Five

Reagan sighed as Ma swept from the room. He downed the last of his coffee and then stood. "Please"—he stretched out a hand—"join me in the parlor."

Zane followed him into the other room and sank down onto the settee. There was a twinkle of humor in his eyes. "She's got spunk, that one."

Reagan rested his elbow against the fireplace mantel. "That she does." He stared into the fire and scratched his thumbnail over his brow, thinking over Ma's earlier reminder. "But we have dangerous jobs, you and I. Wouldn't quite be fair to a woman to saddle her with a man who could be killed each time he went to work."

Zane pursed his lips and made a noise of disagreement. "Then women shouldn't marry farmers, or cattlemen, or doctors for that matter. Any man alive can walk out the door in the morning and be carried back through it in a box in the evening. For that matter..." He cleared his throat. "At one moment a man can be happily expecting the birth of his first child, and in the next he can have lost both his wife and the babe."

Reagan spun towards him, taking in the pain etched into the man's brow. "I'm sorry. That must have been difficult."

The marshal looked up and blinked, as if coming back from

a faraway place. He waved one hand. "Besides...I wasn't asking for her hand in marriage." Sardonic humor ticked up the corner of the man's lips.

Reagan felt his eyes narrow. "I should hope not. You're twice her age."

Zane blinked. Then gave a short bark of laughter. "I was speaking of your mother."

"Oh." Reagan tilted the man a scrutinizing look.

Zane lifted his palms. "Don't worry. Something tells me your ma can more than hold her own when it comes to a rascal like me."

Deciding the man was mostly harmless, Reagan grinned. "That she can, Marshal. That she can." He considered offering a warning about Ma's feelings towards lawmen, but then decided the man had probably gotten a fairly good picture of those feelings over dinner.

Reagan brushed away the conversation with his hand. "Tell me what sort of murderers you are looking for and what makes you think they've arrived in my town?"

The marshal gave him a look that said Reagan was not going to like what he was about to say. "I don't think they've just arrived. I think they've been living here for quite some time."

Reagan frowned in disbelief. "There is not a soul in this town whom I would suspect of murder, Marshal."

"Ah, but that's what makes their deception so genius. I believe you know the two I'm looking for—Rose and Dixie Pottinger."

Reagan could not have been more shocked if the marshal had drawn his gun and shot him, but Ma bustled in just then with the dessert tray. Reagan waited until she had served them pie and coffee and then left the room before he pinned the marshal with a frown. "There must be some mistake."

The lawman shook his head. "I'll need to question them, of course. But I'm quite certain that they are the two women I've been searching for. I've come all the way from South Carolina. The younger woman, Dixie, was the wife of the murdered man. The older, his mother. He was the mayor of a small town called Birch Run. The sheriff of the town reported that he'd observed both women boarding the morning train out of town, and that they'd seemed suspicious. When he went by the mayor's house to investigate, there was blood everywhere, and though no body was found, the man is presumed murdered and the women wanted for questioning. I wasn't there to see the scene at the first. I was only brought in later." Zane waved a hand. "As stated, I have questions because some of the story doesn't seem to add up. And the sheriff of Birch Run...well, it's not my job to conjecture, I suppose. But it is my job to return them for an inquiry."

Reagan lost the will to stand. He sank into the chair next to the settee and clasped his hands between his knees, staring at the braided rug beneath his boots. What had happened to his nice quiet little town? First the hurricane named Charlotte Brindle had arrived. A hurricane that had quite literally turned his world upside down and made him feel things that a man with a job like his had no business feeling for a woman. And now this marshal was here claiming that two of Wyldhaven's most upstanding citizens might be murderers? He shook his head, the shock still taking its toll on him.

This was bound to rouse all sorts of trouble, and that right on top of Charlotte already getting her heart set on upending the men's routines. The timing couldn't be worse—

A shadow passed below the parlor door and his eyes narrowed. Had Ma been listening just outside this whole time? That wasn't like her, but if she'd heard the Pottingers mentioned...

He drew his attention back to the marshal. "I can't stop you from questioning them, of course. But I would like to ask you one favor."

"Yes?"

"I'm asking you not to jump to a hasty judgment. I think if you give Dixie and Rose some time, you'll see they are upstanding and honest. I'm not asking for you to go against the law. But the people of this town are hardworking folks, and I don't want to put a damper on the Christmas season for them."

Zane spread his hands. "I'm a reasonable man, Sheriff Callahan. I've spent months hunting them down. I promise not to rush to judgment. What are a few more days in the scheme of things?"

That lifted Reagan's burden, but only slightly. "For that, I thank you. Now"—he stood—"I have to head back to my rooms above the jail, so I'll walk you back into town. Do you have a place to stay?"

"Indeed, I do." Zane's expression took on a calculating air. "I thought I would see what the accommodations at Dixie's Boardinghouse were like."

Chapter Six

ixie Pottinger was standing at the front desk of the boardinghouse when the bell above the front door rang. The moment she looked up and saw the tall, lanky man in the long brown leather coat striding across the entry, her heart leapt into her throat.

Something about him made her feel like a noose had just been slipped over her neck. She swallowed and forced her voice to be steady. "Good evening, sir. How may I help you?"

The man swiveled his Stetson through his fingers. Likely in his early forties, he had a nice face and gray-blue eyes with laugh lines at the corners. So what was it about him that had set her immediately on edge?

His gaze raked her up and down, but not in the way of a man looking at a woman. It was in the way of a lawman assessing a criminal. She wasn't sure what made her realize it, since she'd never been a criminal until recently, but there was something in his scrutiny that made a shiver run down her spine.

"Just need a room for a few weeks. Happen to have one available?"

If she had doubted her fears up to that moment, his accent affirmed them all. There was nothing quite like a Carolina drawl.

Dixie willed her hands not to tremble as she lifted a key from the back wall and turned the ledger toward him. She offered him a smile she hoped didn't look too stiff. "Yes certainly. A room was recently vacated. If you'll just sign here?"

Settling his hat onto his head, the man picked up the pen and scratched his name across the paper. He peered up at her from beneath the brim of his Stetson, then pushed the book back towards her. "Y'all been in these parts long?"

Dixie swallowed again. Tempted as she was to lie, she knew he'd easily be able to learn the truth from the other citizens of Wyldhaven. And that would only make her look guiltier in the end. So she forced the truth through her lips. "My mother and I run this boardinghouse. We've been here for just over a year."

With a calculating glint in his eye, Marshal Zane Holloway— as he'd signed his name—picked up the key from the counter and gave a little bow of thanks. "Thank you kindly for the room."

Dixie clenched her hands into her skirt, knowing he couldn't see the motion beneath the counter. She offered a nod, hoping he would just go up to his room and not ask her any more questions. She wished Ma wasn't so sick, because then they could pack up and make a run for it. And yet just the thought of leaving Wyldhaven sent a shaft of pain through her heart. They had made a life here. Many of the people were like family. She stamped one foot in frustration. It wasn't fair. Steven's brutality had interfered with their lives once already. Now it was set to do so again.

She should have known that their past would catch up to them eventually. Steven had been too powerful a man for people to simply forget about his death. Of course, he had kept such a perfect line between his private persona and his public persona. Would anyone even believe them when they said the man had been shot in self-defense—by his own mother!

Dixie watched the lawman make his way up the stairs to the

second floor, and absentmindedly rubbed her hand over her forearm. Beneath the material of her long sleeve she could feel the welts where Steven's cigars had left their marks. She could smell the scent of her own burning flesh. Hear the sizzle that always accompanied the grinding of the stubs into her skin.

All her hopes deflated, and weariness washed over her. Had she truly thought they could escape and never be caught?

No. If she were honest, she'd known this day was coming for a long time.

She was only glad that she'd finally worked up her courage to tell Flynn the story on her own before he heard it from some stranger on the hunt for them.

That, at least, was a blessing.

❧⸎⸎❧

He'd found them. After a cursed year, six months, and ten days, he'd finally found them. He'd known Mam wouldn't be able to resist writing a letter to her best friend Dolly Macon at some point. Of course, Dolly would never have told him anything, but Prissy Singleton who worked the post office in Birch Run was another matter altogether.

It had taken some doing to arrange a "chance" meeting with Prissy and then convince her that she must tell no one he was still alive. But with a good measure of his considerable charm, and a few well-timed secretive rendezvous, he'd pulled it off. Prissy had been like putty in his hands. Still, he'd been a little more than surprised when she'd brought him the envelope today. Postmarked with a stamp all the way from Cle Elum Washington.

Thankfully, he wouldn't need to hide out in this seedy hotel in Beaufort any longer. He grinned as he tossed the last of his things into his traveling case and retrieved his cane from the foot of the bed. Hefting the case, he stepped to the door and then paused to survey the room. Dash it, Prissy's skirt still protruded from under the bed! He hobbled over and used his cane to push the material back beneath the low frame. Satisfied that he'd hidden her well enough that she wouldn't be found for several days, he headed for the stairs. He'd paid for the room through the end of the week, so they wouldn't find her at least until then. That is if the South Carolina heat didn't get to the body and raise a stench sooner. Even in December it was warm enough for people to go jacketless here.

No matter. He'd used an alias, and he would be on this afternoon's train headed west under another alias, so all would be well.

In the foyer, he skirted around a bellhop dragging a chest toward the creaky old elevator and strode toward the doors. A cramp seized him when he was only halfway across the room. He pulled up with a gasp and a curse. How many times had he suffered the humiliation of working a cramp out of his thigh in public? He cursed again as he massaged and stretched the leg. After a long mortifying moment where several in the entry paused to see what he was doing, he limped the rest of the way out onto the walk and gestured for a hansom cab. He offered the man a forced smile along with instructions to take him to the train station, and gritted his teeth against the pain as he climbed the steps into the carriage.

Mam's aim had been faulty enough to save his life, but accurate enough to maim him for the rest of it. On most days that morose thought tormented him.

But not today.

Today he was able to set it aside.

Because he would soon enough have his revenge.

Chapter Seven

Liora spread her coins out on the bed and counted them again. Her stomach cramped with hunger, but she didn't dare spend the twelve cents for Ewan's devil hot chili and a roll that would likely be rock hard, or even the ten cents that Dixie charged for a bowl of oatmeal, an egg, and a slice of bacon over at the boardinghouse. Just the thought of bacon and eggs had her settling one hand over the ache in her midsection as her mouth watered.

She might not work for Ewan anymore, but she hadn't had a place to move to and he still expected his rent to be paid right on time. One dollar every week, or she would be out on her ear in the cold. And with the blustery way this December had started off, she didn't relish the thought of trying to find shelter through the worst of it. And she was still twenty-five cents short for this week's rent, due in two days.

Ewan was still upset that Deputy Rodante had forced him to sell her contract, and Liora knew that he wouldn't hesitate to evict her without any warning if she was even a penny short come Monday. The only reason she was allowed to stay here was because he didn't have another woman working for him yet. He figured getting some money from her rental of the room was better than letting it go empty and getting nothing.

So far she'd been blessed enough to be able to come up with the money each week, but the odd jobs were getting harder and harder to come by. She knew everyone in town was tight on funds this time of year. And she didn't want to accept charity. She had the regular job for Mr. King at the post office. She delivered letters for him out to the logging camps for fifty cents a week. But other than that, any money she made was from small jobs she could talk townspeople into letting her do for them. This week Mr. Hines from the mercantile had let her organize his store's back room. He'd paid her fifty cents, which she'd been elated about—especially since she'd gotten to work indoors out of the cold for two whole days.

Between that money and the pay Mr. King gave her every Friday evening, she would have had enough to pay her rent, but her cupboards had been bare of nearly everything. So she'd spent two bits on some food. A quart of beans had cost her ten cents. Adding three potatoes for a penny a piece, a small packet of salt, another of lard, and a one pound loaf of bread, had left her with just enough to buy a pound of stewing meat for five cents. This she'd asked Mr. Hines to wrap in eight one-eighth pound packages for her, which he'd most generously done. The meat was currently sealed inside an old tea-tin which she'd suspended out her window to keep cold. Thankfully, the freezing temperatures would keep it from going bad. She'd been allowing herself to use one packet of meat every three days.

And tonight she could take out another packet—her stomach rumbled at the pleasant thought. But that still didn't solve her problem of what to do in the next two days so that she could pay Ewan his dollar come Monday evening.

With a sigh, she opened her window and extracted a packet of meat from the tin as quickly as she could, then slammed the window against the blast of northern air that could nearly take one's breath away.

She added two sticks of wood to the small stove in the corner and set her one remaining pot onto it. She scooped half a teaspoon of lard into the bottom of the pot, let it melt then added the frozen chunk of meat.

She sighed and sank back on her bed, pulling the Bible that Joe had given her closer. The meat was going to take a while to thaw. She would add half a potato and a few of the soft beans she'd been boiling all day after a while, but for now, perhaps it was best she quit fretting. Ewan kept hinting that he'd be happy to give her back her old job, and she didn't want to get so discouraged that she even started contemplating that idea.

Tomorrow she would see if the sheriff had any work for her at the jailhouse. Tonight she would pray that God would see her plight. That He'd let her know what to do with her future. And that He'd send her enough work to pay her rent for another week.

Eyeing Dixie's door, Flynn paused at the head of the boardinghouse stairs and took a deep breath. The fact that his heart thundered in his chest when he was just here to make a medical call, had frustration coursing through him.

Especially now that she'd made her confession of marital status.

He had no business loving a woman who was still married—or even *maybe* still married—no matter what manner of ruffian that man might be. It was a good thing the man might already be dead, because if he ever ran into the reprobate there were any number of medical ways he could think of to induce pain and suffering.

Flynn swept one hand down the front of his jacket and angled a look toward the ceiling. *Father, forgive me. I know that attitude is not what you would want me to have. But, so help me, when I think about what he did to her...*

At that moment Dixie's door opened and she stepped out with a food tray balanced on one hand. "Oh, Flynn—Doctor Griffin. I'm glad you are here. I was just running Ma's dinner tray back to the kitchen." She pulled a face. "I'm afraid I wasn't able to entice her into eating much."

"Even eating a little helps. Just a few bites at each mealtime will go a long way to helping her regain her health." Flynn set his bag down to one side of the doorway and reached for the tray. "Here,—let me get that for you."

"Oh, no. It's okay. Why don't you go in and check on her and I'll be right up after I wash these things? I'm actually glad that you are here to sit with her till I get back. I'm concerned about her breathing. It has a strange sound to it."

She didn't give him a chance to protest, but brushed by him and trotted down the stairs without so much as another glance his way.

He loosed a breath and let her go without protest. Each time he'd come to check on Rose this week, Dixie's attitude toward him seemed to have grown more strained. Something was bothering her, but he hadn't been able to get her to confide in him about it. He supposed he should be thankful that she'd trusted him enough to finally tell him her whole story, yet that trust obviously didn't go too far if she wasn't willing to confide this seemingly new concern. Perhaps he was misjudging and it was simply her anxiety over Rose that had her so tense and on edge?

Whatever it was, he wasn't going to figure it out by standing here staring at the last place she'd vacated.

He took up his bag and started into the apartment, but a door across the way opened, drawing his attention. A middle-aged man with long dark hair stepped from the room and tipped his hat to Flynn. "Evening."

Flynn nodded and returned the greeting. When had this man arrived? He generally knew about any newcomers to town, but he hadn't heard that Dixie had a new guest staying at her place. Could this man be part of the reason Dix had been so uptight lately?

The man scrutinized him with a piercing assessment. "How do you know the Pottingers?"

The question raised Flynn's hackles. Shouldn't *he* be the one asking the questions?

Nevertheless, he had nothing to hide... "I'm the doctor in these parts. Name's Griffin. Flynn Griffin." He took two steps and offered the man his hand.

The man's grip was firm when they shook. "Pleased to meet you, Doc. I'm Zane Holloway, US Marshal."

Flynn's curiosity piqued at that. What was a US Marshal doing in Wyldhaven? "You just passing through?"

Zane rubbed his jaw. "No. I think I'm going to be here for a while. Say...who's the barber 'round these parts?"

"Isn't one by trade. Most people pay Mrs. Jacinda Callahan. Two bits a cut. She's been cutting my hair for years. You'll find her over on Second Street. Third house down to the—"

"South."

Flynn blinked, wondering how the man had known. Then nodded.

A glint of humor entered the marshal's eyes. "Mrs. Callahan and I have met. Pleasure making your acquaintance." The man tipped his hat and disappeared down the stairs.

Pondering the reasons that a US Marshal might be in town did nothing to make Flynn feel better. He thought of Dixie's story. How she and Rose had left her husband bleeding on the floor. Could the marshal be here about that? A knot that would surely turn to indigestion if he didn't quit his worrying tightened in the pit of his stomach. He sighed. He didn't suppose it was likely his business, so he decided to put the matter from his mind.

He pushed into the apartment and crossed the room to Rose's door, tapping lightly. "Rose? It's me, Doc. Okay if I come in?"

Dixie lingered at the bottom of the stairs, guiltily eavesdropping to see if she could learn anything more about the marshal. Disappointment surged when he didn't reveal anything other than what she already knew.

His footsteps began to descend the stairs, and Dixie rushed into the kitchen on quiet feet and plunked the tray down next to the sink. Between the hurt lingering in Flynn's eyes and the marshal popping up at unexpected intervals, she doubted she would have a moment's peace over the next few days. She flattened one hand against the panic that tightened her chest. She flicked a glance toward the door. Would the marshal follow her in here? She scooted into the pantry. Thankful that she'd insisted on a room large enough to house all her supplies, she pressed her forehead to the front of one shelf.

A breath dragged deep into her lungs didn't do much to calm her.

Everything seemed to be piling on top of her at once. Rose's sickness, the need to come out with the truth to Flynn to stop him from advancing his suit further, the marshal showing up.

She blew the breath out slowly between pursed lips.

She'd known in the back of her mind that one day the past would catch up to her. But she hadn't been prepared for the loss she'd felt the moment she'd laid eyes on the marshal. She hadn't realized how much she'd come to care about her friends here in Wyldhaven. She loved this town. She loved providing meals for people each evening. She loved offering clean lodging to those in need.

And now she was about to lose everything.

Rose's life hung in the balance.

Flynn's sense of propriety would have him keeping his distance—not that she'd ever let him get close.

Her freedom would certainly be taken from her once the marshal determined what they'd done to Steven. And that in turn would sully her reputation with her friends here in town.

The band that cinched around her chest impinged on her desire for another deep breath. Each inhale was short and shallow. Each exhale wheezy and weak.

She longed for a release of the pressure. *Cast all your cares on Him, for He cares for you.* The verse came unbidden to her mind. She used to believe that God actually cared. But that had been a long time ago. Before Steven. Somewhere in the middle of those horrifying years, she'd lost her faith. She couldn't point to a day when she'd given it up. It had seeped out a little here and a little there with each new trial she'd faced, until one day it was gone altogether.

And yet now she longed for the peace she used to have. She longed to trust that someone cared even more for her than she cared for herself. However, her life had proven that simply wasn't true. Where had God been in the years when she'd needed Him most? When she'd prayed for relief from the torment, not only for herself, but also for her mother-in-law? If only He had heard her cries, perhaps things would be different now.

Dragging in a fortifying breath, she pushed away from the

shelf and reached for the sack of potatoes. Last week Flynn had bagged a deer that he'd shared with everyone in town. The last of the meat would make a nice roast for tonight's diners. She gathered a jar of carrots, another smaller one of dried onions, and a clove of garlic.

As she made her way back into the kitchen, she rolled her neck in an attempt to release tension, and mentally ticked through a list of what else she needed to accomplish. With a little sigh, she set to scrubbing the potatoes.

A good portion of the day still remained, and there were certainly plenty of tasks to complete. It would be best if she quit lingering in longings and returned herself to the concrete tasks at hand.

Chapter Eight

Jacinda was bent over the dress pattern on her dining table, several pins clamped between her lips, when the knock came at her front door. She frowned. Was Mrs. King here early for her dress? Jacinda still had to get the last section of the hem finalized.

Her mind was still trying to decide the best lay of the material for this particular pattern when she opened her door.

The marshal stood on her porch, Stetson in hand, his long dark locks wafting in the chill December breeze.

Jacinda's eyes widened, and she quickly set to snatching the pins from between her lips. She miscalculated and one stuck fast into the tip of her first finger. She gasped, but quickly withdrew it and pressed her thumb over the area that was sure to bleed. "Marshal. What can I do for you?" Her pain made the words emerge with more harshness than she intended.

The man's eyes dipped to her fingers and filled with a touch of mirth that heightened her irritation. "Heard you were the barber in these parts and I wondered if I might trouble you for a haircut and a shave? But I'll hope you are handier with scissors and a razor than you appear to be with pins." He winked.

And for some reason, though she knew he was simply attempting to ease her tension with a little levity, the teasing only riled her more. But she wouldn't let him see that. "I'm in the middle of something right now, but if you give me half an hour you can return and I'll be prepared for you. The cost is two bits."

He dipped a small bow, hat pressed to his chest. "I'll be back then. And much obliged."

She felt only a little guilty as she watched him stride back into the icy snow that had started to fall a bit ago. Any other citizen of Wyldhaven, she likely would have invited in and offered coffee and small talk while she'd finished pinning her pattern, but this man set her on edge for some reason she couldn't quite put her finger on. Well, no. She *could* put her finger on at least one part of it. Her eyes narrowed as she remembered the conversation she'd overheard. She hadn't meant to linger so long by the door. But when she'd heard the Pottingers mentioned, she'd wanted to know what the marshal had to do with them. Guilt over her eavesdropping weighed heavy as she closed the door against the wind.

Belle appeared from where she'd been organizing the back room. "I'm finished in there. What else do you need me to do?"

Jacinda's worry pinched. She really ought to let the girl get home to help her own ma fix dinner. Yet propriety dictated that Belle needed to stay until after she'd cut the marshal's hair. It wouldn't be proper for him to be in her home alone with her.

She glanced around, wondering what else she could have Belle do. Her gaze landed on Mrs. King's unfinished hem. She'd planned to finish it herself this evening and save the expense of hiring it done, but now she had no choice. "If you don't mind, could you work on the hem for Mrs. King's dress? The marshal who's in town will be stopping by for a haircut and then you can leave as soon as he's gone."

Belle's eyes sparkled. "I heard he's fearsome handsome!"

"I don't suppose I noticed." Jacinda whirled and pretended to focus on the dress she was cutting out before the heat in her face gave away the lie.

Belle lifted Mrs. King's gray wool and sank into the sewing chair in the corner of the room. "Will you introduce me when he arrives?"

Jacinda suppressed a smirk. She might have known that Belle's interest in the man would come 'round to more than curiosity. "Yes, I can introduce you. But I wouldn't set my cap for the man, were I you. He's twice your age, and not likely to remain in these parts long. Besides that, he's a lawman."

"What's the problem with him being a lawman?" Curiosity underscored Belle's question.

"You would be wise to marry a man with a safe profession so you don't lose him before his time."

Belle seemed to think on that for a bit. "I suppose anyone could go before their time. Just look at my pa. I mean, we are thankful that he seems to be doing a little better now, but it was touch and go there with him for a while. And I suppose farming is about as safe a job as one could have in this modern day and age."

Jacinda sighed. "Yes. I suppose you are right." She didn't really want to carry this conversation further. She'd done her part to warn Belle away from both the man and his profession. What the girl did with that information was up to her.

For all the work Jacinda got done in the next thirty minutes, she may as well have invited the marshal to stay and simply cut his hair immediately. In the time he was gone she should have been able to pin the pattern and get it all cut out. However, she couldn't seem to focus on the task at hand, and realized twice that she'd laid the pattern on the wrong slant of the bias.

So she was just pinning the last piece of the pattern into place when she heard his knock on the front door once more.

She quickly folded the pattern and material onto the side table in the dining room, dragged a chair into the kitchen, and set the kettle over the hottest part of the stove, then hustled to answer the front door.

She hadn't quite realized how large the man was until the moment he stepped past her in the entryway. He towered over her by a good ten inches and his shoulders were twice again as broad as hers. He paused just past the entry and glanced back at her, obviously waiting for instructions on where to proceed.

Jacinda quickly stepped to his side and motioned him past the table and through to the kitchen. On the way, she paused by Belle in the corner of the dining room. "Marshal Holloway, may I present Miss Belle Kastain. Miss Kastain, Marshal Holloway."

The marshal pressed his hat to his chest and gave a courtly bow accompanied by his charming smile. "Miss Kastain, it's a pleasure."

Belle's cheeks turned a pretty pink as she demurred, "A pleasure indeed, Marshal."

Jacinda resisted a smirk. Perhaps Reagan would finally be free from the girl's cloying attentions. She led the rest of the way into the kitchen. No sound of footsteps followed her. Had Belle's flirting captured his attention? She turned to see what was keeping him, only to discover that he was directly behind her. She squeaked in surprise, and he nearly bowled her over.

Lightning quick, he captured her elbows and held her steady so she wouldn't tumble backward.

The blue of his eyes was even more captivating from this close proximity. They were actually more of a gray, shot through with silver shards that splayed out from the black center. Steel-dust blue encircled the edges, adding a hint of hardness. She didn't envy any outlaw who might cross this man's path.

One of his brows quirked upward, and his upper lip slanted into a sardonic smirk. His focus slipped leisurely over her features.

Her hands were still pressed to his chest. The man was lean and hard, seemingly chiseled from stone, despite the fact that most men his age carried at least a small paunch of extra weight with them. How long had they been frozen like this? Would he think she had thrown herself into his arms? The only thing still keeping her upright was his grip.

Jacinda felt heat sear her cheeks, and she scrambled for balance. "I'm sorry. I didn't hear you. I thought you might have—I might have...left you behind."

He gripped her arms until she was stable, then released her and retrieved his hat from where it had fallen to the floor. "I apologize. I've had to learn to be light on my feet over the years. Just sort of comes natural now."

Jacinda smoothed her hands over her waist and searched for the composure she so rarely lost. She spun in a full circle before she remembered she needed him to sit in the chair. Her hands trembled when she scooted it farther into the center of the room. "Just sit here, if you would. Your hat and coat can go on the peg there by the back door." She strode toward the stove.

She heard the soft swish as he hung his duster and Stetson and then the groan of the chair when he settled his weight onto it.

Pouring the warm water from the kettle into a bowl, Jacinda took a breath. This was just a haircut like any other haircut. There was no need for the butterflies that seemed to have taken flight in her stomach. She lifted the comb and scissors from the drawer where she kept them and faced the man, forcing a smile. "Tell me how you would like your cut, Marshal Holloway."

He blinked at her. "Don't rightly know as I've ever been asked that before. Short will do. Never know when I'll get to see a barber again."

Proof right there that the man wasn't planning to stick around for long.

"Very well." She said the words, but inside she cringed. The man's curls were pretty enough to grace the shoulders of a baroness. It was a shame he wanted them all cut off. She set the bowl of water on the table next to his right shoulder and the scissors and comb next to that. Then she draped her largest towel around the man's broad shoulders and took a slow breath. She'd always averred that for a proper cut, hair should be wet, but the thought of running her hands through his curls, especially after the tension-fraught scrutiny they'd just exchanged, had her quaking inside.

She rolled her eyes at herself. She was acting worse than Belle over her latest crush. Thrusting her hands into the water, she commenced dampening his hair with enough force that he glanced back at her over his shoulder. The impact of those gray-blue eyes did nothing to calm her. She curled her palms around both sides of his head and turned him to face forward once more. "Keep looking that way, please." Perhaps if she could get him talking that would distract her. "So, tell me how long you've been a marshal?" She lifted the comb and set to parting his hair into manageable sections.

"My father was a marshal. I never wanted to be anything else. He started having me travel with him when I was fifteen. I've been working the law ever since."

As he talked, Jacinda pulled in a breath and made the first cut. A long lock of curls drifted to the ground. The marshal didn't miss a beat as he continued to tell her about one of the first cases he'd worked with his father.

Jacinda kept her scissors snipping, chastising herself for lamenting so much over a few locks of hair.

The more he talked, the more she realized that once he took on a mission to capture a criminal, he didn't give up.

Her thoughts flitted to Dixie and Rose. The man was in for a surprise this time, because there was not even a possibility that those women were criminals. She worked her way from his right to his left and then paused before him to finish up the front. His story about an outlaw who had escaped and then been recaptured trailed to an end, and his studious gaze settled on her face. She found his scrutiny unsettling, so she voiced her question. "Seems like you are a man who doesn't give up until you catch your man, Mr. Holloway. But what happens if you are wrong? What will you do when you find that Dixie and Rose Pottinger aren't the criminals you suspect them to be? For I know you will find them innocent!"

He quirked a brow.

Jacinda winced. She hadn't meant to mention that.

"Your son told you why I'm here, did he?"

Her face blazed proof of her indiscretion. And no matter that she would rather not admit her eavesdropping, she wouldn't have this man think that Reagan had talked out of turn. "I overheard your conversation the other night."

He chuckled at that, but politely let the matter drop. "First, I never go into an investigation with a preconceived notion about my quarry. I always try to keep an open mind. Our system, after all, is based on 'innocent until proven guilty.' However, considering the fervency of your defense of your friends, Mrs. Callahan, perhaps we should wait to discuss this till you no longer have scissors in hand."

Refusing the smile his teasing tried to coax from her, she made the last few snips and then set the scissors down with a clunk, giving him a look. "Very well, the scissors are down, Marshal. You may proceed."

He scooped his hands back over the trim cut and shifted a bit on the chair.

Losing the length of his locks had certainly not harmed the man's good looks, though she would admit to leaving it a bit longer on top than she did with most men.

Jacinda swallowed and turned her focus to working up the lather for his shave. First she shaved a few small curls of soap into the bowl. Then added just a splash of warm water. The lathering brush made a soft swishing sound as she beat it. She returned her focus to the marshal, who still hadn't answered her question, and lifted her brow to let him know she awaited an answer.

He only grinned at her. "You'll forgive me if I don't reply just yet, Mrs. Callahan, since only momentarily you're going to have a straight razor to my throat."

She sighed and plunked the bowl of lather onto the table next to him. She tugged a fresh towel from the drawer. "Chin up, if you please." When he complied, she draped the towel below his neck. The lathering brush made soft scratching noises as it passed over the thick stubble lining his angular jaw, and Jacinda tried not to take notice of the way her legs brushed against his when she got too close. Most men closed their eyes while she shaved them, but not this man. His eyes remained open, and he watched her every move as though at the ready to defend himself should she decide to cut his throat.

On her last nerve, she snatched a breath, stepped back, and

plunked her hands onto her hips. "You needn't keep watching me like I'm one of your criminals, Marshal. I assure you that I don't normally linger outside doors to eavesdrop. Nor have I ever slit anyone's throat, and I don't intend to start now—no matter how irritating a man might be."

Humor crinkled the corners of his eyes. "I assure you, ma'am, I'm not watching you because I'm afraid of my throat being slit."

He didn't elaborate, but the connotation he gave to the words, and the way those gray-blue eyes drifted slowly down the length of her and back up again, had fire licking at her cheeks. She went back to work, but her hand was trembling so that she feared she might nick him. Thankfully, he must have taken pity on her, for he closed his eyes and she managed to finish without such an embarrassment. She stepped back. "Done. There's a mirror there by the back door. Take a look and tell me if you want anything changed." She strode to the sink and set to rinsing the lather and the brush.

He returned to her side after only a moment, hat in hand. "I assure you Mrs. Callahan that I'm not here to simply catch *any* criminal. I want *the* criminal. And if that's not either of the Pottingers, who everyone in this town seems to love so much, then it's not. But if it is one—or both—of them, then I won't hesitate to do my job." He set a quarter on the sideboard next to her, pushed his hat back onto his head, and tugged the brim in her direction. "Obliged, and good day."

With that, he swaggered from the room, leaving her staring for the longest time at the place where he'd left her sight. She prayed for Dixie and Rose's sakes that neither had been the one to shoot the missing man.

Steven Pottinger stepped from the train onto the Cle Elum platform. Despite the bitter cold that created billowing clouds of each breath, he was ever so thankful to be able to stretch his leg. Using his fist, he pressed hard on the knot of muscles that always seemed to form when he sat for too long. The platform beneath his boots was slick with thick sparkling frost. He'd have to watch his step and use his cane judiciously.

The conductor stopped next to him with a concerned expression. "Is there anything I can do for you, sir?" The conductor smiled as though he understood what Steven was going through, which only made Steven's anger simmer closer to the surface.

Yet he was *this close.*

She had mailed a letter from this town.

He needed information and he wasn't likely to get it if he started making enemies first thing.

Steven put on his best smile. "You can point me to the nearest watering hole." He could surely use a drink about now, both to relax and to warm him.

The man pointed down the street. "Harding's Saloon is just around the corner on Elm."

"Obliged." Steven tipped his hat and limped away before his pain made him do something he might regret.

Everything in this town seemed gray, from the frozen dirt streets to the weathered frosty cedar-shingle roofs. Even the windows of each building he passed were coated with the intricate lacy gray patterns of winter's hoar.

Thankfully, the walk from the train to the saloon loosened up his cramp a mite, and by the time he pushed through the batwing doors he was feeling almost human again. That didn't stop him from ordering two fingers of scotch.

The bartender just looked at him. "Whiskey? Or beer?"

Steven huffed. Of course they wouldn't have a gentleman's drink in these parts. "Whiskey," he grunted.

He downed half the potent brew as soon as it was placed in front of him, then waited for it to abate the pain. After several calming breaths he glanced around. How to go about finding them... That was the question.

Mam hadn't changed her name on the envelope she'd sent to Mrs. Macon. So it was likely both she and Dixie were still going by Pottinger. And if this saloon were anything like saloons in the rest of the country this was going to be the best place to get information.

He motioned for the saloon keeper's attention. "Looking for a couple of women. My mother and...my sister. Know of any Pottingers in town?"

The barman's lower lip protruded in thought as he polished a shot glass. "Pottinger... No. Can't say as I know anyone by that name around here."

Steven suppressed a growl. Now what?

Just down the bar, a man turned toward him. "Pottinger, did you say?"

Steven's anticipation leapt back to life. After all this time could it be that he had actually found them? He nodded to the man, taking a casual sip of his whiskey.

"There are Pottingers who run a boardinghouse over in Wyldhaven. A woman and her mother."

Steven's sense of accomplishment had his heart rate soaring. Finally he was going to have his justice! He was careful to keep all that he was feeling from his face, however. He only nodded to the man. "Much obliged. Does the train run to Wyldhaven?"

Both men shook their heads.

"Stagecoach leaves first thing in the morning," the barman offered. "Only runs through Wyldhaven on Saturdays."

They're not in this town. Steven resisted the impulse to dash his shot glass against the wall. He scrubbed fingers over the headache that had started to pinch his forehead, and finished off his whiskey, then motioned for another.

One more night. But just one. By this time tomorrow he would be smiling at the shocked look of terror on Dixie's face. And Mam's. Definitely Mam's.

What kind of woman shot her own son?

Chapter Nine

Charlotte stood ready and waiting for Reagan in front of his mother's house Saturday morning. It had snowed mid-week, and then the temperatures had plummeted. Though the sun shone with passion this morning, Charlotte's breath still clouded the air before her, and everywhere she looked the snow glistened as though the Creator had scattered handfuls of leftover star-bits over their mountain valley. Charlotte hunched into her coat with a shiver. She was glad she'd decided to give her students a few weeks off. Much as she loved them, she was looking forward to the break for the holiday as much as they were. With the weather being as cold as it was, and many of the students having to walk several miles to the school, it only made sense. She prayed the weather would be a little better after the first of the year when school resumed.

"Morning," Reagan called as he pulled the wagon to a stop. He helped her to the seat and then climbed up onto the buckboard beside her. Pulling a fur robe from beneath the bench, he tossed it across her lap. He also handed her a fur hat with ear flaps that could tie under her chin. "Best put that on," he said roughly. "Wind chill is picking up."

Charlotte was a little taken aback by his gruff mood, but she could already feel the sting of winter's chill nipping at her ears, and she was comforted by the warmth of the fur hat when she pulled it on. "Thank you."

Reagan only nodded. He slapped the reins against the horses' rumps and clucked to them to giddy up.

"How far is it out to this logging camp?"

"Fair bit" was all he replied, his breath clouding the air in a frosty puff before him.

Charlotte pressed her lips together. It seemed it was going to be a glacial ride out to the logging camp, in more ways than one.

They rode together in silence for five minutes before she finally glanced over at him. She couldn't help but wonder what had happened to the easy camaraderie he had been seemingly set on promoting between them just a few days before. "Something troubles you, Sheriff?"

To her surprise, he hauled on the reins and pulled the team to a stop right in the middle of the road. He turned on the bench to look at her.

She swallowed as the full force of his soft blue gaze landed on her.

He studied her for the longest time. His focus drifted leisurely over her features, and a muscle in his jaw bulged in and out. "This is no good, Miss Brindle. No good, at all."

Charlotte searched her memory for something she might have done wrong, but to no avail. "I'm sorry. I do not follow."

He released a lungful of air that clouded the space between them, then faced the road and slumped forward to prop his elbows against his knees. After a moment, he lifted his head to study the snowy field beside them. "What if we go to Mr. Heath and make our case? He's arriving in town today, you know."

Charlotte sucked in a breath. Make their case. Did he mean...?

Reagan turned his full attention on her once more.

She swallowed, hating to disappoint him, but... "We could lose our jobs."

He nodded. "That's true."

Her heart beat up into her throat. She would hate to be the cause of him losing his job, and yet it touched her deeply that he would be willing to approach Mr. Heath. "What would we say to him?"

Reagan scrubbed the back of one gloved hand over his jaw. "We would say we grew...attracted to each other before we knew about his rules."

Charlotte thought to the future. "If you lose your job as sheriff there are any number of other jobs that you could put your hand to. But what would I, whose only skill is teaching, be able to do about finding more work? We really mustn't risk it." At the hurt that flashed in his eyes, she hurried to add. "Though I wish we could."

The glimmer of a thought crinkled the corner of his brow. "I can't think why you would need to be employed were you my wife."

"Sheriff!" Charlotte gasped and twisted herself on the seat to face exactly forward, giving him only a view of the side of her face. A face that was likely blazing red if the heat pumping through her cheeks was any measure. She lifted her chin. "We've only known each other for just over four months. And I don't recall being *asked* if I wanted to be your wife!"

From her peripheral vision, she saw him squirm a little on the seat. He clucked to the horses and gave the reins a smart snap. "So you've just been toying with me then?"

"I have not! How could you say such a thing?" She loosed a most unladylike growl of irritation and clenched her hands into fists in her lap.

He was quiet for so long that she risked a quick peek to see what he was doing.

He angled her a glance that at first she thought was angry, but then his mouth slanted up into a grin. He leaned close and bumped her with his shoulder. "Good. Because I haven't been toying with you either."

Charlotte was on the verge of snipping that he hadn't been doing much of anything with her for the past several weeks, but she knew that wouldn't be fair, since he'd explained the situation with the telegram just last week. She let the silence stretch, but couldn't help grumbling to herself inside. Had he really thought that would suffice as a proposal? Men! The truth was, she might be tempted to give up her teaching if it meant she could become Mrs. Reagan Callahan, but he was going to have to do a sight better with his asking if he expected her to say yes.

The silence had stretched for a long while when Reagan finally spoke again. "Something the marshal said after dinner the other night has been bothering me all week." Reagan glanced over at her, one corner of his mouth tipped down in puzzlement. "How much do you know about Dixie and Rose's history?"

So they were done talking about themselves and Mr. Heath, were they? "Dixie and Rose?" Charlotte couldn't help the surprise that shot through her at his choice for a change of topic. "Not much, I suppose. Why do you ask?" Charlotte clenched her hands tight beneath the lap robe, feeling a tension she didn't quite understand because it had nothing to do with the conversation they'd just had.

Reagan jostled the reins. "The marshal claims that Dixie and Rose killed a man back east and came here to hide."

Charlotte gasped, all thoughts of proposals and matrimony fleeing. "Of all the insidious—he's obviously mistaken!"

Reagan shrugged. "That's what I told him, but he seems certain he's right."

Indignation straightened every muscle in Charlotte's back. "What do we even know about that man? Do we even believe he's a real lawman?"

Reagan jutted his jaw to one side and massaged it with one hand. "Yes. I checked into him. First thing the next morning I had Ben send a telegram to his office back east to make certain."

"He'll ruin Christmas!"

"I asked him to approach his investigation with an open mind, and he assured me he would. That was the best I could do."

Charlotte felt a small measure of relief at that. "Well that's something, at least. Poor Dixie!"

They settled into silence after that. The only sounds that broke the stillness were the jangle of the trace chains, the occasional snapping of a snow-weighted branch in the forest, and the squeak of the wheels over the skiff of fresh snow that had fallen the evening before.

By the time they arrived at the logging camp, however, the sun was high and warm enough that it had turned the snow into rivulets of mud and ice.

As Reagan handed her down from the wagon, Charlotte grimaced and tried to pick the driest spot for her feet to land. She lifted her skirts immediately upon touching the ground, but to no avail. The bottom inch of her hem was already befouled with mud and evergreen needles.

Reagan leaped down beside her, splattering mud even higher on her skirt. His brow furrowed as he took in the splotches. "Sorry about that." Placing one hand to her back, he guided her around a large pile of limbed logs. "The foreman's office is this way."

Charlotte felt her stomach begin to tighten as she followed Reagan's lead. She'd written out her speech and practiced it all week. She only hoped the foreman was a reasonable man..

Reagan pushed open the door on a tiny log cabin and allowed her to step through before him. A desk sat immediately before the door, and a grizzly bearded man looked up from the paperwork he was bent over. Surprise lit his eyes when he took note of Charlotte stepping through the door. By the time Reagan stepped in after her and pulled the door shut against the chill outside, there was barely room for the two of them to stand without bumping into each other.

Reagan took a step forward to stretch a hand out to the camp foreman, but in doing so his boot tromped on the hem of her skirt, jerking her off balance.

Charlotte collided into his side, giving a soft gasp of surprise and embarrassment.

"I apologize," Reagan said, settling his hands on her arms to steady her and set her back. "Are you alright?"

Oh for crying in her buckets. Why did this room have to be so small and the man before her so good looking, and her boss so adamant that she not be allowed to have callers?

She was saved from the heat blazing up her neck when the man behind the desk stood. "It is I who should be apologizing." He held out his hands in a rueful manner. "The room is not set up for visitors. How may I help you?"

Reagan gave Charlotte one more assessing look as if to really make sure she was okay before he turned towards the grizzly logger. "Tom Harris, may I present Miss Charlotte Brindle, the new schoolteacher in Wyldhaven. Miss Brindle has something she would like to discuss with you about a Christmas festival."

Tom's eyes narrowed slightly. He turned his look on Charlotte. "A Christmas festival?"

Charlotte supposed there was nothing for it but to launch in with her prepared speech. "Good day, Mr. Harris."

The man nodded.

"It is my understanding that Wyldhaven does not have a Christmas festival each year because your loggers protest it. Is this true?"

Reagan stepped back, not that he had much room to do so as the door in the tiny log room was only inches from him. But he wanted to be able to assess the emotions he knew were going to be crossing Tom's face during this conversation. He gripped his hands behind his back and waited with anticipation.

Even now Tom's face had paled slightly at Charlotte's question. Tom looked like he would like to sink into his chair, but since there were no chairs to offer his visitors, etiquette dictated that he remain standing. "I-i-if my men protest a Christmas festival, Miss Brindle, it is only because they protest not getting paid. We do not get paid unless we deliver logs to the mill. Unfortunately, the Christmas season is one of the best times of the year for making quick work of hauling logs. This year especially, since we've had such a light snowfall."

"Yes, I understand that. And of course no one would deny the men an opportunity to make the money they need so desperately to keep feeding their families."

Reagan tucked a grin away in his cheek. He'd give her credit for diplomacy.

"Well then you understand." As though he assumed the conversation finished, Tom started to sit.

But Charlotte motioned for him to wait. "And yet on the other hand, Mr. Harris, what if we could accomplish both things at the same time? A Christmas festival *and* getting logs to the river so they can be floated to the mill?"

Tom regained his feet and folded his arms across his chest. He tilted her a look that said he would like to see how she was going to explain this.

Reagan did the same, for he had yet to hear Charlotte clarify how she planned on accomplishing her mission.

"When Sheriff Callahan escorted me in," Charlotte said, "I noticed a pile of limbed logs lying just outside the door. And I confess I was quite pleased to see it, Mr. Harris. Because it fits in rather nicely with the plan I have concocted. Well, concocted might not be the right word, but planned. The plan I have planned." Charlotte's face seemed to pale a little.

A grin did slip free this time before Reagan could check it, but he quickly swallowed it and was thankful to note that Charlotte hadn't seemed to notice. He ought to be more sympathetic to her plight. But they'd been doing just fine for several years without a Christmas festival. So she was going to have to win this battle on her own.

"My idea is this, Mr. Harris," Charlotte pressed on. "You form your men into two teams, or three, or four, if you feel that would be better. Each team will prepare their own pile of logs ahead of time as per usual. But on the night of the festival, we will all meet here. Adult spectators will each pay two bits to watch. Part of the festival will be a contest to see which team can load the logs onto their wagons the fastest. Then the race will continue in a second stage from here to the creek. Whichever team gets to the creek at the Wyldhaven Landing the fastest will win that stage of the race. From there a third stage of the race will commence with the men unloading their logs into the creek, and whichever team unloads their logs the fastest will win that segment. After this I will beg you to encourage your men to allow the logs to float for the night and come to the Town Square, where we will have a Christmas festival. Competition is proven to be good for productivity. And I think the men will be quite pleased with the amount of work that gets accomplished even while taking a couple of hours to spend honoring our Lord and enjoying their families."

Well... He did believe she had done it. Reagan pinched his lips between his teeth, lifted his brows and rocked up on the toes of his boots as he studied Tom Harris.

Tom's mouth hung open slightly, and Reagan could see the cogs whirring in the man's head. He grinned. The man would likely be hiring Charlotte to provide productivity ideas after this. For Reagan had no doubt that the men would go all out for the next two weeks in advance preparing their wagons and their crews for quickly loading logs and winning the races.

Tom stroked a hand the length of his beard, and Reagan could tell that he actually liked the idea but was leery of stating so too quickly. Finally after a long moment, he dipped his chin in a nod. "I do believe that might be plausible, Miss Brindle."

Charlotte was so elated that she actually gave a little hop. "Oh bless you!"

Reagan grinned at the red flooding the burly foreman's face.

Charlotte didn't seem to notice. "Thank you, Mr. Harris. I think this will be a lovely time. Thank you, thank you, thank you for agreeing to urge your men to participate. And please do remind them to put safety first during the competitions. I'd hate for someone to be hurt on account of me wanting to bless the children with a festival."

Tom nodded. "Yes, ma'am. Happy to oblige. You have a good day now."

"Oh yes, we will, I'm sure!" Charlotte spun to exit the room and crashed fully into Reagan. She gasped. "Oh, I'm sorry."

Reagan grinned and reached behind himself to open the office door. Too bad he couldn't find some reason to delay their departure a little, because standing this close to the beautiful Miss Brindle was no hardship at all.

Even with Tom laughing at him from beyond her shoulder.

Chapter Ten

Saturday at noon, Dixie was cleaning up the last of Ma's and her lunch dishes and putting away the leftovers when there was a knock at her back door. She quickly rinsed her hands and dried them on her apron as she moved to see who was there.

Kincaid Davis stood at the base of her steps, hat in hand. His dark mop fell in unruly waves across his head, and his brown eyes were always a bit broody, but my, the boy was going to be a lady-killer in just a few years. She marveled that though it seemed she'd been his age only a couple years previous, in reality seven years separated them. She felt like an old woman at twenty-two.

"Kin." She smiled at him. He was probably here looking for work. She liked to hire him because he worked hard, was always appreciative, and was ever willing to do her chores in exchange for food. Despite that, when she could afford to give him money for his work, she tried to do so, because she knew how desperately he needed it. Well she remembered the days when her own father had spent every spare—and sometimes not spare—penny on drink. "Looking for some odd jobs today?"

His feet shuffled. "Actually, ma'am, I was wondering if you might be interested in some fresh fish for your diners?"

Fresh fish sounded lovely. "Absolutely! What are you charging?"

He glanced down and kicked at a frosty clump of grass in the shade by the back steps.

She could see his mind working, calculating.

He lifted his gaze to hers and gave his hat a twist. "Truth is, I'm going fishing with Washington Nolan anyhow, so…what price would you think is fair?"

Dixie suppressed a smile. This boy was going to go far. Creating enterprise out of something he would have done anyhow. The lad was quite the mischief-maker about town, but Dixie liked his entrepreneurial spirit that never seemed to be quashed by his father's neglect.

She pretended to think, but she already knew the generous offer she was going to make, and she had work to finish, so she didn't ponder for long. "How about twenty cents for every brace you bring me? And I'll take up to six braces each week, for as long as you keep them coming. To serve a meal, however, I'll need at least three good-sized braces at a time."

She saw his mind calculating and knew only a moment later that he'd realized he could be making a dollar and twenty cents each week.

His eyes widened, but only for the briefest of seconds before he carefully recomposed himself and spoke as though this were an everyday business transaction for him. "Yes'm. I think I can do that."

"Lovely. I'll have money waiting for you this evening if you think you can bring me six today?"

He nodded. "Yes'm." He slid his hat back on his head and tugged the brim toward her, and then he turned and casually strolled in the direction of the footbridge.

Dixie closed the door, but nudged the curtain to the side just enough so she could still watch him. The moment her door clicked shut, the boy leapt into the air with a pump of his fist, and then took off running as fast as his legs could carry him.

Dixie smiled.

"That's a nice thing you did for the boy."

She gasped and spun around, one hand flying to her throat.

The marshal leaned in the doorway between the kitchen and the dining room. He lifted his hands, one of which clasped his hat by the crown. "Sorry. I didn't mean to startle you. I know I'm late, but I wondered if I might trouble you for a plate of the lunch that smells so good?"

Dixie smoothed her hands over her apron. "I'm sorry, but ever since school started, I haven't been serving luncheon to guests. McGinty's next door usually has some chili on the stove."

His face twisted into a scrunch. "I've had McGinty's Devil's Chili every nooning for the past week." He glanced longingly at the chicken-fried steak and mashed potatoes she was ready to put into the ice box. "I'll make it worth your while."

Everything in her resisted feeding the man who was here to steal her life from her. And yet... She plunked her hands on her hips. "Very well, but the only thing I want is for you to let me tell you my side of the story." If God wasn't going to help her, maybe she could help herself by getting out in front of this.

The marshal blinked at her. "Your side of what story?"

Dixie hesitated. Could it be that he really wasn't here to investigate her? Or was he bluffing? She narrowed her eyes. He was bluffing. "Marshal, I've known from the first moment you walked in the front door of my boardinghouse why you were here, so please let's not play games." She set to dishing up his plate. "Why haven't you questioned—or even arrested—me before now?" She thrust the plate into the warming oven. Five minutes and the food ought to be piping hot again.

The marshal pointed to the small kitchen table in the corner. "May I?"

She nodded and set about to wash the two dishes she'd just emptied.

He eased into one of the chairs and hooked his hat over the spindle of another. Folding his hands atop the table, he looked at her gravely. "I haven't questioned you because I never rush to judgment, Mrs. Pottinger. I wanted to observe for a while before I set in to questioning you. Also, Sheriff Callahan let me know that he felt both you and your mother-in-law were fine upstanding citizens and that I should give you every benefit of the doubt."

Dixie's hands stilled in the sudsy water. Reagan had known, and hadn't warned her. Yet, what did she want from him? She certainly didn't want him to play favorites for her and jeopardize his duty to the law. She returned to scrubbing the bowl. "That was kind of him."

The marshal nodded. "I thought so. As for arresting you...I'll not hide the fact that it's certainly a possibility, if I determine it necessary." He relaxed against the back of the chair that seemed too small for his large frame, and hooked one arm around the spindle so his arm rested on the top of the slats. "So, tell me your story, Mrs. Pottinger."

Dixie's jaw jutted to one side. If she told him their story would that be proof enough of a crime for him to arrest her? Was it even a crime to defend the life of someone who was about to be killed? "Is self-defense, or the defense of someone who is about to be killed by another, a crime, Marshal?"

The marshal scrubbed one hand over his jaw, studying her with serious eyes. "Mostly no. But there are always extenuating circumstances."

Extenuating circumstances... Dixie released a breath. How

well she knew about that. How often had Sheriff Berkley back in Birch Run told her she was living under extenuating circumstances?

Still... She was tired of running. So maybe she should tell all and plead mercy for Rose who had only been trying to save her life.

With that decision made...where to begin?

She'd just told Flynn all the sordid details only a few days ago, so she decided to simply stick with the same order of events. When she delivered his plate to the table, she rolled up her sleeve and showed him the scars where Steven used to stub out his cigars. She strode to the sink once again and stood looking out onto the frosty riverbanks as she finished the telling. She told him how she had tried every avenue available to her, including showing the sheriff back home her fresh burns and begging him to bring her before a judge so she might plead her case there. But the sheriff had only told her she would be wasting the court's time because South Carolina didn't allow divorce for any reason. She told him how she knew that even if the state had granted her the divorce, Steven wouldn't have stood for it. He would have taken his retribution whether she was seen as his wife or not. And so in the end they'd been left at his mercy—of which he had none.

After she told of the way Steven had taken the baseball bat to her and how Rose had shot her own son, she turned to face the marshal.

The food on his plate remained untouched.

"If Rose takes any of the blame for stepping in to save my life, I should take more, because I'm the one who talked her into running. I knew that if fresh burns and purple and gold bruises around my neck—which I kept hidden from others with a high collar—couldn't induce the sheriff to help me, nothing would. Certainly not the fact that Steven was lying in a pool of his own blood. I had no reason to think this time would be any different, and I couldn't bear to think what Steven might do to Ma—or to me—if he recovered. So we ran. Lord, forgive us, we left him there bleeding on the floor and we never looked back. So you see, his death was my fault."

The lawman shifted in his seat. "Actually, your husband's body was never found. We thought you two might have buried him somewhere."

Cold terror slithered down Dixie's spine. "You mean to tell me he's gone missing?"

"He was not in the house the next morning when the sheriff went to the house after seeing you two boarding the train." He looked up and assessed her with those hard gray eyes that seemed to be able to see to the very marrow of her bones. "Are you sure you told me the whole story, Mrs. Pottinger?"

Dixie felt a rush of lightheadedness and pressed fingers to her temples. "H-his body was n-never found?" She knew she was repeating his words, but needed to hear them again to comprehend them.

The man nodded. "Indeed, he hasn't been seen since the day you two fled town. The house was nearly destroyed, and there was blood everywhere, but no body."

Dixie lost all the strength from her legs and collapsed into the chair across the table from him.

The marshal only studied her.

"The broken tables and the lamps and the holes in the walls were from Steven's bat. He'd chased me through the house for"—she rubbed her fingers across her forehead—"I don't know... Quite some time before he caught me and... We left him lying by the door. He was bleeding badly, but we never touched him after we shot him. And that's the truth of it."

Marshal Holloway rubbed one hand down the lower half of his face in a weary gesture. "After *we* shot him?"

Dixie waved away his pointed question, realizing that he probably thought she was changing her story. "What I said was the truth, Marshal. Rose shot her son, but I've always thought of the incident as something we did together. A...horror we escaped together. The truth is, if I had found him beating his mother like that, I would have shot him too."

She massaged her thumb into the palm of her opposite hand. "What will I do if he comes? It seems as a woman I have no legal recourse. And now, from what you say, he could even at this very moment be on his way here." She threw her hands into the air. "I have told you my story, and now I am at *your* mercy, Marshal. I know I'd rather face trial for attempted murder than ever go back to living with that man again, so maybe it is best that you arrest us and cart us back home for trial."

The marshal pushed his still-untouched plate back. He folded his hands on the table before him and hung his head for a moment. "You understand that despite the evidence on your arms, I can't just take your word for it?"

Dixie felt exhausted. She sank against the slats of the chair. "Yes. I suppose I do know that."

The marshal simply looked at her for a long time, searching her face. Dixie let him look. She was tired of hiding. Tired of fearing. Tired of worrying every single day that Steven might be coming after them.

Finally, he slid a half dollar across the table and tugged the plate closer.

Dixie stood. "Half dollar is too much. I'll get you some change."

"Keep it." He lifted his fork.

She eyed the coin for only a moment, then decided not to fight him. "Want me to heat that up for you again?"

One of his lips quirked upward. "This would beat McGinty's Devil's Chili if it were frozen solid and laced with nails."

Dixie returned his smile with a tired one of her own. "I'll leave you to it then. Thanks for listening to me."

He nodded.

"I need to go check on my mother-in-law. Please just put the plate in the sink when you are finished."

He nodded again, and with that, she left him there.

If she still prayed, she would have asked God to help him see the truth in her words. But she didn't see the point in asking God for help when He'd never helped her in the past.

Chapter Eleven

~⟡~

Washington Nolan met Kincaid Davis at the river, pole in hand. Worms were hard to find this time of year, but Pa had let him take a chicken leg, which was almost just as good. He couldn't wait to get his line in the water. There was nothing like the taste of fresh trout pulled direct from an icy river.

Kincaid greeted him with a grin. He was perched on their usual log with a fire already burning cheerily in the carefully rock-framed firepit. Everyone round these parts knew that if a fire got out of hand it could be the death of them all.

Washington settled on the other side of the fire and worked some of the chicken onto his hook, using a bit of extra fishing line to ensure it didn't come loose.

"What took you so long?" Kin needled.

"Had to do chores. Don't you have to do chores?"

Kin snorted. "My pa ain't never home to care one way or the other."

Wash tossed his hook into the current, pondering on that. Pa might be raising them on his own since Ma's passing two years back, but at least Pa was there for him and his brothers when he wasn't at work. He bought food when it was needed. He cooked. He even made them keep the house in a semblance of order and read to them from the Good Book every night. Wash had often envied Kin his freedom to do whatever he pleased, but he couldn't help but be thankful that Pa at least made it clear he cared for his boys. The thought of food reminded him... He dug through his satchel and pulled out the paper-wrapped package.

"Brought you a couple ham and egg sandwiches." He tossed it over.

Kin snatched the missile in midair. He set to unwrapping the string in the blink of an eye but, like always, he made his appreciation known. "Much obliged."

Wash nodded and pretended great interest in adding another stick of wood to the fire. Often Kin's hands trembled from hunger when he gave him food, and it pained him to see it. Thankfully, that didn't happen as often now that they were older, because Kin had gotten better at hiding his stashes of food from his pa so he couldn't sell it for booze. Even so, Wash tried to bring his friend food whenever they got together. Hopefully, they'd get a good enough catch today that Kin could take some home and cook his pa a decent meal tonight.

The sun rose above the tree line and steam lifted from the snow-covered riverbanks like wisps of fairy dust. This was his favorite time of year. He loved sitting on the banks of a river, pole in hand, simply soaking in the quiet beauty of nature all around him. The large maple above them stretched bare branches toward the winter-blue sky. Icicles dripped from the branches in several places, and the sun caught them now and fragmented into silver sun-spots on the snow at the boys' feet. Golden-crowned sparrows chirped lustily from a branch where they fluffed and sunned themselves, and out on the river a fish jumped as though to taunt them with its intelligence.

Beside him, Kin sighed in satisfaction and tossed the paper wrappings and strings from the sandwiches into the flames.

Wash pulled in his line to check his bait. "Nice that Miss Brindle gave us a couple weeks off."

Kin grunted. "It's gonna be boring. We should do something to liven things up around here."

Satisfied that his bait was still in place, Wash tossed his line back into the water. "I hear there's gonna be a Christmas shindig this year."

A roll of his eyes revealed Kin's thoughts about that. "Bunch of adults standing around yammering about this and that. Not my idea of fun. I was thinking of something exciting."

A premonition of impending trouble tickled the back of Wash's neck. "Kin, you ain't gonna do something stupid, are you?"

Kin grinned, his dark eyes sparkling. "It'll only be stupid if I get caught."

Knowing his friend's penchant for causing trouble, Wash eyed him warily. "What are you planning?"

Kin's brows pumped mischievously. "So I was in the post office the other day dropping off a letter for Pa. Ben King got a telegraph message while I was in there. Turns out old man Heath is arriving on this afternoon's stage."

Wash swallowed. Mention of a stage could not be good. "Yeah?" He felt his heart bump against his ribs, but he kept his features masked and pretended the need to check his bait once more.

"So...? Just think how fun it would be if we robbed the stage and got away with it? And all with Old Man Heath right there on board!"

Washington pursed his lips. How was he going to talk Kin out of this one? He'd heard that special note of determination in his voice before, and he knew that when Kin got that level of excitement pumping through him, there was almost never anything he could do to talk him out of his stupid plans. "Kin! We can't rob the stagecoach! Mr. Heath is the one who's made it possible for your pa to have a job! Mine too!" And that was when it hit him like a bucket of ice water to the face. Kin's pa was mostly sober when he didn't have any money to spend, but the minute the man had even a handful of pennies, it was off to the bar for him, and Kin was left to fend for himself. "You ain't aiming to get your pa fired, are you?"

Kin blew out a breath of disgust. "Naw. I'm just funnin' with you."

Wash eyed him suspiciously. "Kin!"

Kin grinned. "Okay, maybe I really am thinking about doing it, but I don't expect you to come with me."

"If that ain't the dumbest thing I've ever heard!" Wash pushed Kin's shoulder.

"Hey!" Kin laughed. "You're disturbing my line, if you don't mind."

"Well you just tell them when you are standing trial that your pal, Washington Nolan, tried to talk you out of your stupid plan."

Kin chuckled.

Wash decided to try and change the subject. Maybe Kin would forget about the whole plan if he got him to think about something else. "Saw you eying Belle Kastain in class the other day."

Kin snorted. "Belle is one of those girls that is like a poisonous flower. She's pretty to look at, but all her flashy colors are a warning sign to anyone paying attention that they better stay away. Far away. Besides, doesn't Deputy Rodante have his cap set for her?"

Wash pondered on that. "I'm not so sure. He's taken her to a few socials, but I ain't never seen the love struck look in his eye like the sheriff has for Miss Brindle."

Kin socked him in the arm. "Or like you have for Zoe."

Wash felt the heat of that truth burn through him like a brushfire. Thankfully, just then Kin's line was taken, and all Kin's attention turned to hauling in his catch.

And Washington was easily able to change the subject after they had spitted the trout over their fire. "What kind of bait are you using? My chicken meat obviously ain't working."

Kin nudged an old coffee tin toward him with the toe of his boot. "Dug some ol' grubs from a rotting tree 'tween my house and here. Help yourself."

They fished for most of the morning, and by the time they left, they'd not only eaten a fish each cooked over the fire, but they each had a stringer of trout to take home for their dinners and Kin had a whole extra creel that he said he'd promised to Miss Pottinger at the boardinghouse.

They parted ways without ever mentioning the idea of robbing the stage again, but Washington couldn't seem to shake a heavy foreboding that Kin's intentions had not changed.

His spirit was weighed down with a melancholy that couldn't be lifted. Not even when he came across Zoe picking rose hips in the field just outside of town.

<hr />

Weariness weighted Dixie's eyelids as she sat next to Ma's bed inside the steamy tent. She dipped the cloth into the cool water, wrung it out, and carefully dabbed the moisture from Ma's sweat-dampened brow. Her inhales and exhales rattled in a way that made dread crawl into Dixie's bones.

"Ma, can you hear me? Would you like a sip of water?"

Ma's eyes opened slightly, and her tongue darted across dry lips.

Relief relaxed Dixie's shoulders. "It's good to see you awake. I'm sure you are thirsty."

Panic had been building ever since her talk with the marshal. She wanted to gather Ma up and run again. Leave this place behind. Steven's body, never found! That meant he really was somewhere out there, just as she'd feared.

But Ma was in no shape for flight, so instead she reached for the cup. "Here—this will help." She held the spoon to her mother-in-law's lips and was thankful to see that Ma apparently had enough strength today to lift her head, if only slightly. Dixie coaxed five teaspoons of water into her before she waved away any more and her head fell back to the pillow.

Thinking Ma would immediately return to sleep, Dixie set the cup down and stood to straighten the bedding, but the older woman's hand clutched Dixie's forearm with a surprisingly strong grip. Dixie's gaze flew to hers.

Ma tugged her closer, earnestness in her eyes. "Forgive me. Please?" There was such an urgency to the words!

Dixie frowned. "Forgive you? Whatever for?"

Ma's grip slackened, and her gaze drifted toward the sheets draped over the string above her. She stared as though seeing into the past, her chest barely rising and falling with each rattled breath. "I...didn't...kill him. I should have...protected you better. He...will—" A wracking cough seized her, and Dixie helped her sit up.

Ma had known? All this time she'd known he was alive? Did she know where he was? If he was coming? Dixie drew in a breath meant to abate the hysteria that threatened to capsize her. She couldn't let Ma see any of her trepidation. Not in her present state.

Dixie's concern mounted as the coughing continued. "You mustn't fash yourself so. You're going to wear plumb out." She did her best to keep her voice steady and the chiding gentle as she rubbed circles on Ma's back.

For a long moment, she wondered if this was to be Ma's end. But then the coughs stopped and Ma was finally able to take a full breath.

Dixie carefully eased her back down.

Ma clutched for her once more. Her eyes held insistence that Dixie listen. "I aimed low. He will come."

Another crest of panic surged, but Dixie again did her best to keep it hidden. She soothed one palm over the plump veins and angular bones of Ma's age-spotted hand. Forced words that she didn't really believe past her lips. "If he was going to come, he would have come after us by now, don't you think? We'll deal with him if the time comes. For now you just worry about getting yourself better, hmmm? And let's remember that Sheriff Callahan is nothing like Sheriff Berkley back in Birch Run."

That thought seemed to ease some of Ma's tension, and she relaxed further into soft feather pillows. After an extended minute where Dixie waited to see if she would say more, Ma's eyes drifted shut, and her breathing even seemed a little easier now.

Just like that, the strength left Dixie's legs and she collapsed into the chair.

Ma's breathing deepened to that of sleep.

Dixie scooted the chair back from the bed and let the sheet fall between her and her mother-in-law so she didn't have to guard her expression so carefully. When Dixie lifted her palms to cover her face, both hands quaked. She gritted her teeth against the press of panic that bade her to give in to tears. First the marshal said Steven's body had never been found. And now Ma insisted that Steven was most likely still alive. Just the thought sent a cold wave of terror through her.

She would not cry! That man had already taken more than his share of her peace and tranquility. She would not give him another moment of space in her mind!

But the desire to banish him from her thoughts and actually accomplishing such were two entirely different things.

Despair drained the last of her energy. She was tired of trying to be strong on her own. Tired of wondering what she had done—what Rose had done—to deserve the treatment Steven had doled out to them each day, while at the same time knowing there was no logical answer.

Though she had assured Rose that Sheriff Callahan wasn't anything like Sheriff Berkley, she also knew that even Reagan would be bound to the laws of the land. If Steven came, there wouldn't be much Reagan could do to intervene on their behalf.

She pushed the tenting sheets back from one corner of the bed, then slumped forward until her folded arms could form a pillow. If only she could retreat into the oblivion of sleep. She glanced at the contraption of sheets currently keeping steam close to Ma, and guilt nagged. She shouldn't be longing for retreat or sleep when Ma needed her so much—when she had plans to make about what to do if Steven did come.

If he came, she would have to face him again. She would have to be strong. She would have to make sure that he could never hurt her or Ma again. That realization filled her with icy resolve, and for the first time since her talk with the marshal, she felt like she could breathe again.

There was so much work to do. She needed to fetch new hot water for the steaming pots. The marshal's bedroom needed to be cleaned, and the evening meal needed to be prepared and served. There was no time for slumber. And yet with her decision made, it was as though all her energy had drained out of her.

How long would they have to wait?

It could be years.

It could be moments.

For Dixie knew something with absolute certainty. If Steven was alive—and both the marshal and Rose seemed to believe he was—he would come. His sense of revenge wouldn't let him live any other way.

And this time when he came she would be ready for him. She refused to live with the terror he invoked for even one more day. The soft quilt welcomed her weight, and she gave in to the tug of slumber.

Chapter Twelve

Flynn leaned over his patient in the back of the wagon that sat before McGinty's. The wounded man's friends had brought him in from Camp Sixty-Five when the tree he'd been sawing had split up the middle and kicked back into his sternum. "Widow Makers," they called such trees. A fairly rare occurrence, yet common enough to warrant a label. And sadly in this case, though the man was single without a wife and children to leave behind, the tree would indeed come out the winner. The man's chest was so crushed there was nothing Flynn could do but keep him comfortable. The logger also had a large concave dent on the side of his head, and hadn't come around since the incident. He wouldn't make it through the night.

Heart heavy, he reached for the laudanum bottle in his bag.

"Can you fix him, Doc?" This from one of the man's anxious friends.

Flynn sighed. He hated this part of his job. He took his time uncorking the laudanum before he looked up at the man. "I'm sorry. No."

All three men shuffled their feet. Varying expressions of sorrow cloaked them. One man folded his arms and worked the toe of his boot into the dirt at his feet. Another tipped his head back and blinked rapidly at the sky while his jaw worked from side to side. The third gripped his neck and studied the wounded man, seemingly unable to grasp that they would never have another conversation. "He stopped for a drink from his canteen about ten this morning, and gave me a hard time because my missus had brought out the lunch I forgot. I haven't even eaten the lunch yet."

Flynn understood the shock. After doling out some laudanum into a smaller, bottle, he jumped from the back of the wagon and handed it to the man who had spoken. "If he starts to come around, you can give him as much as thirty drops from the dropper." Flynn squeezed the man's shoulder and picked up his bag. "I'm right sorry for your loss. Please let me know when he passes so I can fill out the death certificate for the sheriff and for Heath Logging."

"How long—" The man couldn't seem to finish the question.

"I'll be surprised if he makes it through to morning." Flynn made sure to make eye contact to ensure that he understood the short timeframe, and then he walked away and left the men standing there. He'd long ago found that the best way to help people realize it was time to say goodbye was to give them the bad news and then leave. It somehow made the truth more real in their minds, callous as it might seem.

He strode into the boardinghouse and took the stairs up to the second floor, pausing to knock on Rose and Dixie's door. He prayed he wouldn't soon have to give Dixie similar news about Rose. He hadn't liked the sound of the woman's lungs when he'd checked on her earlier today. He prayed the poultice he'd prepared would work to break up some of her deep congestion.

When there was no answer at the door, he tapped again. Usually if Dixie was inside she would have answered the door by now. He must have missed her downstairs. Perhaps she'd already been back in the kitchen preparing dinner.

With still no answer, he turned the handle softly and stepped inside. "Rose, it's just me, Dr. Griffin." He spoke the words softly as he crossed the main room so he wouldn't startle her, but loud enough to let her know she had nothing to fear. Then he pushed open her bedroom door.

He stilled, his heart constricting in his chest. For there was Dixie, with the tenting sheet pushed back from the foot of the bed, sound asleep with her head propped on her arms, and clear evidence of tears glistening in her lashes. He pulled a clean handkerchief from his pocket and stepped closer to her. Knowing he probably shouldn't and yet somehow unable to stop himself, he bent and ever-so-gently dabbed the tears from her eyes. A brush of the backs of his fingers over her cheek revealed that her skin was cold to the touch, so he tugged the extra blanket from the slats of the ladder-back chair where she sat and draped it carefully around her. She slept on, undisturbed. The poor woman was probably in danger of extreme exhaustion, trying to take care of Rose and keep the boardinghouse running too. Were her tears ones of weariness? Perhaps they had something to do with the new marshal in town? Or were they due to something else entirely?

He wished he had the freedom to ask her. To prod her to rely on him.

Instead, he stepped back and made his way to the other side of the bed. He pulled aside the sheets, pleased to see that Dixie was keeping the water hot and that plenty of steam dampened the air. After applying the poultice to Rose's chest, he left his bag on the side table and stepped to the indoor lavatory that Dixie and Rose shared to wash his hands in the sink. He marveled that he could get clean running water with the turning of a tap. If only every home had one of these sinks, sanitation conditions throughout the country could be much improved. He was in the middle of drying his hands when he heard the first whimper.

His brow furrowed. Was that Rose? Or Dixie?

He draped the towel over a hook, and this time the cry was more than a whimper and he was able to distinguish the voice as Dixie's. He had no right to go to her, and yet, wasn't it human duty to make sure someone was alright when you heard them crying like that?

He pushed the door to Rose's room open, gripped the edge, and peered in at the woman.

Dixie was obviously having an unpleasant dream of some sort, for her breaths were rapid, her eyes, though still closed, rolled and scrunched, and her arms kept flinching as though in her dream she might be fighting someone off. Fresh tears dampened her lashes.

Flynn's jaw hardened. Was her sleep often tormented like this? He squatted next to her and spoke quietly, not wanting to startle her, or wake Rose.

"Dixie, It's me, Flynn. It's alright." He brushed her hair back from her sweat-dampened neck and squeezed her shoulder.

Dixie lurched to her feet, arms swinging, eyes wide.

Caught unprepared for such a reaction, Flynn felt a sharp pain slash through his skull as her elbow connected with his eye. He grunted and squinted the eye shut, then held his hands out to her, trying to break through the fog of her sleep.

"Dixie, it's okay. Everything's alright. It's just me. Flynn."

Through the one eye he could see out of, he saw her slim hand press to her throat as she took stock of the room. The blanket he'd folded around her had fallen to her feet, and he bent to retrieve it, giving her time to regain her composure.

"Flynn—Doctor, I'm so sorry. I don't know—" She gasped. "How did you cut your eye?"

He was bleeding? He draped the blanket over the back of the chair, then gingerly touched his brow bone. His fingertips came away bloody. "How's your elbow?" He winced at the amount of blood. He probably should do something about that before it dripped everywhere. He strode to his doctor bag on the table in the corner.

"My elbow? Did I—oh! I'm so sorry."

Flynn pulled a wad of clean cotton bandages from his bag and folded them into a tight square before pressing it to his brow. "Think nothing of it. I shouldn't have startled you."

"No, it's my fault. I shouldn't have fallen asleep. Here let me look at that." She stepped right up into his personal space and gave him no choice but to give way when she tugged the cloth away from his eye.

With her skirts brushing his ankles, the warmth of her breath puffing gently against his cheek, and the gentle probing of her fingers, he willed his breathing to remain steady, and reminded himself he had no rights here. He kept his focus steadfast on the doorframe just beyond her shoulder.

She winced and eased back. "That's going to need stitches."

Relieved to have some extra space between them, he pressed the cloth to the cut once more and wrapped his hand around the handle of his bag. "It'll be fine. I've given myself stitches before." He meant to immediately take his leave, but something kept his feet rooted to the ground, and he studied her face, willing her to confide in him.

Palms pressed together before her, she rubbed them in circles. "You needn't look at me with such worry. Something...a discussion I had just before I drifted off, brought the nightmare. Most nights I sleep...okay."

His jaw flinched. She hadn't said "fine" or "wonderfully" or even "well." And he'd seen the strain of weariness cloaking her, especially lately. He couldn't offer the comfort of his arms, or the promise that if she ever needed to divert her mind on a long, lonely night he'd be happy to sit and idle away the hours talking to her—that one wouldn't have been appropriate to offer even if she wasn't married, he supposed. But what he could offer her was the truth of God's Word.

"Have you been waiting on the Lord, Dixie?"

She blinked, her brown eyes not quite able to meet his. "Whatever do you mean?"

Flynn quoted from memory one of his favorite scriptures. It had gotten him through many a weary long night tending to patients. "Even youths grow tired and weary, and young men stumble and fall; but those who hope in the Lord will renew their strength. They will soar on wings like eagles; they will run and not grow weary, they will walk and not be faint."

Dixie only looked at him. She appeared to want to say something, but then decided against it.

It was time for him to take his leave. "It's from the book of Isaiah, chapter forty."

Still she didn't respond.

He tipped her a nod and left her standing there staring out the window, with one hand toying with the buttons at her collar like she might have just had a revelation.

He hoped so.

Everyone ought to know just how much the Lord could give to them if they would only let Him.

❦

Liora Fontaine just wanted some time to be alone. She sank onto the large root at the base of the huge oak tree in the wildflower field just outside of town.

She felt such relief that the sheriff had let her scrub the

jailhouse floors. And he'd even paid her fifty cents, so she already had money to go towards next week's rent, or towards food. Since she still had some food left over, she hadn't decided what she was going to do yet.

For now, she was enjoying the relief of not having to worry about where she would sleep this week.

She liked to come to the field to pick rose hips to mix with her tea, though it was getting quite late in the season for them now. But it had been a very mild autumn this year, so a few of the little bulbs were still ripe for the picking and she'd already gathered all she needed.

She would need to head back into town soon, but ever since Charlotte Brindle had pointed out the verse that spoke about God loving her more than He loved the sparrows, she had found a certain peace when she came to the wildflower field outside of town and just sat and soaked in the creation around her.

She huddled into a tighter ball inside her thick wool shawl. Even on a cold day like today, nothing gave her a greater measure of serenity and reassurance than just sitting in the quiet of God's creation and marveling over all the things that He had done for her.

The scar on her forehead was easily hidden with a careful swoop of hair now, but sometimes at night she took a moment to look at it—really look at it—before she fell into bed. The fact that God had loved her enough to send Joe to save her life when she'd been so intent on taking it still filled her with wonder. She was so unworthy of God's consideration. And yet, that was the wonder of it. That He'd loved her enough to save her even when she had spurned His existence.

A week after he'd saved her physical life, Joe had given her the gift of that Bible, and the Truths therein had saved her soul. She brought it with her to the field to read often.

And so when she heard the footsteps approaching, she didn't come out of her little hiding place near the oak tree. She had discovered the place quite by accident one day when she'd been following the antics of a rabbit through the field. The oak had a large protruding root that offered the perfect chair surrounded by rose bushes that kept her from sight.

She knew within a moment that it was Zoe Kastain by the humming and chattering she did to her dog Jinx. Liora thought Jinx might sniff her out, but he seemed content to frolic and sniff the bushes near Zoe.

Tipping her head against the oak, she smiled softly and just listened to the girl chatter, and it only took her a moment to realize that Zoe wasn't talking to the dog, but to God. Liora released a wistful sigh, and thanked God that the young woman had such a lovely family, and not a family like she'd been raised in. She prayed that Zoe would never take God's love for granted or doubt it. And then she prayed for continued healing for Zoe's father who had been shot by Patrick Waddell—the man who had sired Liora but never been a father to her in all her years.

Zoe had only been at the field for a few minutes when another set of footsteps entered the meadow.

For one moment Liora tensed. Had Ewan followed her to try and convince her to come back to work for him?

Zoe greeted, "Washington, you're a good ways from home."

Liora released the breath she'd been holding.

"Went fishing with Kin." The clatter of a bucket handle was probably Wash holding up his catch.

Liora's mouth watered at the thought of fresh fish. Perhaps she'd use her extra quarter to pay the boy to bring her a brace one day this week. But she'd have to think on that and see how many odd jobs she could get this week. If only funds weren't so scarce. And here she was already worrying about money again. She wrinkled her nose and lifted a gaze to the sky that was visible through the bare branches of the oak tree. *Forgive me. You've provided for me week after week. Help me to be able to rest in the fact that You will never leave me or forsake me. And that I can trust Your plan for me, even if it turns in a direction I'm not ready for.* She returned her attention to the conversation between the two young people.

"You're looking rather down in the mouth for having spent the morning fishing," Zoe noted, the soft *tink tink* of rose hips plopping into her pail.

Washington's sigh could be heard all the way across the field in her hiding place. "Kin's got a notion in his head that it might be fun to rob this afternoon's stagecoach."

Zoe gasped. "He doesn't!"

"'Fraid he does. I tried to talk him out of it. But you know how he gets when he has a challenge that's niggling at him. It's like he don't feel alive unless he takes a big risk every so often."

"You oughta tell the sheriff."

"Can't. He took Miss Brindle out to the logging camp this morning. He won't be back until late this evening."

Zoe sighed morosely. "They oughta never have moved the stage day to Saturdays. If it was on a Thursday like it used to be, Kin would be in school where he'd stay out of trouble."

Washington snorted. "Unless he was skipping."

Zoe chuckled. "True enough." Then her tone turned serious again. "We have to do something!"

Go to Joe.

Washington's bucket clanked again. "I don't want to get him in trouble!"

"He brings his own trouble on himself, Wash. What about Deputy Joe?"

Relieved that one of them had finally thought of it, Liora held her breath so she could better hear what they'd decided.

"It's not his day to work law. I think he's out helping old man Jonas chop the rest of his winter firewood. What if you and I just went to Kin's place and tried to stop him ourselves?"

"You said you already tried that."

"I think he might listen to you better than he does to me."

Zoe released a long-suffering sound that let Washington know just how much he was demanding of her. "Fine, but first I have to run these rose hips home to Ma so's she can start drying them. Doc says they might help Pa improve faster."

"Fine, I'll come with you. Your ma might like a couple of these fish for dinner. I caught more 'n we can eat at home."

Liora waited until their footsteps faded into the distance and then stood from her oak hideaway. Old Man Jonas just lived a mile the other side of town. She'd best get on her way and let Joe know what she'd just heard.

Chapter Thirteen

oe Rodante swung the ax high and hard. He was almost done with this pile of wood and then he just had the stacking to do. Homer would be thankful for the ease of simply being able to bring in an armful of wood each morning instead of having to face the task of chopping enough for the day. He'd already made that point very clear to Joe. Joe hoped that Homer didn't feel too inept with him stopping by and offering to do the work. He knew the old coot prided himself on a hard day's labor—had since Joe was a kid in these parts—but he also knew that old Homer was shaky enough that it was dangerous for him to be swinging an ax. He made a mental note to check on him more often.

As he set up the next log, sweat trickled from his forehead and he swiped at it with the back of his hand.

Footsteps sounded behind him. "Joe?"

He lifted his head. His heart seemed to still at just the sound of her voice. Or maybe it was his name on her lips. His eyes fell closed. Of course she showed up when he was dripping with sweat and probably smelled like the south end of a northbound mule. He turned to face her. "Liora, what can I do for you?" He cleared his throat. He hadn't meant to sound so gruff. He swiped his forehead with his sleeve.

She pressed her palms together. "I'm sorry to bother you,

but I overheard something that I really thought you needed to hear too."

Today she was wearing a beautiful blue dress that brought out the distracting color of her eyes. Why couldn't the woman wear a gunnysack once in a while? He turned to the pile of tumbled logs scattered around him and started gathering an armful. "What is it?"

She stepped forward. "Here—let me help."

"There's no need."

Ignoring him, she bent to heft her own load. "I don't mind."

He swallowed when the sweet scent of her perfume wafted to him—something that always reminded him of citrus and cinnamon and brought to mind California orange groves. He'd probably be envisioning them all afternoon. He withheld a grunt and started toward the backdoor where he was stacking the wood within easy reach for Homer. Who was he kidding? It wouldn't be orange groves lingering in his mind's eye, and that was certain.

Liora stopped directly behind him. Back arched, she held out a double armful of logs for him to remove and stack. "I was up in the wildflower field reading the Bible you gave me."

Joe was careful to keep a neutral expression on his face. If only his heart beat faster when she told him she was reading the Word because he cared deeply for her soul. He did care, but he'd be a fool trying to deceive himself if he thought that was the only reason her comments made his pulse thrum. Ever since she'd started asking him questions about the Word, he hadn't been able to get the woman from his mind. He'd thought she was beautiful before, but when her blue eyes were shining over a new Truth she'd discovered, it was almost breathtaking.

Careful not to touch her, he removed the last log from her arms, tossed it into a slot in the neat stack he was making, and then brushed past her to get another armful of wood. "So what did you hear?"

Liora dusted dirt and splinters from her sleeves, but then bent to fill her arms with another load. "Zoe was up there picking rose hips for her pa when Washington stopped by. He'd just been fishing with Kin and it seems Kin has gotten it in his mind to do a little mischief to today's stage into town."

Joe froze at that. His gaze snapped to hers. "What kind of mischief?"

Liora swallowed visibly. "Wash seemed to think Kin was going to...hold it up."

"Did you let Reagan know?"

She shook her head. "He took Charlotte out to one of the logging camps earlier and isn't supposed to be back till after the stage arrives this evening. That's why I came for you."

Joe's gaze sought out the angle of the sun as he darted to the stack and hastily unloaded his armful. "Homer!" he called.

The old man poked his head out the back door, adjusting his suspenders. His rheumy eyes lit up when they landed on Liora. "Well hello, pretty miss. How do?"

Liora dipped a curtsy beneath her armload of wood. "Mr. Jonas."

Joe set to snatching the pieces from her arms. "Homer, I have to run into town to deal with something that's come up. But you leave that wood alone, you hear? I'll be back to finish stacking it before the week is out."

Homer rubbed his grizzled jaw, eyes narrowing in a way that let Joe know his comments had been taken as impertinent. "I ain't so far gone that I cain't stack a few sticks still. Don't you worry none about me."

Joe tossed the last length from Liora's arms against the side of the house and brushed off his hands. "I didn't mean it like that. Just meant to let you know I'm happy to come back in a day or two. Just can't finish today."

Homer waved a hand. "You go on. I 'preciate what you done already. And thank ye, kindly." He tipped an invisible hat in Liora's direction. "Ma'am." And then he disappeared into his house.

Liora glanced toward the mess of scattered logs in the yard. "I could stay and keep stacking them."

"Not a chance. I don't want you riding back to town on your own after dark."

Her chin lifted and her eyes narrowed. "I walked. And I can more than take care of myself."

He couldn't help the grin that tipped up his lips. He took her arm. "I don't want you walking back to town alone after dark even more than I don't want you riding." He nudged her toward his mount, tied on the sunny side of Homer's laurel bush.

Her steps dragged. "Are you ignoring the fact that I said I can take care of myself?"

He grinned down at her. "Mostly. Now"—he gestured to his horse—"do you want to mount up? Or should I toss you aboard?"

She narrowed her eyes at him and leaned closer. "What if I want to walk back, just like I arrived?"

He shook his head and gestured to where the sun was sinking into the afternoon sky. "Don't have time for that, and I'm not leaving you to walk back on your own, even this time of day."

Liora loosed a breath. "Joe, I've been taking care of myself for a lot of years before you ever came along. There's no need for me to go all soft now."

"It's not going soft to let a man who ca—" He broke off and cleared his throat. Had he really been about to tell her he cared for her? Had he even thought that through? The consequences of starting a courtship with a former whore? "Just"—he motioned to the horse—"we need to get going."

Liora seemed to have lost her fight, for she turned to mount without so much as another word, and didn't protest when he swung up behind the saddle and settled in.

He tried to ignore the soft brush of her arms as he reached around her to gather the reins, willed himself to banish the scent of her from his mind, and made a concerted effort to keep his gaze from the slim expanse of her calves exposed by her lifted skirt. He failed miserably at all three.

He hauled the horse's head around more roughly than he normally treated the poor beast and swatted one haunch with the end of the reins. "Come on. Get up now."

They set off at a trot for town. And Joe endeavored to set his mind to figuring out where Kincaid Davis might think was a good place to rob the stagecoach.

⁂

By the time Zoe got home and left the pail of rose hips with Ma, and she and Wash trekked through the sleet that had started to fall, crossed the creek, and made it down to Camp Sixty-Five to Kin's house, a couple hours had passed.

And they were too late.

Kin's pa wasn't home, but they knew Kin had been there because two of the fish he'd caught this morning had been paper-wrapped and were lying on the ice in the Davis's ice box on the back stoop.

Zoe studied the worry on Wash's face as he stood in the Davis's yard, hands propped on his hips. He hefted a clump of ice-crusted pinecone, and chucked it into the woods with a cry of frustration. His face was tightly furrowed.

She'd known they should have gone straight to Deputy Joe, but she didn't suppose now was the right time to say so. Still, they had to do something. "What're we gonna do?"

Wash shrugged.

Zoe imagined Kin riding down on the stage and Old Don Brass pulling his big Winchester and filling Kin's hide with lead. Her hands trembled, so she clasped them together to keep Wash from seeing how worried she was. Kin's life could very well be in their hands.

Wash looked around at the run-down lean-to that the Davises called home, and Zoe followed his gaze. Zoe knew that pretty much anything of value Mr. Davis ever received was sold for drink. Why, just this year he'd sold the school supplies that Kin had purchased with money he'd worked all summer to earn. So Kin came to school that first day empty handed. He acted like he didn't care, but Zoe couldn't imagine that was actually true. She would have been madder than a mama bear whose cubs were threatened if Pa had done something like that to her.

Zoe had heard what happened before school started—the whole class had known what happened since word traveled so fast 'round these parts—but it had taken her a week to think of her plan, and she could only wish she'd thought of it sooner. But she'd been real proud of all the kids in the school when she'd gone to each of them and asked for a small donation of school supplies and each one had given something. Some a few sheets of paper. Another a pencil. Wash had donated a ruler and an eraser. She and Belle had had Pa help them fix up an old slate. They'd painted it deep blue and added two pieces of chalk. And when Kin arrived for the first day of the second week of school it had been to find a neat pile of necessities on his desk.

Zoe remembered the way his jaw had worked and his eyes had blinked real fast. He'd looked up and caught her watching him, and before she could spin away he'd given her a nod. So much had been said without him ever saying a word at all. She'd nodded in return and then faced the front of the room.

Now as Zoe remembered the incident, she was even more determined than ever to save Kin from himself. If her pa treated her the way Kin's pa treated him, she might be tempted to take out some of her anger by doing stupid stuff too.

Zoe reached out and grabbed Wash's arm, tugging him after her. "Come on. We have to hurry. We're going to stop Kin from doing something stupid."

Chapter Fourteen

s the coach rolled toward Wyldhaven, Zebulon Heath felt like a child the day before Christmas. He tried not to fidget. Though the air outside could crystallize breath, the interior of the coach was warmed by the hot bricks beneath their boots and the thick leather curtains that hung over each window. Next to him sat Preston Clay, his newly-hired minister, and across the way the other man who had joined them on the coach at Cle Elum scowled glumly at the passing scenery through the small gap of his window's curtain.

Zeb adjusted his cuffs. He'd been gone much too long. He couldn't wait to see how things had progressed since he'd last been in town, and to get started building the church—for Sheriff Callahan had informed him in his last letter that the schoolteacher and Miss Pottinger had organized a box social to raise funds towards the building.

He glanced over at Preston, who had also fingered his curtain slightly to one side so he could watch the countryside roll by. The man was young. But Zeb had chosen him because he carried a serious, almost melancholy expression with him that had, if the truth were told, tugged at Zeb's heart. It made Preston seem much older than his actual years. And Zeb supposed that wasn't a bad thing for a man of the cloth. But after traveling across the entire country with the young man, he couldn't help but wonder if he had made the right decision.

He'd tried on more than one occasion to get Preston to open up, but the man's solemnity couldn't seem to be penetrated.

Zeb, however, had never been the type to give up.

He nudged the parson with his elbow. "Only a few more miles. We don't have a church building just yet, but our new schoolteacher, Miss Brindle, and our boardinghouse owner, Miss Pottinger, helped—"

A loud snort from the man across the way interrupted, and Zeb's gaze flew to his, even as his hand fell instinctively to the pistol strapped to his side.

The man's lips twisted sardonically as he released his curtain. "*Miss* Pottinger, is it?"

Seeing the man only had words in mind, Zeb relaxed. "Indeed. Miss Pottinger and her lovely mother, Rose."

The sneer transformed into a snarl. "She's not a 'Miss.' She's my wife. And the woman you call her mother is actually *my* mother." He folded his arms over his chest.

Zeb's brow furrowed. He'd never met two finer women, and he had no doubt that if the man across the coach was telling the truth that the women had possessed a very good reason for leaving him behind when they moved west. "I'm sure you'll be able to iron out your differences once you arrive in town."

"Oh yes. I'm sure we will." The man turned his attention outside the coach once more.

Despite the tension raised by the surly man's accusations, Zeb's excitement grew. Almost home! He made a mental note to search out Sheriff Callahan first thing when the stage came to a stop in town to let him know of the potential trouble.

For now, he decided to ignore the man and continue his talk—one-sided though it might be—with the minister. He pulled out the plot of the town which he'd had printed up on a pamphlet and nudged Preston to pay attention. "The sight for the church is all picked out. There is a flat area just here to the north end of town next to Wyldhaven Creek that will be the perfect place for the church. There's plenty of room behind the plot for a parsonage in a nice grove of trees just here. And the town cemetery will be located on a hill about a mile outside of town where it will be high enough to avoid any flood damage."

Preston nodded. "Parsonage can wait. I can sleep on a pew for a while."

Here again was something that impressed Zebulon about the younger man. He obviously wasn't in the business of saving souls because he wanted the luxuries of life lavished on him by others. "Nonsense. Won't take but a month to get the parsonage built and until then, you can stay with one of the townsfolk."

A gust of wind blew open the leather flap over the window and Zeb caught a glimpse of winter-blue sunlight that let him know the dark forest that had been pressing close to the road for the last several miles had now given way to the rolling plains that led into Wyldhaven.

The coach slowed to take the sharp curve that lay just a mile outside of town.

Kin sidled across the high ridge just south of Wyldhaven and peered down into the gulch where the stagecoach always had to slow down before making the turn toward town.

Something like a handful of fishing worms squirmed in his gut, but he could do this. He had to do this. He was going to cover his face with a bandana and ride down there and give the folks aboard a good scare. And then he was going to keep on riding right past the stage and over the hill on the other side of the road. He'd thought everything through. Old Don

Brass packed a rifle under his seat atop the stage, Kin knew. And he was only going to have a split second before the old man pulled that old Winchester and aimed to make a sieve of him. He didn't actually plan to steal anything. He didn't need any trifles. Just the ride by would be enough to catch Pa's attention.

Because he was going to get caught, that much he knew. He'd purposely told Wash, because he knew Wash wouldn't be able to help himself. Wash was probably in town telling the sheriff all about his plans right at this moment and worrying himself sick over the fact that he was a turncoat.

But it was that very trait that made Kin admire his friend so much. Wash always seemed to do the right thing, even when it was hard.

Yep, he was going to get caught. He had no delusions about that. And Pa was going to lick him but good. But that was okay too.

At least the old man would be paying attention. Maybe this would keep him out of the saloon when he wasn't working. And keep him from nipping at the bottle so much when he was.

It was the only thing left that Kin could think of to try. Because if he didn't do something, Pa was going to drink himself to death. He'd heard Doc Griffin tell him so the last time he came by when Pa was feeling ill. Doc had told Pa in no uncertain terms that he needed to stop drinking. And Kin had tried everything he could think of since then to help Pa comply.

Pa was always so drunk when he passed out each night that Kin knew he'd never remember how much liquor was left in his bottle. So he'd poured Pa's drink down the drain so that when he went to fetch his bottle it would be empty. But Pa would just ride into town, then come home in debt to Ewan McGinty, who had come around several times aiming to collect.

Next, Kin tried pouring only most of the whiskey out, but leaving just enough to get Pa into his cups. But when he was drinking, Pa passed through a stage of anger just this side of totally drunk, and Kin had quickly realized that just getting Pa to that point was a fairly dangerous proposition. Even now he winced and rolled his shoulder. Pa was big and when he swung, he swung hard. And the wood walls of their lean-to were none too soft when one crashed into them, even if the house did shake like it was set to fall apart.

After that, when Pa woke up mostly sober one morning, Kin had tried pleading with him to recognize that the doc's words were true. That time the punch sent him into the dresser. He fingered the scab that still clung to his scalp just above his ear. Thankfully, it was hidden by his hair.

In the distance a plume of dust revealed that the stage was just leaving Stone Cutter Gulch. It would be here in twenty minutes. The hairpin turn just ahead ensured that the coach would have to slow down. It was the best place to make his run, because Old Don would be going slow enough to recognize him as he raced by.

Kin glanced at the sky. He wondered if Ma was up in heaven looking down on him right now. If so, what would she say? Would she be proud of him for trying to get through to Pa? Or would she be angry with the way he aimed to do it? He tugged too tight on his horse's reins and the animal shifted backward. Loosing a breath, Kin forced his hands to relax, and bent forward to pat the horse on its neck. He wondered if there might be something he hadn't thought of that might get Pa's attention better? But nothing ever got Pa to listen to him like when he was acting up.

Kin rolled his eyes at his second guesses. Ma would likely tan his hide for what he was about to do. But Ma wasn't here.

Hadn't been for a long time. God had taken her and his whole life had changed. And no one seemed to be able to tame Pa like she had.

This was the best way he knew how.

Something had to break through to the old man.

He pulled his focus back to the road. The fog was thick, but not so thick that Kin couldn't see the coach pull into view on the road below him. It was already starting to slow for the turn towards Wyldhaven. His mouth was as dry as year-old sawdust. But he'd come too far to turn back now.

He kicked his heels into his horse's side and urged him to a trot. He planned to hit the road at a full gallop behind the coach. Give a good yell, and then barrel past, glancing back just long enough for Old Don to get a glimpse of him before he disappeared up the ridge and into the trees. The timing was critical. He had to be slow enough for Don to recognize him, but fast enough to evade one of Don's bullets.

Kin's mare was a sturdy mountain-bred mustang that Pa had won in a poker game—the one and only time he'd won anything. And for some reason he'd never tried to sell the horse. She was the one thing Pa seemed content to let Kin keep.

He'd delayed long enough. Kin kicked his heels one more time. "Git up now." The mare responded to his urging and leapt from the embankment onto the road right behind the stage's boot.

Pulling in the biggest breath he could muster, Kin let loose with the wild screech he'd mastered on one of the many nights he and Wash had slept out under the stars the year they'd turned ten. Wash had claimed the screech could make the hairs on a frog stand up and salute before they fainted dead away.

Even now, Kin felt the wondrously pleasant shiver the yell

sent down his spine. His mare laid her ears back and surged forward with a speed he hadn't known she possessed. The coach slipped by on his left side as his mare's strides ate up the ground. This was all going just as he'd planned! Except—! They were much closer to the hairpin turn than he'd realized!

Old man Brass must be trying to outrun him, thinking he planned to go for the strong box.

They were going too fast!

There was no time for him to ride past the coach and give Don a look at him. In fact if they kept going at this speed—

Kin pulled his mare up, his heart thundering in his chest. The mare danced in the middle of the road, but Kin couldn't seem to take his eyes from the looming disaster.

The coach started into the turn, tipping up onto two wheels!

"Slow down," Kin breathed, hardly able to talk at all. "Please, slow down."

But his pleas went unheeded.

The hitch snapped and the coach crashed onto its side, sending Old Don sprawling into the field next to the road as the horses galloped away.

From inside the coach there came the loud report of a gunshot.

Then all fell quiet.

Kin swallowed. What had he done?

The blood curdling screech cut through the quiet outside, and the thunder of approaching hoofbeats shot Zeb's pulse into his throat. Were they being robbed? Zeb thought of the money he'd put in the strong box atop the coach. Dash it all! That money was meant for improvements to his town! Not to line the pockets of some scallywag!

His Colt six-shooter was already in his palm before he'd even thought what he was doing. As he thumbed back the hammer, he noted with satisfaction that Preston had also palmed his pistol, and appeared to know how to use it.

From outside at the front of the coach, Don Brass whistled sharply and called loud encouragement to the horses. The coach lurched forward and Zeb knew Don would negotiate the hairpin turn just ahead as quickly as the coach could move.

Zeb yanked aside the curtain on his side to peer out the window, but saw nothing. He was just turning to urge Preston to search for a target to shoot at on his side when he felt the coach begin to tilt.

His arm shot out for balance, and reflexively his finger tightened on the trigger.

Outside, Don cursed loudly from the driver's bench.

Preston clutched at the window frame in an apparent attempt to keep from sliding across the slick leather seat into Zeb's space.

Across from them, the unpleasant man's eyes were wide as he slipped toward the sidewall. He grabbed wildly for any handhold he could find.

The coach lost the battle with balance and crashed onto its side. Preston slammed into Zeb, knocking the air from him in a whoosh. One of the warm bricks crashed into him, sending a jagged shard of pain slicing through his ribs.

An explosion of sound pulsed against his eardrums, and Zeb had the fleeting realization that he'd pulled the trigger on his Colt. But then his head slammed into the side of the coach and all went black.

Chapter Fifteen

Zoe's side pinched with a sharp pain as she chased Wash through the woods toward the road. At least she was no longer cold. Perspiration dripped from her forehead and stung the corners of her eyes. She stumbled to a stop and propped her hands on her knees. She used the hem of her skirt to dab at the sweat on her forehead, not caring how unladylike Belle would accuse her of being. "Wash..." She gasped for air. "I can't...keep going." She waved him forward. "Go on...without...me."

Washington spun from looking down the trail where he wanted to be, to looking back at her. He must have turned a full circle at least twice. Finally he stomped back toward her. "I'm not leaving you. But hurry up and catch your breath."

That was when they heard Kin's signature blood boiling screech.

Zoe jolted to her feet. How many times had Kin terrified her or Belle with that very scream after he'd snuck up on them in the berry patch, or even on a lunch break at school. She stumbled forward and broke into a run again. "We have to help him! Run, Wash. I'll be fine. I'll stay as close as I can."

Washington grabbed her arm before she'd gone more than two steps. "Not on your life. I'm not leaving you in the woods alone. Here, get on my back." He squatted down before her.

Zoe hesitated. Even though she was already twelve and almost a full-grown woman, she was small for her age. Wash might be fifteen but he was already as tall as her pa and broader through the shoulders. She knew he wouldn't have any trouble carrying her, but should a lady let a man pack her through the woods on his back? She didn't relish getting her backside tanned later if Ma found out she'd done something improper.

"Come on, Zo! We don't have time for this!"

In that moment, they heard a gunshot reverberate in the distance.

Zoe didn't hesitate another second. She leapt onto Wash's back and clung for dear life as he leapt through the last quarter mile of the woods to the road.

⋯≫✶≪⋯

After dropping Liora off in town, Joe was still a good quarter mile from the hairpin where he figured Kin would likely mount his attack, when he heard the bone chilling screech.

"Ha!" He slapped his horse's flank with the end of the reins.

A shot rang out only a few moments later.

He was going to be too late!

By the time he pulled up at the top of the ridge overlooking the turn, the coach was on its side, thick fog billowing in a great cloud all around it, and the Clydesdales were bucking their way down the road, fighting the unfamiliar flap of the singletree against their hocks. The traces dragged in the road behind them.

Joe trotted his horse down the ridge and emerged before the Clydesdales. "Whoa there. Steady." He leaned down and captured the cheek strap of the nigh horse. "Easy there." The horses seemed to calm some, though their heads still bobbed in agitation. He dismounted and released the traces from the singletree, then led the horses back toward the toppled coach.

A gust of wind cleared some of the fog and there in the middle of the road sat Kin Davis, wide-eyed, with perspiration dotting his brow.

Joe released the horses' reins and pulled his gun, leveling it at the boy's chest. "Hands up, son."

Kin blinked at him, and then slowly lifted his hands above his head. "I only meant to ride by and give them a bit of a scare."

Joe's jaw clenched. "I don't have time for your excuses right now. Get down off that horse, nice and easy."

Kin moved ever so slowly. "I ain't armed. So don't go and shoot me."

Joe gritted his teeth and reminded himself that he'd once been a stupid fifteen-year-old boy too. Instead of giving the boy a speech about how if he didn't want to get shot, he probably oughtn't go chasing stagecoaches, he kept his mouth shut.

The boy's feet landed in the roadbed. His hands were still above his head.

Joe motioned with the gun toward the roadbed. "Face down. And spread 'em."

The boy hesitated for a moment. "Can I at least tie off my mare to that tree there? She ain't trained to a ground-hitch."

The kid had some nerve. "Should have thought of that before you decided to go robbing a stage." Joe dipped the barrel of his pistol toward the ground again. "Don't make me ask you another time."

The kid did sprawl out this time, but he stubbornly refused to release the reins of his horse.

Joe snatched them from him and, keeping his gun trained on the kid, strode to the side of the road and looped them over the low-hanging branch of a frosty tree.

With a sigh of relief, the kid seemed to relax, even though

Joe knew the ground where he was lying in his thin coat had to be as cold as an ice block. It only took him a moment to get the kid's hands manacled behind him and yank him to his feet. He pushed him into a sitting position in the middle of the road and hobbled his ankles good and tight in case he tried to make a run for it.

Moans were emanating from the coach now.

That was when he heard the call. "I've been shot! You shot me!"

Joe's heart leapt into his throat as he let the kid go. "Sit here and don't move! Did you shoot someone?" He kept his gaze on the kid even as he moved quickly toward the stage.

The kid's face was a perfect match for the patch of snow on the hillside behind him. He shook his head and swallowed. "I didn't even have a gun. I swear!"

Thumps and groans from inside the coach were louder now.

Joe finally allowed himself to take his eyes off the kid. "I'm Deputy Joseph Rodante from Wyldhaven," he called as he scrambled up onto one of the large back wheels. "Everyone okay in there?"

"Deputy Rodante. Zebulon Heath here. I'm afraid there's been an accident. I've shot a man. He's bleeding rather badly from his upper right abdomen. What should I do?"

Joe pushed the thick black leather curtain up above one of the windows and peered into the chaos inside the coach. Three men lay sprawled inside. Blood seeped from the side of one of the men, forming a pool beneath his side. The other man still seemed to be unconscious. A brick lay very near his head.

Zebulon Heath used one arm to drag himself through the debris of broken benches, feather stuffing, and shards of wood toward the man who'd been shot.

Thinking quickly, Joe yanked off his coat, then ripped at

the buttons on the front of his shirt as he hurriedly removed it "Here. Use this." He lowered the shirt into the coach, and then tugged his coat back on. "Try and get the bleeding stopped while I see what I can do about getting you three out of here."

Zeb nodded, wincing at the movement. "What about Don? He all right?"

Joe lifted his head. Right. Where had the old whip gotten to?

His heart thundered in his chest. This was a bad situation, and getting worse fast. He needed Doc Griffin, but could he trust Kin to ride to town to fetch him? That was when he saw Washington Nolan and Zoe Kastain peering down at them from the ridge above.

When they topped out on the crest of the ridge near the hairpin turn, Zoe's eyes widened.

Deputy Joe had his gun leveled at Kin's chest. They exchanged a few words she couldn't hear from here, and then Kin spread-eagled himself in the middle of the road.

"No. No. No. No." Wash paced three steps one way, and three steps back, even though he never took his eyes off of what was going on in the road below them. "I told him not to. I tried to tell him, Zo."

Zoe didn't bother correcting Wash's use of the shortened version of her name. She could only stare, wide-eyed, at the scene below them.

One of the stagecoach's front wheels was spinning a lazy circle, as though it relished the freedom of being released from the confines of the ground. Up the road a ways, the Clydesdales had wandered over to munch frosty grass from the embankment.

Deputy Joe was up on the top of the sideways coach now, peering into one of the windows at the passengers who must still be trapped inside. He took off first his coat, and then his shirt, before putting his coat back on. He passed the shirt in through the window.

"What happens to Kin if somebody is dead in there?" Though the words were barely audible, Wash must have heard her.

He shook his head. "I don't know. But it won't be good."

Just then, Deputy Joe lifted his head and focused on them. "Washington Nolan, come down here, son. Quickly! I need you to fetch Doc Griffin."

Washington ran down the hillside, his long legs carrying him over boulders and logs that took Zoe longer to maneuver. Zoe followed as quickly as she could. By the time she reached the road, however, Deputy Joe already had Wash mounted on Kin's mare. "Bring him back quick as you can. Tell him the man's lost a lot of blood." With that Deputy Joe slapped the rump of Kin's mare, and Wash started at a gallop for town.

Zoe swallowed and looked at Kin. This wasn't good. Wasn't good at all.

Relief swept through Joe as Wash headed down the road toward town on Kin's mare. Now to find Don. He jogged to the other side of the coach.

The old man lay face down in the tall grass by the road. *No.* "Don!" He clambered up the embankment to the man's side. The frozen ground had no give beneath his fingers. "Don?" He squatted next to the man and forced himself to go slow and assess wounds before he tried to move him, just like Reagan had taught him.

Gently, he ran his hands down the man's neck, shoulders, arms. Then his ribs, hips, and each leg. There were no bumps or abrasions. Joe rolled him over. A small lump on Don's temple indicated he'd probably whacked his head when he hit the ground, but other than that, his pulse was strong, and his breathing seemed even.

Joe released a sigh. It might take him some time to come around, but the man would likely be just fine. Keeping him warm would be key, however. He could use his own coat, but Reagan had pounded into him time and again the importance of keeping his own needs in mind during critical situations such as this. He would do no one any good if he gave up all his warmth to help others and put himself in danger. Since he'd already given up his shirt to help stop the bleeding of the man in the coach, he didn't dare give up the coat.

He scrabbled atop the carriage once more and this time he hauled open the door and let it crash back against the side of the coach wall. Snagging the knife from his belt, he leaned in as far as he could and slid the knife into the leather of the bench seat. As he worked at stripping off a length of the leather that would be wide enough to lay Don on, he spoke. "Hang in there Zeb. I just need to get Don off the frozen ground, and then I'll be back to help you all out of here. How is he?" The gunshot man must have passed out, because other than Zeb's ragged breathing, the inside of the coach rang with silence.

"He's bleeding bad." Zeb's voice trembled.

Joe tore the leather off the seat in a long thick strip, sending a shower of feathers floating through the air like snow cascading from a weighted tree branch in a windstorm. "Give me five minutes. Maybe less. I'll be right back. Keep the pressure on that wound!"

"Hurry!" Zeb called after him.

Joe ran to the kid who was still seated where he'd left him. Zoe was standing by his side looking toward the coach with an expression filled with disbelief. Grabbing Kin's arm, Joe hauled him to his feet, shucking his knife from its sheath. "I'm going to need your help. But, so help me, if you try and escape, I won't hesitate to shoot you. Do you understand?"

Kin nodded.

"Good. Zoe, come on, I need your help too."

Chapter Sixteen

ixie stood staring out Ma's window for the longest time after Flynn left. One finger toyed with the collar of her blouse as her vision blurred against the roof-peak of the post office across the street.

Those who hope in the Lord...

Hope...

Her conscience squirmed.

She had *given up* hope, hadn't she? She used to believe. Long, long ago, it seemed, though in reality it had only been a couple years. She used to believe in God. In the fact that He'd sent His Son into the world to die for the sins of all mankind. She'd even put her hope in that sacrifice.

And yet... Somewhere in the long year and a half that she'd been married to Steven, her hope had somehow drizzled away, until now it was barely a memory on the horizon of history.

Longing seeped into her soul. She closed her eyes. Oh to have hope once more. Was it too late for her?

Hoofbeats thundered into town with an urgency that drew her attention to the street below. Washington Nolan leapt from the back of the horse as soon as it skidded to a stop in front of McGinty's Alehouse. "Doc!" He was yelling before his feet even touched the ground.

Something was terribly wrong. Had something happened to his father, Butch, or to one of his brothers?

She'd better go down to find out so she would know where to send a meal.

She took only a moment to check on Rose, thankful to see that she seemed to be resting a little easier this afternoon, and then hoisted her skirts and hurried down the stairs.

By the time she reached the front of the boardinghouse Flynn was already shrugging into his coat and on the run for the livery where his horse was kept.

Washington stood with his hands propped on the hitching rail by Kin Davis's horse, his head hanging down between his arms.

Dixie's heart threatened to stop in her chest. *Not Kin!* "Wash?" She stopped by his side and folded her arms against the cold, wishing she'd remembered her shawl. "What happened?"

He started a bit at her nearness, but didn't reply right away. "Is it Kin? Is he hurt?"

Wash shook his head, sending a wave of relief through Dixie. He scrubbed one hand down the length of his face. "It's my fault. I couldn't talk him out of it. Kin….he wanted to…well, I'm not sure what he wanted to do, actually. But he rode down on the stage, and they must have thought he intended to rob them because Old Don took the hairpin too fast and the stage tipped over. Someone got shot. I think by another passenger inside the coach. Deputy Joe said he was bleeding real bad." Washington looked like the weight of the world had fallen on his shoulders. "I'd best get back, and take a couple mounts with me. There are going to be a few people who need rides back into town. Will you send the sheriff on out, if we aren't back by the time he gets in?"

Dixie nodded. "Of course. Take a wagon too. Some might not be able to ride. And I'll make an extra-large supper tonight. Kin brought me enough fish to make a large chowder.

You let everyone on the stage and those helping know they are welcome to the diner tonight—on the house."

Wash nodded. "Yes, ma'am. Will do. And good idea about a wagon."

With that, he swung up onto the tired mare and trotted down the street toward the livery.

In the distance, Dixie could see Flynn just galloping out of the livery yard, with his doctor bag and rolled-up stretcher tied to the saddle behind him.

Kin Davis, what have you done? With a sigh, Dixie hurried back into the warmth of the boardinghouse. She'd best put on some extra pots of water to boil too. Doc was sure to need plenty of hot water tonight if he was going to be doctoring several hurt patients.

Charlotte was thrilled that the foreman had agreed to her Christmas festival plans. Her mind had been whirling through all kinds of ideas for preparations that would need to be made before that night.

She would have the children put on a theatrical stage-show of sorts that would portray the birth of Christ. There would be shepherds, and wise men, and sheep. Someone would need to play the star, and there would of course have to be a Mary and a Joseph and a Christ-child.

They could use some of the long empty days between now and Christmas to practice the production. A thrill of excitement rushed through her simply at the thought.

Her gaze wandered to the silent man beside her. He had visited amiably with her for much of the ride home. But now his brow was pinched and she could tell he was back to worrying about Dixie and Rose. And who could blame him? If she wasn't so excited about Christmas, she would be worried sick over Dixie and Rose being accused of murder by a man none of them even knew. Surely he couldn't arrest the two women without proof?

She worried her underlip with her teeth. Perhaps if she could just get Reagan talking about *something* she could ease some of his tension. "What made you decide to become a lawman, Sheriff?"

A muscle bunched along Reagan's jaw, and an indecipherable emotion crossed his face. "What made you decide to be a teacher?" He turned the question back on her.

Charlotte's fingernails bit into her palms. But very well. They couldn't just sit here in total silence for the next hour into town. So if he refused to converse she would do the conversing.

"My choices were homemaking, nursing, or teaching. Since I wasn't ready to set up housekeeping, and since blood makes me feel rather faint, I chose teaching. Don't get me wrong, I do love children, and I do love helping them learn. So it wasn't chosen out of hardship but chosen because I felt it was the best match for my skills."

Reagan nodded.

For a long moment, Charlotte feared that she was going to have to come up with another topic if she wanted to keep the conversation going. But then Reagan spoke.

"My father was shot by an outlaw he'd been chasing for months when I was still a teen." The muscles in his jaw bulged in and out. "I had so much anger bottled up inside me. Took me a few years to work through that, but eventually I realized that, if it were in my power, I wanted to keep things like that from happening to others as much as possible. The only way I could see to do that was to become a lawman myself, much to my mother's chagrin." The corner of his mouth tipped up into a sardonic grin. "We lived in Seattle at the time and I went to the sheriff in town." The sardonic grin grew into a soft chuckle. "Let's just say the man was familiar with me, but not because of any reason you might think." He winked. "He was mighty leery about training a boy who'd up till that point mostly been on the wrong side of the law, but he took me under his wing despite his misgivings and taught me everything he knew. Even made me a deputy for a short time. But then I saw Zeb's advertisement in the paper seeking a sheriff for his new town. Ma and I were ready for someplace a little quieter than Seattle by that time, so I applied." He shrugged. "And here we are."

"Well, I'm glad you are here, Sheriff." The words emerged before she could think better of them.

His gaze darted to hers, then he nodded. "And I'm glad you are here."

Forbidden emotions surged to life in her chest. Before she could give them foothold, she turned to study the patches of snow that glistened in the shaded areas along the road.

Beside her, Reagan blew out a breath. "I'm afraid I haven't been very good company today and for that I apologize.

Charlotte waved a hand. "Think nothing of it. I'm worried about them too, now that you've told me about the marshal's accusations."

He nodded. "Seems so contradictory to their character, and yet the marshal doesn't seem like a frivolous man."

Charlotte didn't want to dwell on what kind of man the marshal might be. "How much farther back to town?"

Reagan cleared his throat. "We should be there inside thirty minutes now."

The silence descended again, but this time it felt more companionable than oppressing, and Charlotte let it rest. Her worry for Rose and Dixie returned to the fore and she niggled at the inside of her lower lip. Finally, she released a long slow breath. It was best she take these worries to the Lord in prayer before she worked a hole clean through her skin.

Flynn pushed his mount as fast as he would go, but it still took him twenty minutes to reach the site of the accident.

Zebulon Heath paced the edge of the road near two unconscious men, the tip of his cane making a rhythmic tick, tick, tick, against the ground. Flynn offered the town founder a nod as he swung down from his horse. "Mr. Heath, good to see you again."

"Likewise. I wish it was under better circumstances."

"Indeed." Flynn turned his focus toward the two men laid out in the grass beside the road. One was Don Brass, the stagecoach whip. The other man he didn't recognize. He was glad to see that Joe had put a barrier between them and the frozen prairie sod. A rapid assessment showed that neither man was bleeding, and he should turn his attention to the one with the gunshot wound. He flicked Zeb a look. From what Wash had said, Zeb had been the one to accidentally shoot another passenger when the stage had overturned. "The other man?"

Zeb jabbed his cane toward the coach. "They're working to get him out now."

Zoe Kastain and Kin Davis both balanced on the toppled coach, leaning through the door to each take the arm of a man. Flynn couldn't see the extent of his injuries from here. Joe must be lifting him up from inside. Since there was no moaning or howling, the victim must be unconscious, which was a mercy. Wash had said the man was shot in his midsection and abdominal wounds were often severely painful.

Flynn yanked the rolled-up stretcher from where it was

strapped behind his saddle. With a quick flip, he unfurled it onto the roadbed. He wanted to ask for details about what happened, but his patient's health always came first. He would need to see the man before he knew what questions to ask. Besides, he knew that Reagan and Joe would sort out all the details of today's event.

"Joe, I'm here," he called into the coach. "What can I do to help?"

Joe didn't hesitate. "Zoe, thank you. You can get down now and let Doc take your place."

Flynn hauled himself atop the carriage, and as soon as he had a hold of the wounded man's arm, Zoe scrambled out of the way.

The patient was a dark-haired man who appeared to have been in good health prior to today's accident. Good. That would be a benefit to his recovery.

"Ready? And...lift!" Joe instructed.

Flynn was even more glad for the patient's sake that he was unconscious, because it took the three of them a lot of heaving, and pulling, and pushing to extract his dead-weight from inside the carriage. He, Kin, and Joe were covered in the man's blood by the time they got him down and laid out on the stretcher.

Washington Nolan rode up only moments later with a buckboard and Flynn thanked the Almighty for his good sense. They were certainly going to need that wagon with three unconscious men to haul into town.

As they worked at loading the wounded into the wagon, Flynn thought ahead. There wasn't enough space in his room at the alehouse to quarter all three patients. He was going to have to requisition a room at Dixie's place. He checked the gunshot wound while Joe and Kin worked to lift the other two men into the wagon. The bullet had penetrated high on the man's right side. He didn't notice any frothing around the wound, so maybe he'd been lucky enough for the bullet to miss his lung. If the bullet had only damaged the man's liver, then there was a very slim chance he would live. Flynn felt relief. But a dusty road in the middle of nowhere was not the place to conduct a surgical exploration for the bullet. There was nothing more he could do for the man here. They needed to get him back to town as quickly as possible so a better look could be taken in a more sterile environment.

A soon as they got the wagon loaded—which included not only the injured, but the satchels and lockbox from the boot of the stage—Joe took hold of Kin's arm. "I'll ride into town with Kin and the rest of you can ride the mounts or sit in the wagon."

Washington swung down from Kin's mare and handed over her reins. "If it's all the same to you, Deputy, I'd like to get Zoe home to her parents' place."

Flynn tied his horse off to the wagon and helped Zeb up to the box seat at the front, halfway listening to the conversation taking place near the tailgate.

Joe pierced Wash with a hard look. "You have anything to do with these shenanigans, son?"

Wash swallowed, but it was Kin who spoke up and right quick. "He didn't have nothing to do with it, I swear. In fact, he tried to talk me out of it."

Wash only studied the ground, kicking at a ripple of dirt that had been mounded up by the frost.

Zoe cleared her throat and looked at Joe earnestly. "Wash and me was coming—were coming—we were coming to try to stop Kin, not to help him."

Joe gave a nod. "Very well. You may head home. But I

might have more questions for both of you, so expect me to pay you a visit."

"Yessir," both young people chimed together.

Flynn pulled himself up to the driver's seat and slapped the reins against the horses' flanks. "Get up," he clucked to them. He needed to find the balance between getting the wounded man to surgery as quickly as possible and not jarring him so much that he expired between here and town. He set the horses to a trot that would hopefully be the middle road between the two.

Relieved to be on the way, he could finally ask Zeb for more details. He glanced over at the man.

Hands folded one atop the other and resting on his cane, Zeb leaned heavily on the prop as though his legs had just been kicked from under him.

"Care to tell me what happened back there?"

Zeb loosed a tremulous breath. "We were riding along just as quiet as you please, when from out of nowhere comes this banshee screech that liked to have shaved the hair clean off my neck. Both the parson and I shucked our weapons. I was trying to get a good glimpse of the bandit so's I could get a shot at him, but Old Don tried to outrun him. Likely to protect the cash I had in the lockbox. Next thing I know, the whole shebang is going wheels over top railings and the parson crashed into me and that's when I shot him."

Flynn tossed a glance into the back of the wagon. "So the gut shot man is a parson?"

Zeb seemed startled. "Oh, no. I apologize. The 'him' I meant was the other passenger who boarded the carriage with us. The new parson—Preston Clay—he's the one that took a conk to the head and is lying next to Don there."

"I see. So do you know anything about this man you shot?"

Zeb sighed. "'Fraid not. Other than he said he was Dixie Pottinger's husband. Now don't that beat all?"

Flynn's blood seemed to freeze in his veins, and then in the next moment his temperature surged till it could have rivaled the bubbling water of the hot springs just outside of town.

Dear Lord Almighty.

Flynn twisted on the seat to give the man a better look.

For the first time ever, he considered whether it might be better *not* to save some patients.

Chapter Seventeen

team hung heavy in the boardinghouse kitchen by the time Dixie heard the hoofbeats that indicated Doc and the rest of the party had returned from the site of the accident. Swiping at her forehead with the back of one hand, she quickly put the bread rolls that had been rising on the warm sideboard into the oven. Fifteen minutes and they would be a perfect golden brown, a tasty accompaniment to the fish and potato chowder that bubbled fragrantly at the back of the stove.

Tugging off her apron, she hung it on the hook behind the kitchen door and then hurried out to let Flynn know she had plenty of hot water on to boil.

Flynn was already rushing through the boardinghouse door when she stepped into the entry from the dining room. "Dixie." He strode straight to her. His face seemed a shade paler than usual. His hands fidgeted with the brim of his Stetson as he twirled it through his fingers.

Concern surged, and she glanced past his shoulder. A wagon was parked just outside; she could see it through the door's windowpanes. "What is it?"

"Listen, first of all there were three men injured and I need a room to put them in. Can we use one of yours?" There was something strained about his tone—tight like it was ready to break.

She nodded. "Of course. Room five is available. It already has two beds in it, and I have an extra cot that's not being used. I'll get it right now and bring it in." She started to turn, but Flynn's hand shot out to grip her arm.

"Dixie, wait." He released her as soon as she gave him her attention again.

She searched his face.

He swallowed. "I'm afraid I have bad news."

Her heart thundered. Had he gone up to check on Rose just now? Her gaze darted to the stairs. "Is it Rose? I've been so busy cooking. I should have check—"

"No." He shook his head. "It's your husband."

Dixie's hand flew to her throat. At just the mention of Steven she felt a wave of nausea. She swallowed it down, trying to make sense of the confusion swirling through her. Steven... Her focus slipped to the wagon parked outside.

Flynn's feet shuffled, drawing her attention back to him. He peered at her from beneath his brows. "He was the one who was shot in the accident on the stage."

Dixie felt her knees go weak, and she took a stumbling step backwards. "Steven? Is in Wyldhaven?"

"Yes. Here, sit down." He nudged her toward the leather bench that sat against the wall next to the boardinghouse's front desk. "He's very badly injured and might not make it."

Uncertainty swirled through her. She didn't know whether to be happy or sad about that news. She gave her head a little shake.

Flynn took backward steps toward the door, still studying her face. "I need to get him and the other two injured men brought in, but I wanted you to hear the news from me first." He paused with his hand on the door handle. "Are you going to be okay?"

She nodded. "Yes. Thank you for letting me know." She waved a gesture back toward the kitchen. "I have hot soup for everyone, and the bread rolls will be done soon."

He simply nodded.

When he went out, he propped the door open with the large rock she kept on the stoop for that purpose. A chill breeze swept in, running icy fingers across her neck. Dixie shivered.

Only a moment later, Flynn and Ewan hauled Steven through the front door. One held his ankles, while the other clasped him around his ribcage. Steven was moaning and cursing, obviously in terrible pain. It had been over a year since she'd seen him, but even incapacitated and bleeding as he was, just the sight of him filled her with terror and queasiness. His gaze latched on to her as they carried him past her. He snarled and reached out, his bloody fingers grazing the material of her blouse before Ewan noticed what he was doing and jerked him away from her.

Steven shrieked in pain. "Devil! You are a devil of a woman!"

"Be silent!" Doc gave Steven a little shake.

Steven screeched again, but seemed determined to continue his bombardment. "Curse you...for...ever..." A fit of coughing seized him, and the men hauled him up the stairs and out of sight.

Dixie stared at the smear of blood on her blouse. Only a few hours ago, she'd thought that maybe she had a chance at renewing her hope in a Savior. But now it was as if those tender shoots of hope had been trampled by a stampede of futility. All prospects of hope had been obliterated in the blink of an eye.

Taking a calming breath, Dixie gave herself a shake and forced herself to action. They would need that extra bed. And she needed to don a clean blouse.

But as she moved to retrieve it, her legs trembled to the point of near uselessness.

Steven was here.

Under her same roof.

And Rose was too sick for them to run.

Another chill breeze swept through the door.

She didn't understand how it could still be so cold when hell had just arrived in Wyldhaven.

Reagan knew something was terribly wrong the moment he turned the carriage onto Wyldhaven's main street. He'd planned to ask Charlotte once more if she would be opposed to him talking to Mr. Heath about them courting, but he could see that the conversation would have to wait. A wagon sat before Dixie's Boardinghouse, with a bevy of activity happening around it.

Beside him, Charlotte gave a little moan. "Oh, Kin! What has that boy gotten himself into now?"

Reagan followed her gaze to the place where Joe was just hauling Kin Davis through the front door of the jail.

Charlotte flapped a hand. "Just pull over anywhere. I'll see if Dixie needs my help with anything, and then I can see myself home."

Reagan pulled the wagon to a stop in front of the jailhouse. "Wait for me at Dixie's and I'll walk you home. Might be a bit before I'm free, though. Not sure what's going on here."

Charlotte nodded. "Yes. Fine. I'll wait for you there."

Dixie's was only two doors down from the jail, but Reagan waited until he saw Charlotte disappear inside the boardinghouse before he pushed into the warmth of the jail. He needed to make this quick. With all that had been on his mind, he'd driven the horse a bit hard today, and it wasn't good for it to be left out in the cold for long without a rubdown.

Joe was locking Kin inside one of the jail cells and speaking when Reagan stepped inside. "I'm sorry, but for now, you are going to have to stay in here. Leastwise until we get a straight story about what happened today. And I don't have time to listen to it right now. I need to go help Doc get the injured settled into their beds. Make yourself right at home, kid." He gave the bars of the cell a good thump with his fist, driving home the boy's new lack of freedom.

Reagan lifted his brows at his deputy, waiting for an explanation.

Joe tipped his head. "Walk with me and I'll tell you what I know on the way to Dixie's."

By the time he and Joe had helped carry Don Brass and the other man, who Zeb said was the town's new parson, to the upper room at Dixie's that was the town's newly-dubbed hospital, Reagan had heard the whole of what Joe was certain of. And there were plenty of details that Joe admitted still needed investigation. But Reagan knew one thing with absolute certainty—he needed to find Marshal Holloway, and he needed to find him quickly.

If they could get Steven Pottinger to admit who he was, that would eliminate all murder charges against Dixie and her ma.

⁘⤳⤳≀⟨≀≀⤲⤲⁘

Flynn gritted his teeth as he and Ewan set Pottinger on the bed closest to the window in room five. The man was still spewing invectives against Dixie between bouts of coughing and cries of pain. He writhed on the bed, obviously unable to get comfortable.

Dixie bustled in with a large feather tick in her arms. Flynn noted that she'd changed her blouse. It had been almost his undoing when Pottinger had smeared blood on her as they passed. Almost like a picture of what the man had done to her life in the past.

Dixie worried her underlip. "I don't have another frame, so this one will have to go on the floor."

Flynn nodded. "Don't worry about it. I think Don is already coming around. I'm more worried about the minister. He might need a bed for a couple days."

"I'm coming for you, Dixie," Steven rasped from his bed. "Don't think this is going to slow me down."

Flynn snatched a towel from his doctor bag and clamped it onto Steven's bleeding wound. He pressed down hard.

The man yowled like two cats in a fight.

"Don't mind me. I just need to get this bleeding stopped."

Steven went slack. And for one heartbeat Flynn thought that he'd killed him. He felt a swirl of lightheadedness that was quickly relieved when he found a pulse in the man's throat. When he looked up, Dixie was gone and Joe and the sheriff were depositing the still unconscious minister on the next bed, while Ewan was supporting the upright but still woozy stagedriver, Don Brass.

Flynn glanced down at Pottinger. He loosed a breath and sent up a prayer of repentance. He reached for a light. He would never be able to live with himself if he didn't try to do everything in his power to save the man. He reminded himself of the truth that every person was created in the image of the Creator, whether they chose to live worthy of that honor, or not. He would do his best to save the man's life. Despite the fact that a gunshot wound like this was almost always fatal. If the man did die, Flynn wanted his conscience to be clear in the matter.

And if the man recovered, Flynn was going to do everything in his power to ensure that he stood trial for the injuries he had caused to his wife and mother.

Flynn set to rolling up his sleeves. "Ewan, I need you to bring me a pot of boiling water. Dixie said she had some ready in the kitchen."

The bartender nodded.

While Ewan headed down to get the water, and Joe and Reagan set to asking Old Don questions, Flynn hurried across the hall and pushed into Dixie's living quarters. He took a lantern off the shelf in her front room, and another from the side table in Rose's room. A brief check showed that Rose was sleeping peacefully, probably for the first time in days, and blissfully unaware that her devil of a son had just arrived in town. Her body needed the rest, so he left her to sleep and hurried back to room five. Turning the lanterns up as bright as they would go, he set them so that they worked in tandem with the first lantern he'd already placed on the dressing table by Steven's bed.

He assessed the man's weight, then dripped twenty-three drops of chloroform carefully onto a cloth and inserted it into the dispensing cone. This he placed carefully over Pottinger's mouth.

While he waited for the chloroform to take effect and drag Steven into a deep sleep, he ran his hands over the minister's scalp, giving it a more thorough check than he'd been able to afford out at the scene. An egg-sized lump protruded from the man's skull just above and behind his left ear, but Flynn was thankful to feel no loose bones or soft spots. The man would probably be fine and coming around at any moment now. But he would need watching over the next couple of days.

Flynn quickly mixed two cups of headache powders. One he

gave to Don and urged him to drink it all. The other he set on the table nearest the second bed. He might be in the middle of removing Pottinger's bullet when the minister came around, and he would want something to cut the pain that was bound to be pulsing in his head tonight.

With that preparation done, he set to stripping Pottinger of his shirt and laid out his surgical instruments on the clean, boiled cloth, on the side table. When Ewan brought the pot of boiled water, fresh from the stove downstairs, Flynn dropped the instruments into the water one at a time.

Right. He was ready to work. He offered the prayer he always prayed before he undertook a surgery. *Lord, guide my hands and keep them steady.* And then he got to work.

Charlotte found Dixie and helped her carry a basket of bandages up to the hospital room. Don Brass had already come around and was chatting with Joe and Reagan quietly in one corner of the room. Charlotte pushed a chair over to the group. It took a lot of talking from Reagan to even get the old hostler to rest himself on the seat. He insisted that his clothes were unworthy of meeting with the fine linen of Dixie's embroidered cushion. They finally had to bring in a towel to cover the cushion so the man would sit down and rest.

Dixie seemed morose and jumpy, startling at even the most mundane of sounds. Charlotte's concern grew as the minutes passed and Dixie's nerves didn't seem to be settling.

"I've some cleanup to tend to in the kitchen," Dixie declared, and hurried down the stairs.

Charlotte followed her.

Once in the kitchen she tugged Dixie to a stop and took both her hands in a firm grip. "What's wrong? Out with it." She knew Dixie had been facing a lot of concern and worry lately, what with Rose's sickness and having to run the boardinghouse all on her own. But Charlotte wasn't prepared for the tears that burgeoned on Dixie's lashes, or for the sob that caught in her friend's throat.

"Oh darling, come here." Charlotte pulled Dixie into a warm embrace. "You've gone and worn yourself to a frazzle, but I get the feeling there is more to this than just being tired?" She gripped Dixie's shoulders and set her back so she could get a good read on her expression.

Dixie huffed a sound that was half laugh and half despair. "You have no idea."

"Here, sit. You need to eat." Charlotte dished up a good portion of the fish chowder and set it in front of a chair at the table. Pushing Dixie into the seat, she then turned and helped herself to a small portion, and snagged two piping-hot rolls for each of them.

"Thank you," Dixie nodded.

After grace was said, Charlotte tore a chunk from her bread, but kept her focus on Dixie's weary face. "I actually have *some* idea."

Dixie's brows rose in question, and Charlotte confessed that the marshal had come to Jacinda's house close to a week past and shared with Reagan his reason for being in town.

"Mind you, Sheriff Callahan told the man he couldn't possibly know the truth, but I'm guessing some of today's kerfuffle has to do with the marshal?"

Dixie sighed. "In a roundabout way, yes." She blew on a spoonful of stew before tasting it. "It's rather a long story. Are you sure you have time for it?"

"For you, I always have time." Charlotte hoped her expression conveyed the sincerity of her words.

Apparently it did, because Dixie launched into her tale. By the time she got done with the telling, Charlotte was swiping tears from her eyes with an utterly damp handkerchief. "You mean to tell me that the man Zeb shot on the stage is your no-good husband who the marshal thought you'd killed nearly two years ago, but who in reality lived after Rose shot him? And he was coming to drag you back home with him?"

Dixie's lips twisted. "I doubt he wants to go back home. Because of all that's happened there would be too many questions about his character now. But yes, I'm sure he had plans for Rose and me."

The way she said the word 'plans' sent a shaft of horror straight down Charlotte's spine. She had been taken captive once and forced to squeeze into a trunk in the back of a wagon. Reagan had caught the man and rescued her inside a quarter of an hour. Yet, that experience had made her hesitant and untrusting for days. She couldn't imagine what it must feel like to have a man who was supposed to have your best interests at heart treat you with such contempt and disdain.

She offered Dixie another gentle squeeze. "Well, maybe something good will come of this. God's plans are always to prosper us, and not to harm us, right? At least that's what Jeremiah says. So perhaps this was part of God's plan all along?"

Dixie's hand stopped halfway to her mouth. She blinked at Charlotte for a moment, but then pushed her barely-touched bowl of chowder back and stood. "Perhaps you are right. But if you'll excuse me, I really should take Ma some food while I have a moment."

Charlotte shot out a hand and laid hold of Dixie's arm. "Dixie, you can't go on like this. I can see the weariness weighting your shoulders like a cloak."

Dixie rubbed the back of her neck, but didn't meet Charlotte's gaze. "It's only for a few more days."

"You and I both know that Rose isn't going to be up to helping you for a month at the very least!" Charlotte purposely gentled her tone. "I could come by and help you for a few days, but once school starts up again I would be no good to you. Can you afford to hire someone?"

Dixie tilted her head. "I hadn't thought of that. Yes, I suppose I could. Business has been good. I practically ran myself ragged at dinner last night."

Charlotte smiled. "That's because you are the best cook inside of ten counties."

Dixie rolled her eyes. "I suppose I could put out an advertisement in Seattle."

"You let me worry about that." Charlotte tapped her arm. "And don't fret about cleanup in here. I'll have it done in no time."

Dixie sighed, and the very fact that she didn't protest revealed just how tired she must be. "Thank you."

"Yes. Of course," Charlotte offered, but as she watched Dixie load a tray and then hurry from the room, she couldn't help but wonder why her comment about God only planning good for us had upset Dixie.

It didn't take her long to wash the dishes and tidy up the kitchen.

She was just finishing up when Reagan appeared and asked if he might walk her home. "It's going to be a long night, and I'll feel better knowing you are tucked away safe and warm in Ma's house."

Charlotte appreciated the gesture of chivalry, and reached for his arm. "Much obliged, Sheriff."

At the entryway, Reagan helped her on with her wraps

and then they stepped out into the frigid wind that blew tiny ice crystals with it. Charlotte shivered and clutched her coat closed more tightly at the neck. "Reagan, what do you think about Liora working for Dixie at the boardinghouse?"

Reagan leaned away to get a better look at her face. But then he resumed walking with a contemplative expression. "I know she needs the work. She even came by the jailhouse offering to scrub the floors for me the other day, which I let her do, but I can't afford to pay her to do it every week." He massaged one hand over the lower half of his face. "Is Dixie looking to hire someone?"

Charlotte nodded. "Rose won't be on her feet again for quite some time, and Dixie can't cover all of the boardinghouse's needs on her own."

"Well"—Reagan directed their steps into the alleyway between the jail and McGinty's, and Charlotte felt the instant relief from the biting wind—"I'm not sure how Dixie would feel about employing a woman of Liora's former profession, but I suppose it couldn't hurt to ask."

Charlotte gave a little bounce as they hurried up onto his mother's porch. "My feelings exactly, Sheriff. And thank you for walking me home."

Reagan only nodded. He swallowed and his gaze drifted over her features for a moment before he took a swift step back, tipped his hat, and then hurried off into the night.

Charlotte felt like a little part of her heart had just been torn from her chest. She sighed and pushed into the house.

Chapter Eighteen

fter taking Rose a tray of the chowder, Dixie stood quietly looking down at her husband, who was lying, pale and still, on the bed closest to this room's window. Evening had fallen, so the only light in the room came from the dim glow of the turned down-lamp on the dresser.

Steven's breaths were low and shallow and every once in a while, he moaned, shifted, or winced in his sleep. Flynn had assured that he hadn't felt pain during the surgery, but that he would be in a lot of discomfort once he awoke from the effects of the chloroform. Laudanum would need to be administered so he could rest and recover.

Flynn said the bullet had gone through Steven's liver and then lodged too near his spine to be removed. Only time would tell if Steven retained the use of his legs, or if he recovered at all—he'd said the chances of Steven living through this were about one in ten. Flynn had left the wound open so that infection could drain out of it if it set in.

Dixie's guilt mounted as she looked down at him. She should want him to live. She should at least feel sorrow, maybe worry, or concern. But she felt only numbness. The familiar numbness that she'd learned to surround herself with whenever Steven was around. It was better not to feel or think; that way she wasn't likely to voice an opinion he might disagree with.

Both Don Brass and the parson had come around now, but

Flynn had refused to let them leave their beds—he'd forced Don into a bed as soon as he'd finished his surgery on Steven, giving Don no leeway to dodge the order. When Don had said he was too dirty for the linen sheets, Flynn had said sheets were made for washing. When Don had declared that he needed to go take care of his horses, Flynn had told him that Joe had already taken care of them. And when Don had insisted that he was feeling just fine, Flynn had told him that he'd once known a man who hit his head, declared he was feeling just fine, and had been dead by the next day. Don's face had gone a little pale, but he'd climbed into the bed after that. Flynn had instructed both Don and the parson that they were under watch for at least one night and the parson for likely two. He'd elaborated again that injuries to the head could often turn dangerous without a moment's notice.

Now, both men chatted quietly with each other from where they lay in their beds, though to Dixie's estimation, Old Don was doing most of the talking. Wyldhaven's new minister seemed to be a quiet man of very few words.

Flynn had just stepped down to the kitchen to get a bowl of chowder and some bread, since he hadn't had a chance to eat with the others.

Dixie gave herself a shake. Don and the minister were probably hungry too. She pivoted toward the door. She could worry about what she was going to do about Steven another time. Right now she had things to attend to.

Charlotte had apparently gone home, for she was no longer in the now tidy kitchen. Flynn, however, was sitting quietly at the table, looking weary as he spread butter on a piece of bread. He stilled when she entered, his gaze scrutinizing her slowly. "How are you doing?"

She waved away his concern and pasted on a smile. "Fine.

Fine. I'm just getting Don and the minister some soup." She set to gathering a tray and bowls, plates for some bread, spoons, two tumblers of fresh water. Flynn just watched her solemnly all the way until she ladled the chowder into the bowls and put two warm rolls on each plate. She hefted the tray.

"Dixie." The word was soft and low.

She stilled but didn't look at him. She couldn't handle his gentle concern right now. "I'm fine, Dr. Griffin, truly." She inserted the formality to remind herself of the need for distance and left quickly, before he could see how her hands trembled against the handles of the tray.

When she reached the room and pushed the door open with her back, she stilled. Reagan and the marshal both stood by the far bed with Zeb between them.

The marshal was speaking. "His identification says his name is"—he consulted the papers in his hand—"Orin Wells. Are you sure he said his name was Pottinger?"

Zeb leaned over Steven's bed, and thrust a finger at him. "I'm telling you this man told me plain as day that his name was Pottinger and he was Dixie's husband and Rose's son."

The marshal tapped his hat against one leg and looked over at her.

She swallowed and nodded. If Steven never came around, or refused to identify himself, would they believe her? Would charges be dropped? Or would they still be in trouble for shooting him back in Birch Run even though he'd lived?

Ewan, standing in the shadows of one corner, shuffled his feet and cleared his throat. "He did seem to know Dixie when we carried him past her downstairs. Cussed her, even."

Relieved to see from the marshal's expression that his suspicions about the story she'd told him earlier seemed to have been allayed, Dixie stepped the rest of the way into the room and set the tray on the table between Don and the new minister. "I thought you gentlemen might be hungry. I can bring up coffee or tea, along with some cake once you've finished with this, if you like."

Appreciation shone in the minister's eyes, and he dipped a nod of thanks.

Don touched his forehead and squirmed uncomfortably in the bed. "Much obliged, Miss Pottinger."

The word 'miss' sent a shard of guilt through Dixie. These were all such good people, and she'd deceived them for long enough. "Actually it's 'Mrs.'" She tipped a nod toward Steven's bed. "That man there is my husband who was coming to look for me."

Don's eyes widened, but he had the grace not to comment further. Instead, he tasted his chowder and gave a definitive nod. "Best soup I've had in quite some time. Thank you kindly."

The minister studied her with eyes that seemed to see more than he let on. She wished she could remember the name Zeb had introduced him by, but she'd been in such shock over Steven that it hadn't stayed with her. His focus bounced between her and Steven lying so still on the bed across the room. For a moment she thought he might speak, but then he turned his attention to the soup in his bowl and set about eating it with slow methodical scoops of the spoon.

Kin sank onto the edge of the thin cot in the jail cell and buried his face in his palms. A feeling of despair settled like an eagle swooping in with plans to perch and stay for a while. He'd gotten a man shot and that was the truth of it, whether he'd pulled the trigger, or not. And now he was in jail when he should be home making dinner for Pa and making sure he didn't fall asleep with the door or window open, or with the fire blazing too hot, or even outside in the cold barn, as he had last week.

Worry pinched his stomach.

Unable to sit still a moment longer, he stood and paced the room. It was three paces to the bars of the cell next to his, five paces along the bars to the outer wall of the jail, three paces back to the far end of the cot, and five paces along the length of the cot back to where he started from. And repeat.

It seemed like forever until Sheriff Callahan and Deputy Rodante returned to the jailhouse.

When Deputy Joe slid the tray laden with fragrant chowder and bread beneath the bars of the door, Kin's stomach growled appreciatively. But guilt niggled when he took the first bite. This was made from the fish he'd caught this morning. He should be home right now frying the brace he'd kept for Pa and himself. He swallowed and looked up at the two men who were still watching him. He had no right to ask, but he should at least try. "Do you think one of you would be able to ride out and check on my pa? Sometimes he falls asleep with the lantern on or..." He let the thought trail away with a shrug. Truth was, he never knew what Pa might do.

The two lawmen exchanged a look. Then Sheriff Callahan strode to the stove and poured a cup of coffee from the pot. He returned to the cell and slid the cup beneath the bars.

Kin gave him a nod of thanks, even though he would have preferred plain water. Coffee never had been much to his liking.

Joe cleared his throat as the sheriff straightened to his feet. "We were just coming to ask you if you thought your pa might be home."

Kin snorted. "Unless he's at McGinty's or in a ditch somewhere between there and home."

Deputy Joe shuffled his feet, gripped the back of his neck, and looked at his boss questioningly.

Kin stopped chewing and held his breath, not wanting to miss anything the sheriff might say.

Puffing out his cheeks, Sheriff Callahan tossed his hat down on his desk and sank into his chair. "Why don't you go out and fetch Mr. Davis, while I have a chat with Kin here?"

Kin's eyes fell closed. *Fetch Mr. Davis.* So he was going to end up in jail *and* get the beating he'd been expecting from Pa, to boot.

Deputy Joe nodded. "Sure, Boss."

A bit of trepidation settled in Kin's chest as he watched the deputy head out the door into the blustery snow that had begun to fall. The man had been firm, but not unkind to him. He hadn't struck him, or cinched the cuffs around his hands too tight, or even forced him to run back to town behind his horse, like Kin knew some lawmen would have done.

When the door clicked shut, he transferred his wary gaze to the sheriff. What kind of man was Sheriff Callahan? Kin had gotten into his fair share of mischief, but he'd never run aground of the law before, and he couldn't say that he liked this feeling all that much.

The sheriff slapped his hands against his knees, stood wearily, dragged his chair out from behind his desk, and set it carefully in front of Kin's jail cell. He poured himself a cup of the coffee—apparently emptying the pot, because instead of returning it to the top of the pot belly, he set it on the floor. Taking a quiet sip, the sheriff sank into the chair and propped his booted feet atop one of the brace-bars that ran horizontally through the door of the cell. He tipped a nod to the tray of food that was still by Kin's side on the cot. "Better eat your food whilst it's hot. Would be a shame to waste food as good as Dixie's." There was a gentle light that conveyed kindness in the man's blue eyes, though his face remained serious.

Kin swallowed, relieved to see that he likely wasn't about to have the stuffing pummeled out of him. Still...he'd best do as he was told. "Yessir." He picked up the bowl and dunked one of the rolls into the thick creamy juices. His stomach rumbled loudly. It had been a long time since he'd eaten food that tasted anywhere close to this good.

The sheriff sat quietly until Kin had finished eating and slid the tray back beneath the bars. Kin cupped his hands around the warmth of his coffee cup and waited for the sheriff to speak as he sank back onto the cot. That was one reason to like coffee, he supposed. On a cold night like this, the heat offered a good deal of comfort.

"Care to explain what happened today, son?" the sheriff finally pressed.

Kin rubbed at a patch of sticky pitch on the side of one thumb. He knew he needed to make one thing clear right out of the barrel. "I didn't have a gun."

The sheriff frowned. "So I've heard. Did you think you were going to be able to rob Old Don Brass without a weapon?"

Kin sighed and delayed his answer by taking a sip of the bitter black brew. No one was going to understand why he'd done this. Even he was feeling like he'd been an idiot. He didn't meet the sheriff's gaze. "I wasn't trying to rob the stage."

"That's not what I heard."

Kin resisted a roll of his eyes. "I only told Wash that I was going to rob it so that he'd for sure come tell you about it."

"What was that?"

Kin realized that his words had been mumbled too low for the sheriff to hear, but instead of repeating himself all he said was, "Nothing."

The legs of the sheriff's chair thunked to the ground, a sure sign he was getting irritated. Despite the kindness he'd seen in the man's eyes, Kin was actually kind of glad that a set of bars stood between them.

"So here's what I know so far." The sheriff leaned forward, braced elbows to knees, and pegged him with a stern look that made Kin swallow. "Screaming like a banshee from the grave, you rode down on the stage. Old Don thought you were coming for the strong box and tried to outrun you, which caused the carriage to tip over at the hairpin. Mr. Heath had pulled his gun to try and shoot you." He hesitated. "And the parson too, for that matter. Did you know that?"

Kin swallowed. "I knew I needed to be fast. But I was expecting the shots to come from Old Don, not the passengers."

"Yeah? Well, now a man's been shot. How do you feel about that?"

Kin pushed at the pitch again with his thumb, nearly sloshing coffee over his hands. "Didn't think there was any danger to anyone but me."

The sheriff surged to his feet and snatched up the tray. "'Didn't think' is about right!" He stomped to his desk and plunked the tray down, leaning onto his fists with his back to the cell. "And now I have to decide what to do with you." He spun around and leveled the full force of his narrow-eyed scrutiny on Kin. "Why did you do it? That's what I want to know."

Kin set the coffee cup on the floor and picked at a splinter on one of the boards next to it. "You wouldn't understand."

The sheriff snorted. "You're probably wrong about that. I used to be a lot like you, Kincaid Davis." He nodded affirmatively. "A lot like you."

Kin twisted his lips to the side. He doubted the sheriff knew anything about losing a ma and then having your pa turn to drink and essentially becoming a different man.

Silence hung heavy for a long minute before the sheriff said, "So... You done talking?"

Kin nodded.

The sheriff threw up one hand. "All right." He picked up the tray, blew out the lantern, and left the jailhouse.

With the darkness, the chill wind that crept through the clapboard siding of the jail seemed to grow colder. Kin wished he had a warmer coat, but this one that he'd had since Wash handed it down to him when they turned twelve was the only one he owned. It was nearly worn through in places, and too tight through the shoulders, and the sleeves were too short, but it was better than nothing. He tugged the thin quilt from the cot around his shoulders and curled into a tight ball on his side, wishing there was a pillow.

Kin laid in the dark for a long time. He was too cold to sleep, but too tired to do any of the exercises that he sometimes did at home to warm himself enough so he could sleep. He wished the sheriff had banked the stove with a couple extra logs before he'd left the room. And he kept wondering why the deputy hadn't returned with Pa yet. Had something happened to him?

He tossed and turned long into the night and finally got up and made himself run in place for a time. While he was running, he noticed the cot against the far wall in the other cell. It was dimly lit by the moonlight that slanted through the barred jailhouse window. Another thin quilt sat atop it. Kin's jogging sort of trailed off of its own volition as a thought struck him. He still had a fishing hook and some string in his coat pocket! He tugged it out and uncurled his line. He might have just enough. It took him another fifteen minutes of tossing the hook before he was finally able to snag the quilt deeply enough to drag it all the way across the cell to him, but after all that exercise and with the extra blanket, he was warm enough that he was able to get some fitful sleep.

Despite that, his mind was fuzzy with exhaustion the next morning when Deputy Joe stepped through the creaky front door. Joe told him to back up to the bars of the cell, where he cuffed his hands and then opened the door.

Joe took Kin's arm and urged him across the room. "New minister has some things he'd like to say to the whole town. Figured it would likely be good for you to hear it.

Kin swallowed, only one thing pressing on his mind. "Did you talk to my pa?"

Giving the jailhouse door a push, Joe nudged him out onto the street. "He was more than a bit drunk when I got out there. I couldn't wake him. But I made sure the fire was banked and all the doors and windows were shut tight against the cold. And I covered him with a blanket."

Kin watched the road carefully so he wouldn't misstep and lose his balance, and maybe to keep the deputy from seeing the depth of all he was feeling reflected in his eyes. "Thank you."

He sensed more than saw the deputy nod. "I'll go back out there today."

A group of townsfolk had already started to gather in the field across from McGinty's Alehouse. Kin's stomach rumbled loudly as Joe helped him up the low embankment and into the field. Joe paused and unclasped Kin's hands from behind his back and reclasped them in front of him. Then he tugged a cloth from the large pocket of his coat and handed it to him. Inside were two biscuits and a hardboiled egg.

Kin nodded his thanks.

They had just paused at the back of the crowd, when the minister started speaking.

Chapter Nineteen

ixie stood at the back of the crowd, arms folded against the cold. Steven had lived through the night, and with each passing moment that he lingered on, there was an urging deep inside to protect her future—Rose's too—and to do it quickly before he regained his strength. Because once he regained his strength the upper hand would fall to him. A shiver slipped over her that had nothing to do with the cold.

The clouds that had brought the skiff of snow during the night had cleared and sun sparkled so brightly off the fresh white blanket that it hurt her eyes. She'd much rather be back in the boardinghouse kitchen preparing her supplies and planning the coming week's meals—and what she was going to do about Steven. But she'd felt it might seem rude for her not to show up. As a town businessperson, she wanted to stay in the good graces of all, especially Mr. Heath.

At the front of the gathering the minister smiled, and it transformed his face, making her realize he was much younger than she'd first thought, and actually quite handsome. His dark hair and soft green eyes would soon have all the single ladies of Wyldhaven swooning, she'd bet.

"Good morning, everyone. I'm glad you could join me today." His voice, a smooth tenor, had coaxing overtones that were pleasant to listen to.

A good voice for a minister to have, she supposed.

"I promise not to keep you out in this cold for long. I'm Preston Clay, your new town minister, recently hired by town founder, Mr. Zebulon Heath." He stretched a hand toward Zeb and everyone broke into applause. After the applause died down, he continued. "As many of you know, there was a bit of hubbub with the coach's arrival yesterday"—many eyes turned to look at Kin, who stood in cuffs by Joe's side—"and at this very moment a man lies upstairs in the boardinghouse, fighting for his life."

Dixie's attention narrowed on the man. Surely he wasn't...

"I've gathered us here to seek our maker on that man's behalf."

Murmurs of concurrence traversed the crowd.

Dixie suddenly didn't care if she would be thought rude, or not. She wasn't going to stay here to petition the Almighty for the life of a man who had made hers nothing but torture.

Even though the minister kept talking to the townsfolk as she walked away, she could feel his gaze boring into her back the whole way across the street.

Rose lay gravely ill with pneumonia, and yet no one had called a town meeting to petition the Lord on *her* behalf. Of course, the minister might not have heard yet about Rose's condition, she supposed, since he'd only arrived in town last evening.

Instead of going through the front door of the boardinghouse, she slipped around to the side and took the door that led her straight into the kitchen. Her troubled thoughts were still wrestling with themselves over what to do about Steven.

One thing she knew—she couldn't let him live. She'd been accused of his murder once already, so why not make the accusations true? She didn't have a problem with that.

What she did have a problem with was leaving Rose to care for herself in her elder years. If she got caught, it would be hanging for her, without question. And what would it do to Rose to lose both of her children in such violent manners? For despite the fact that she wasn't Rose's blood daughter, she knew the woman thought of her as one.

No. If she were going to follow through with this, she needed to come up with something that couldn't be traced back to her. She just wasn't sure what that was.

With a sigh, she hung her coat on its peg by the back door, and set to rolling up her sleeves. She had meals to cook for Rose and—

She froze.

Sitting on the small kitchen table was Flynn's doctor bag. And in that moment, she knew exactly the solution to her dilemma.

Flynn must have left it there after he'd checked on Rose and Steven this morning, and before he'd headed over to the impromptu church service. *Laudanum.* When she was a girl, their neighbor had taken her life with an overdose of the medicine. In fact bottles of it were now most often labeled with the warning of "poison!" even though small doses were quite harmless.

A cramp took hold of her stomach. What better opportunity was she ever going to have to find something that would make Steven's death look like it had come of natural causes? He was already on high doses of the opiate. It would only take a little more to ensure that she and Rose never had to face his cruelty again. And yet to take advantage of it would be a massive betrayal of Flynn's trust.

With a tormented groan, she sank into the chair across the table from the bag. She covered her mouth with a trembling hand and stared at the black leather. Thirty seconds. Maybe even less. That was all she needed.

She glanced to the back door. If someone came through from the dining room she would hear them coming, but if anyone stepped through that door they would see her immediately. One more glance at the doctor bag sealed her decision.

She dashed across the room and twisted the back door's lock into place, then hurried back to the table. Her hands trembled almost to the point of uselessness as she fumbled with the clasps on the bag. Her ears strained to hear if anyone might be coming through the dining room, but her heart was beating so loudly that she suddenly knew she'd never be able to hear if someone approached.

Hurry!

The clasp finally gave way to her fumbling, and she pushed the satchel open, scanning the interior. He kept all his medicines in neat rows of pockets and loops of leather. It only took her a moment to spot the large brown bottle with the red label that read "laudanum-poison."

She lifted it, but a thought suddenly stilled her. She couldn't just take his whole supply or he would surely know that he'd been robbed. But what could she store a portion in? She fumbled through the pockets and compartments, doing her best to hurry yet not disturb the orderly contents too much. There! A pocket in the satchel contained empty apothecary jars that he must use for doling out doses of medicine to patients. Since it was full of empty jars of varying sizes, it wasn't likely that he would miss one.

Both bottles rattled against the table as she set them down and worked to unstop first the empty one and then the laudanum.

That task accomplished, she paused. How much would

she need to kill a man? She'd watched Flynn give Steven the equivalent of half a teaspoon last night. So more than that. If she took too much, Flynn might notice it was gone. Yet if she didn't take enough, she might not succeed in her mission.

"Be right with you, I just need to grab my bag!"

Dixie jolted and almost dropped the bottle of laudanum! Flynn's voice and coming from right outside the back door! He rattled the handle. Dixie held her breath.

"Huh." His footsteps retreated.

No time! She didn't even stop to consider further. Her hands shook so badly that she spilled some of the brown liquid down the side of the empty apothecary jar, but she managed to fill it half way.

She heard the bell over the front door ring.

Quickly, she thrust the cork into the top and snatched a towel to wipe the side of the jar. She couldn't have it leaving brown splotches everywhere!

She shoved the apothecary jar into the pocket of her skirt and snatched up the cork for the laudanum bottle. It tumbled from her trembling fingers and bounced to the floor and under the table.

He was going to catch her! Dixie dove under the table, hand fumbling across the shadowy boards in search of the darkness-cloaked cork. She couldn't find it!

Flynn had started through the dining room, because she heard him move a chair out of his path.

Cork still not in hand, Dixie froze and settled her forehead against the floor. She'd failed.

"Doc! Could I speak to you a moment?" That was Joe's voice.

"Sure. What can I do for you?"

Dixie's head shot up. Reprieve! And there was the cork!

She could see it, now that her eyes were used to the dim light under here.

She snatched it up, holding it more carefully this time as she tamped it home. She settled the laudanum bottle into the pocket she'd removed it from, assessed that she hadn't disturbed anything else too much, and snapped the flap closed.

"Alright, I'll stop by in a few minutes." Flynn's voice was coming her way again.

Dash her quavering fingers and the double leather buckles. Her heart pounded in her throat. At last, the final clasp settled into place and Dixie shoved the bag against the wall where he'd left it.

He banged through the batwing doors as she swiped up the faint brown ring of liquid from the tabletop.

Dixie jolted guiltily and hurried to the sink, presenting him with her back. "Morning." Her voice rattled like a marble in the bottom of an empty milk pail. She cleared her throat and tried again, turning to face him this time. "Morning."

He had paused by the doors, one hand still holding one of the wings open. He studied her, concern etching his features. "Everything alright?"

She waved the towel, too late realizing that it held convicting evidence. "I'm fine. I just didn't sleep too well last night." She dropped the towel into the sink and pumped water onto it as though her intent had been to scrub it all along.

"Yes. I'm sure this must be wearing on you. I plan to sit with Rose today, and I hope you will do your best to rest as soon as you are done with this morning's clean-up. It is the Sabbath, after all."

Dixie tensed. He planned to be here all day? She looked over at him. "I can sit with her."

He hefted his doctor bag, and Dixie halfway expected him

to suddenly realize that it was lighter one apothecary bottle and some liquid.

She held her breath and scrubbed the towel all the harder.

"Nonsense. I have to be here all day anyhow to sit with Steven. He's going to be very touch and go today, and I don't want to be far from him. So I can check in on Rose often. I want you to take a walk, or take a nap, or simply lie about and read your favorite book. You need the reprieve. I don't need another patient to attend to." He smiled, but his expression brooked no bucking.

Dixie huffed a breath. "Yes. Fine. I can do that. And thank you."

He nodded. "My pleasure."

When he didn't leave right away, she hurried him on his way with, "I'll bring oatmeal and dried apples up for everyone in a few minutes. And more broth for Steven?"

He shook his head. "Today I only want to give him water. His body needs to put all its energy into healing, not digesting. So if you could just pour a bit of the warm water out when you make tea? And I'll give that to him."

She dared not let her shoulders slump. It was probably best that she not heat the laudanum in a hot broth anyhow. It might change or dilute it somehow. And she couldn't add it to water because the brown coloring and smell would give it away. She would just have to bide her time until she could have a few minutes alone with Steven.

"Yes. Fine. I'll be up in a few minutes."

He nodded and started out the door, but then paused and looked back at her. "Dixie, I'm going to do my very best to make sure he stands trial for what he did to you if he lives through this."

She pressed her lips together and nodded, focusing on wringing the soap out of the towel.

What she didn't say was that she was going to do her best to make sure he didn't have to go through that trouble.

Monday morning, the sheriff pushed into the jailhouse. Kin sat up groggily, but he was afraid his teeth might chatter if he said anything, so he held his silence. He'd spent another night half frozen and huddled into the thin blankets. The sheriff, who hadn't stepped foot into the jail all day yesterday, tossed a surprised double-take at the bare cot in the other jail cell, then immediately set about adding wood to the stove. Though Joe had done some better of a job of banking the fire last night than had been done the night before, Kin looked forward to the first rays of heat that would soon be radiating from the stove. He scooted to the end of the cot that was closest to the pot belly, both thin quilts still wrapped around his shoulders.

The door opened again and Miss Brindle stepped into the room, followed by Deputy Rodante.

Kin's brows shot up. He straightened quickly, and combed his fingers through his too-long hair.

Miss Brindle was saying, "...so I thought I would check with you to see if you would be willing to talk to her and see if she's interested in the job? She could start right away."

Deputy Joe nodded. "I think Liora will be interested, of a certainty."

Even though Kin would have liked to have stayed wrapped in the quilts, he swept them off his shoulders and folded them up while he listened to their conversation.

"I'm so glad!" Miss Brindle gushed. "I'm certain Dixie won't have any objections to her. She's perf—"

Her words severed so quickly that Kin felt his heart give a thump. Slowly, he lifted his gaze to look over the quilt at the three people on the other side of the bars. Miss Brindle was looking at him. Both the sheriff, who was halfway bent over with a stick of wood partway into the stove, and the deputy, who was hooking his Stetson onto a peg by the door, were looking at her.

Miss Brindle's jaw dropped nearly to her collarbone. "Reagan Callahan, what have you done to that poor boy?"

The sheriff jolted, tossing a surprised look toward Kin's cell. Then he chucked the wood into the pot belly, latched the stove door with a clang, and straightened, jaw jutting to one side. He gave Miss Brindle a look that could only be described as wary.

Kin bit back a grin. The sheriff looked exactly like Jefferson Nolan had on the last day of school when Miss Brindle had given him a dressing down for forgetting his homework three days running.

Miss Brindle hurried toward his cell. "This poor boy's lips are almost as blue as cornflowers!" She rounded to face the sheriff and plunked her hands on her hips. "Tell me you gave Kin more than those thin blankets to sleep with in this drafty old place!"

"Actually, he only gave me *one.* I had to fetch the second from the other cell, Miss Brindle." He conjured the most pitiful tone he could muster. "Good thing I still had my fishing hook and line with me, else I might be nothing but a block of ice this morning." Since Miss Brindle's back was still to him, Kin grinned at the sheriff over her shoulder. He was sure feeling some better now that the stove was kicking out a wave of crackling warmth. Course, some of the warmth might have to do with Miss Brindle taking up for him the way she was.

But in the next moment, he lost some of his smugness. Maybe he oughtn't to have taunted the sheriff, because the man narrowed his eyes at him. "Sure would be a shame if I forgot to bring you breakfast this morning, son."

Miss Brindle gasped. "Reagan! You wouldn't! He's just a boy."

The sheriff took hold of Miss Brindle's arm and led her from the room.

Kin's shoulders slumped in disappointment. He sure would have liked to have heard more of that conversation.

In the next moment, however, he forgot all about Miss Brindle and the sheriff, because the door opened and Pa stepped into the room.

Chapter Twenty

When Dixie's alarm clock clanged on Monday morning, she turned over and shut it off with a groan. She had barely slept at all last night, and what sleep she had snatched had been fitful and guilt-ridden. It was as though the stolen bottle of laudanum which she had stored in her nightstand drawer the evening before had prodded her with sharp talons all night long.

Oh my, was she truly going to go through with this? She had a very acute fear that she was about to become a murderer. And for real this time. All day yesterday, Flynn, true to his word, had sat either by Rose's side or by Steven's. And by the time he went home last night, the minister was comfortably ensconced in the room's second bed. No matter how badly she'd wanted the deed done, she hadn't been able to bring herself to do it with a man of the cloth in the room. But now her moment of opportunity may have arrived.

Doctor Griffin had said he would be by to check on the patients first thing this morning but then he had to go out to the logging camps. And she'd heard Zeb ask the minister if he would have time this morning to talk over some plans for building a church come spring, and the man had agreed.

Old Don Brass had insisted he had to get back to work this morning, so he would take off first thing. He'd already requested a traveling breakfast from Dixie the evening before, and she'd packed biscuits and hardboiled eggs into his basket. All she needed to do was fix the parson breakfast and then wait for Flynn to check on the patients and then head to the camps, and for the parson to leave to talk to Zeb. Then she would sneak into the hospital room and make sure she got every last drop of stolen laudanum down Steven's sorry throat. Perhaps the deed could be all done by this evening.

She fumbled with her buttons, eyes fastened on the drawer that seemed to shout her culpability to the world, though it remained steadfastly closed.

Her chest constricted with the guilt that had been plaguing her for hours, but she shook the feeling away. Opening the drawer, she tucked the apothecary bottle into her skirt pocket. Why should she feel guilty for doing the world a favor? It couldn't be considered murder to do away with such a man, could it? No. It would be just like she was acting in self-defense. Just like the marshal had said the other day. Self-defense was an entirely different matter in the eyes of the law.

As if the Almighty were showing his displeasure with her reasoning, an ill wind howled like a lone wolf around the eaves, and when she pulled back the curtains, she saw that a thick blanket of powdery snow had fallen sometime during the night. The wind whipped up mini dervishes that twirled down the street as though begging her to let go her plans and come dance with them instead. A moment of longing ended with a shiver. Dixie dropped the curtain back into place.

A quick check on Rose showed her still resting easily, and Dixie was thankful. It seemed like Rose might be on the mend. And when she had fully recovered, Dixie wanted to be able to offer her the gift of never having to fear her son again. She added a couple sticks of wood to the firebox in Rose's room, thankful that she'd insisted on extra insulation when they'd built this place that first year.

Taking the now-cold buckets of steam-water with her, Dixie hurried down the stairs to the boardinghouse kitchen. She wanted to quickly get the parson his breakfast so he would go to talk to Zeb before she changed her mind. In fact, if she could get him to eat quickly, maybe she could have the whole deed done long *before* this evening—even before Flynn arrived to check on the patients this morning!

She would cook an easy breakfast this morning of pancakes and eggs and fried ham. She used a splash of kerosene and the bellows to quickly bring the fire to life, then started two pots of coffee, good and strong. Between her rush and her trembling hands, she spilled coffee grounds all across the top of the stove. She brushed at them, singeing her fingers in the process. With a gasp, she snatched her hand back. She could clean that up later. Right now, she needed to hurry and get the griddle heating. That meant more wood, but when she went to reach for another stick, she realized that with all the cooking and water-boiling she'd done on Saturday, the indoor rack was nearly empty.

She groaned. It looked like the whirling dervishes would succeed in luring her outside, after all. But not in diverting her from her mission.

A quick glance at the clock proved that time was marching much too quickly for her comfort. What if the minister decided not to wait on breakfast, but just to go and see Mr. Heath first thing while she was cooking for her diners? Then he might return and rest in the room for the remainder of the day. Worrying about the timing of all of this threatened to send her heart into failure.

She yanked a scarf about her head and tugged on the large

thick jacket that she'd purchased from the mercantile her first year in these mountains. She slipped her fingers into the soft kid-leather gloves and then took in a breath and opened the outer door. Even though she knew what to expect on a blustery December morning, the gusts of icy wind still took her breath away when she stepped outside.

She squeaked out a grumpy protest and squeezed the coat closed more tightly at the neck as she leapt through the blowing snowdrifts toward the woodpile. She loaded her arms with as many logs as she could manage and then spun back toward the boardinghouse, only to crash into someone.

Her shriek was more a reflex, and perhaps a reflection of her guilty plans, than a revelation of fear. It only took her a moment to realize it was Doctor Griffin. His eyes peered at her above the edge of a frosty scarf. "Sorry to have startled you. I thought I could bring in a couple loads and save you another trip."

Teeth chattering from far more than just cold, she nodded her acceptance. "Thank you," she said, before dashing back to the warmth of the kitchen. The vial of liquid in her pocket bumped against her leg, and she had a horrifying image of it somehow tumbling out and rolling across the floor to come to a stop against one of Flynn's boots.

Flynn didn't seem aware of her guilty conscience, however. He continued bringing in wood until he had the firewood rack filled to the brim and mounded up.

By the time he was done, Dixie had a plate stacked with three pancakes, two eggs and a thick slice of ham. She set it on the table next to a steaming cup of coffee and added a small pitcher of syrup and plate of butter from the icebox in case he wanted some. Perhaps she could run the parson's breakfast up to him while Flynn ate here at the table. Now that she'd thought about just doing the deed quickly this morning and getting it over with, she'd realized that maybe she could pull it off, even with the minister in the room with her.

"Payment for services rendered." She smiled at Flynn. "I'm just going to fill a tray and hurry it up to the parson and-and maybe give Steven a little something to drink as well." She could make this work!

If he noticed her stutter, he didn't comment. He also didn't sink down at the table as she'd hoped. Instead he remained standing while he tugged off his gloves. "Thank you."

There was a note of weariness in his voice that made her turn to look at him. "Did you get any sleep last night?"

She cracked two more eggs into the hot skillet, and flipped the four cakes on the griddle. As soon as these eggs were done she could take the minister his breakfast and get this over with.

Flynn scrunched his eyes tightly closed and then opened them wide. He reached for the coffee cup first, and took a hearty sip as he tucked his gloves into his coat pocket. "Steven is touch and go. I've checked on him several times throughout the night. So I'm just going to take this up to the room if you don't mind. I'll let the parson know you are bringing his up momentarily."

Dixie felt her shoulders droop.

He dropped a quarter on the table and lifted the plate in one hand, mug in the other.

Doing her best to hide her disappointment, Dixie flipped several pieces of the ham. "You don't have to pay," she chided him. "It's the least I could do since you are doctoring my..." She cleared her throat. "...husband."

"Keep it." Flynn's jaw bunched. "He can pay for his own doctoring, if he makes it."

Dixie looked away from the pain in his eyes and tried not to give life to the hope his words produced. Maybe she didn't need to try and kill Steven. Maybe he would die on his own. A headache flared to life at the base of her skull. What kind of woman wished for the death of anyone, much less her husband? She rubbed at the hollow of her throat and stilled, staring at the bubbling eggs for a moment. If she were any kind of upright woman, she would have been the one by the man's side through the night, not the one who had tossed and turned while planning how she would murder him. But the truth was, it terrified her a little to even be in the same room with him, no matter that he was weak as a newborn mouse. She felt the need to explain herself. "Doctor Griffin, I wish I could, but—"

He blew out a sound of dismissal. "You don't have to explain yourself to me." A muscle in his cheek moved in and out, in and out.

She released a tremulous whoosh of air and scooped the pancakes onto a waiting plate before dropping four pats of butter onto the hot griddle and then ladling more batter over each one. There was some relief in knowing that she'd been too late to carry out her plan, at least for this morning. Perhaps Flynn's untimely arrival was the good Lord's way of closing a door—at least that was what her mother would have said when she was a girl.

Flynn had started from the room, but he hesitated. "How is Rose?"

"Rose seemed to have a wonderful night. She slept clean through. I think she's on the mend."

He smiled a genuine smile. "That's good to hear."

He had started away again when she realized she didn't know what to bring for Steven. "What should I make for Steven?"

Flynn shook his head. "Still no food for him for at least a

couple days. If you could drop a slice of that ham into about two cups of water and let it simmer real low for thirty minutes, we could try to get some of the broth down him. Otherwise, just keeping water in him will be the biggest challenge for the next few days."

He left her then, and her hands trembled as she dropped the ham into the boiling water. Would it be brown enough to disguise the laudanum? She pursed her lips. No. She couldn't risk it. Flynn likely wouldn't force him to drink all the broth at once, and then her whole plan would be shot and all her laudanum gone.

He was still watching her, she realized. "Will that be enough for you to eat?"

"Yes, thank you. I'll just go up and see to the patients now. But remember I have to ride out to the logging camps today. It's my normal day for visiting out there. I'll leave you with the laudanum for treating Steven. But you'll need to dose him very carefully. In his weakened condition especially, too much could kill him."

Dixie felt a prickle creep across her scalp and sweep down her neck. She looked up at him, but he was already through the batwing doors and out of sight. She didn't relax until she heard his footsteps crossing into the boardinghouse entry.

Then she slumped into one of the chairs at the table. All that sneaking and hurry and terror over being caught and he was going to give her some before he left! My, how the tables had turned. Because he was sure to walk her through the dosages, so if she gave Steven too much she would be the first to be suspected.

Chapter Twenty-one

Zane Holloway stood for a long time outside Jacinda Callahan's home, just staring at the evergreen wreath hanging on her door. Holding his Stetson by the crown, he tapped it against one leg. He'd known the moment Steven Pottinger had arrived in town that a trip east to backtrack and investigate the man was in order.

Dixie Pottinger had sure told a convincing story yesterday morning. He'd run into his fair share of liars, and he didn't think she was one of them—especially not with the proof etched into the skin of her arms. That still might not let her and her mother-in-law off the hook for shooting the man and then fleeing the scene, even though he was alive. But if he could prove that they'd needed to act in self-defense, he could probably get the charges against them dropped.

And if Pottinger had been playing dead for the past year and a half, that likely meant he had something to hide. The trick would be in getting someone in Birch Run to verify that the women had indeed been misused.

He grinned at himself. Not a week ago he'd ridden into town set on hauling both women in for the murder of Steven Pottinger. My, how a week had changed his mind.

When Zane had spoken to Zebulon Heath last evening, the gentleman had told him Pottinger had boarded the coach under the name Orin Wells. Traveling under a false name certainly wasn't the sign of an upstanding citizen. And with that detail he had his first clue that would hopefully lead him back to wherever the man had been hiding out before he showed up in town yesterday.

But first, he wanted to say goodbye to Jacinda. And yet he was standing outside her house like a still-green-behind-the-ears lad experiencing his first infatuation.

He rubbed the back of his neck and chuckled at himself. What was he doing here, anyhow? It wasn't like the woman had given him any hope. And it wasn't like he could just up and quit his investigation of this case right in the middle. It was probably best that he just leave town and get on with his business.

He sighed and plunked his hat back on his head, then adjusted it down against the cold blustery snow that had been falling all morning. He needed to ride to Cle Elum by tonight, but first he needed to go see Dixie Pottinger back at the boardinghouse.

He took the alley between the jailhouse and McGinty's and then pushed into the entryway of Dixie's Boardinghouse. The entryway was empty. She was likely in the kitchen or upstairs. A quick trudge through the dining room to poke his head into the kitchen showed she wasn't there.

Upstairs helping to care for the patients then.

Zane trudged up the stairs, feeling every one of his forty-five years. He'd had moments of loneliness over the years since he'd lost Maria, but he'd never considered himself a lonely man. He'd always been able to compartmentalize these feelings and rationalize his reasons for never having taken on another wife. His job was dangerous and required long hours away from home. That was no life to ask a woman to share. At the same time, he met few intriguing women, so it had never been a hardship. Yet now... Jacinda Callahan intrigued him in spades. By the barrelful. By a *train-carful*.

He smirked. Yes, indeed. It was probably good that he'd be riding out of town within the hour before he made a fool of himself somehow.

Once in his room, he packed his haversack with his few extra things and then glanced around the room. What would it be like to have a permanent place to come home to each night? He'd never had that in all his years. Yet, with no family to support, he'd saved up more than a substantial sum of money. And he'd been feeling the weariness of the trail, lately. Maybe it was time to settle down?

He slung the haversack over his shoulder.

Yes. Maybe it was.

He was definitely going to think about that as he concluded this investigation. He would have to return to Wyldhaven at the end of it, no matter what. And maybe settling in this area wasn't such a bad idea. He was definitely going to think about it.

He stepped back out into the hallway that stretched the length of the building. The room the patients were in was just two doors down, but when he looked in, Miss Pottinger wasn't in sight. The minister was finishing up a tray of breakfast, with his Bible open on his lap. And Doc Griffin was leaning over Pottinger, listening to his chest with a wooden stethoscope

Zane tipped a nod of greeting to the minister, then strode across the hall and rapped soundly on Mrs. Pottinger's door.

It was only a moment before Dixie pulled it open just a little and peered around it. When she saw it was him she started a little, but after only a moment she opened the door a little more. He noted that she held a bowl of scrambled eggs in one hand.

"Marshal." She stepped back and invited him in. "I was just feeding Ma some breakfast. Please, won't you come in?"

He cleared his throat and hesitated. He really only wanted to ask her if she had a picture of her husband that he might borrow, but he was reminded that the man was just across the hall. Severely injured or not, Zane didn't want to give him any ideas about running. "Thank you." He took off his hat and stepped over the threshold.

Dixie lifted the bowl. "If you don't mind, Ma doesn't keep her strength long these days. I'd like to get a few more bites into her before she needs more sleep. Can we talk while I feed her?"

"Yes. Certainly." He swept his hat to indicate that she should lead the way.

Dixie performed brief introductions between him and her mother-in-law. And once she was settled by her mother-in-law's side coaxing another bite into her mouth, and he was leaning in the doorway, she prodded him to get down to business. "What can I do for you, Marshal?"

Was her hand trembling? Why was she suddenly so nervous when she'd seemed fine when they spoke yesterday? He was also hesitant to say too much in here. How much did the sick woman know about her son being in town but lying on death's door??

Dixie must have noticed his pause, for she glanced his way. "I've told her everything, Marshal."

He darted a glance at the older woman and noted the trickle of a tear streaking back into her hair. He looked down at the floorboards. "Yes. Very well. I'm here because I wondered if you might by chance have a picture of...your husband...that I might borrow? I need to trace his path back to the east, and I feel the picture will be of immense help."

Dixie used a cloth napkin to dab the tears from her mother-in-law's cheeks. "I'm afraid I can't help you, Marshal. I never had a photograph of Steven." She didn't once look up at him.

Though he was disappointed—it had been a long shot, after all, considering the story she'd told him yesterday—it would have made his investigation that much easier. "Well then, I thank you for your time. I'll be leaving town. I thought you should know that I plan to backtrack your husband and hope to learn what he has been up to for the past year and a half. I don't know if I will be able to clear your name, but I aim to try."

She did look up then, a fathomless depth of emotion swimming in her eyes. "You believe me then?"

He nodded. "I do."

She dashed at her own eyes with the napkin now. "Thank you, Marshal. You've no idea how much just that means to me."

He could understand that. How frustrating it must have been for her to time and again go to the law in her town only to be turned away and disbelieved. And with that he knew just the person to question back in Birch Run. He gave her a nod and turned to head for the front door.

"Marshal." The quiet rasp from the older woman on the bed froze him in his tracks.

Slowly, he turned to face her.

She held a quavering hand out toward her bureau, indicating the top right drawer.

Dixie was on her feet, giving him a questioning look as she moved to the dresser. "This drawer?" she questioned her mother-in-law.

Rose nodded. "Bring me the box at the back."

Dixie peered into the depths of the drawer and withdrew an old biscuit tin. She carried it to Rose.

With trembling hands, the older woman tried to remove the lid, but had to give up in defeat. She thrust it back toward Dixie, who tugged the lid free. Her eyes widened as she looked at the contents. She pulled out a stack of photo plates and sorted through them. Finally, she held one up toward Rose. "This one?"

The woman nodded, seeming to relax back into her pillows like her task was accomplished.

Dixie stepped over and handed him the flat cardboard rectangle.

And he couldn't have been more pleased than to see a very clear image of one Steven Pottinger.

<hr />

Joe had just stopped by the stove and started to make a pot of coffee when the door swept open to reveal Mr. Davis. The man had once again been so drunk when Joe had ridden to his place the evening before to tell him that Kin was in jail, that Joe hadn't thought he would remember to ride in this morning. He felt some relieved to see the man. With all the questions he still needed answers to, namely from Washington Nolan and Zoe Kastain, it would have put a crimp in his day to have to ride out to the Davis place again.

He nodded to the man. "Morning, Mr. Davis, I'm just making coffee. Should be ready in about fifteen minutes. Can I interest you in a cup?"

The man's jaw worked back and forth, his squinted gaze fixed on his son who sat behind the bars across the room. "No. Thank ye, just the same. We won't be here that long."

Kin's feet shuffled, and Joe noticed that he'd scooted to the far end of the cot till he was nearly plastered against the outer wall. Joe looked back to the boy's father. Did the man think he'd be able to take Kin home? "I'm afraid we can't let Kin go home with you just yet. A man was shot. Questions still have to be answered."

Davis nodded. "Very well. Mind opening up the door? Maybe I can get you some of the answers you need." His red-rimmed eyes settled steadily on his boy.

Kin shot to his feet and spread his legs into a wide stance, almost like a boxer ready to take the ring. The boy folded his arms over his chest. Even though Kin didn't say anything, Joe had an uneasy feeling. But the man was Kin's father. The least Joe could do was give them some time together. "Sure, I guess I can do that."

Kin's eyes fell closed, and his jaw pushed first to one side and then to the other, like he was mentally preparing himself for something. Joe's hand hesitated above the keys on his belt. The boy's face was so pale it was a near-perfect match for the frost on the jailhouse window behind him. Joe took another look at Mr. Davis. But the man seemed as calm as could be. What was going on here?

Slowly, he lifted the jangling ring of keys and inserted the one for the cell's lock. The barred door squeaked eerily in the sudden quiet of the room, the hinges begging for oil.

Mr. Davis was through the door with lightning speed. Leveling a string of curses against his son, the man plowed one meaty fist into Kin's face. "What in thunderation do you think you was doing, boy?!"

Kin stumbled backwards, trying to catch his balance, but his calves connected with the edge of the cot. He sprawled into the wall with a thud hard enough to shake the whole building.

"Hey!" Joe waded into the cell, intent on dragging Davis away from Kin.

But Davis was like a bull that had seen a red flag. He elbowed

Joe so hard that he flew backwards and crashed headfirst into the bars of the cell. With a roar, Davis went after Kin again. "What do you think your mother would think of this stunt you pulled?" This time the man kicked a boot at Kin's ankles in a sideswipe meant to take him to the ground.

The boy's feet went out from under him like he'd slipped on a mossy river rock. A loud *crack* rang through the room as Kin's ribs connected with the solid wood frame of the cot.

Joe's heart constricted when he heard the kid grunt in pain, and he tried to get to his feet. But, he must have hit his head harder than he realized, because the ground seemed to dip out from under his boot when he stepped forward. He collapsed onto one knee.

"Pa, please." Kin held up one hand. "I did it for you!"

Davis swung again, but Kin ducked and scrambled out of his way.

"Did it for me, did you?" Davis cursed the boy. "Come here and I'll just show you my appreciation!"

Kin scurried past Joe, and, even with his vision as blurred at it was, Joe noticed blood gushing from Kin's split eyebrow. It streamed over the boy's face and onto his thin coat. The kid swiped one wrist at his eye, obviously trying to clear his vision as he searched the cell in a panic, terror filling his expression because he'd momentarily lost sight of his father.

Joe gave himself a shake and forced himself to his feet. He had to protect the kid! His vision was still blurry, but he lurched into the middle of the fray and pushed Davis away from his son. "Leave him be!" The command sent a burst of pain through his skull. Joe gave his head another shake and blinked hard. His vision cleared enough so that he could at least see more than blurry blobs.

Davis was still cussing, his face almost as red as Mrs.

Callahan's gingham kitchen curtains. The man started to push Joe aside, but suddenly clutched one hand to his chest, eyes going wide, voice falling silent. Davis looked past Joe's shoulder and reached a hand toward his boy, taking a stumbling step.

Joe once more inserted himself between the two.

Davis struggled again to reach his son, but his strength seemed to be gone, and he leaned heavily against Joe's shoulder as he rasped, "You are a disgrace, son!"

Joe gave the man a push in the opposite direction of his son. Though Davis's face was still contorted, Joe couldn't tell if the expression was anger, or pain.

Davis stumbled a sideways step and clutched at the bars of the next cell.

"Pa?" Kin peered from behind Joe.

"Ought to"—Davis's leg seemed to collapse out from under him, and he went down hard on one knee—"tan your...hide." He was gasping for breath now and clutching at his chest.

Assessing that the man was no longer a danger to his son, Joe sprang from the cell and flung open the jailhouse door. He dashed for the street, calling, "Stay with him. I'll get Doc!" The last thing he saw was Kin falling to his knees next to the crumpled body of the man who'd just tried to thrash him.

Joe almost crashed into Reagan, who was running his way, obviously having heard the commotion. He skipped around him, facing Reagan for a moment, even though he was still moving toward McGinty's, where he assumed Doc would be. "Luther Davis just collapsed. I'm going for Doc." As he turned back to continue his run toward McGinty's, Reagan lurched for the jailhouse.

"Doc!" Joe was yelling before he even burst through the alehouse door.

Ewan looked over at him from where he stood behind the

bar, polishing a glass. "Doc ain't here. He rode out to the camps today."

Joe's hopes fell. There was no time to waste then. He needed to get his horse and fetch Doc. He ran back to the jail and poked his head inside. "Doc's out at the camps. I'm going for him now."

Reagan waved him to silence before he even got done speaking. "It's too late, Joe. He's gone."

Joe's gaze flew to Kin as he stepped back into the room and closed the door against the cold.

The kid's jaw was hanging loose, and though he was seated on the cell's cot his hands were propped against his thighs like he needed the support to hold himself upright.

Whatever kind of father Davis had been to his boy, it was obvious the kid was devastated by his loss.

⛤

Kin scooped both hands back into his hair and stared, dumbfounded, at his father. He lost all the strength in his legs and stepped back to collapse onto the cot. Elbows to knees, head still propped in his hands, he just looked.

This was what he'd been trying to prevent. *This.*

Around him he heard the vague buzzing of conversations, and every once in a while, something moved into his line of sight and broke his visual connection to Pa, but he didn't pay any of that any mind. He just sat. Feeling numb. Useless. Hopeless. Lifeless.

The very thing he'd wanted to prevent, he'd caused. He'd only wanted to get Pa's attention. Make him sit up and realize that he was drinking his life away so much that his son was flirting with the wrong side of the law, but now... If Pa hadn't gotten so angry, he wouldn't have had one of his attacks.

Kin had seen them happen before, but usually not as bad as this one. Pa would clutch his chest and stumble to his bed. Generally, he couldn't work for a few days afterward, but he'd always recovered.

He should check his pulse just to be sure.

Kin fell to his knees and scrambled across the cell on all fours. He pressed his fingers to Pa's throat, begging God silently to let there still be life beating in his old man's veins. He felt nothing. He readjusted his fingers and stilled again. And again. And again.

Nothing. Nothing. Nothing.

Someone squatted beside him and settled one hand on his shoulder.

As though in a trance, Kin looked over.

The deputy's eyes were kind. Sorrowful. "I'm right sorry, Kin."

Another movement drew his gaze.

The sheriff draping Pa's body with one of the quilts.

Despair leaked out of him, and he slumped back onto his heels. "I just wanted him to see that he needed to stop drinking. Doc said he was killing himself. I tried everything to get him to stop. But nothing worked. I figured, maybe if I got in trouble with the law he'd pay attention."

Kin felt more than saw the two lawmen exchange a glance.

"Come on, son." The deputy tugged him to his feet. "Let's take you down to Dixie's to get you some breakfast."

Kin followed numbly at his heels.

Chapter Twenty-two

Joe couldn't imagine what the kid must be feeling. He was feeling some shocked himself. Although he hadn't really liked Mr. Davis, it was horrible to watch him die that way. He couldn't imagine what he'd be feeling if that man had been his father.

He knew Dixie's place would be packed at this time of morning. Shanty houses had been springing up like dandelions for most of the fall, and most of those loggers were single men who didn't mind paying for excellent cooking like Dixie's. Which reminded him that he needed to get Liora and tell her about the offer of a job. She could probably start on the spot.

He took Kin into the kitchen through the back door and nudged him into a chair at a small table, knowing Dixie wouldn't mind.

She pushed through the batwing doors that separated the kitchen from the dining room at that very moment, smothering a yawn beneath one hand. "Oh!" She blinked at them. "You startled me." Her eyes widened when she took him in more fully. "Are you all right?"

Joe frowned, wondering why she was asking him if he was okay and not the glum, beaten boy at the table. He waved away her concern and spun his hat through his fingers. "I'm sorry we startled you, but..." He glanced at Kin, who had settled his chin on crossed arms that rested on the table and was staring into nothingness. Taking Dixie's arm, Joe urged her to the far corner of the kitchen and quickly filled her in on the details.

Her face contorted with compassion and her eyes brimmed with tears that she kept swiping away as she alternated between looking at the boy across the room, looking at Joe's face, and looking at the floor by her feet. "That poor child."

Joe nodded. "Could you get him a plate? On the jail's account? And keep an eye on him for a bit? We need to get his father into a coffin and then figure out what the boy wants to do about the burying. Oh, and I'm going to swing by Liora's right now to tell her about the job offer."

Dixie's brows shot up, and she blinked at him. "Liora?"

Joe tipped back his head and scratched under his chin with three fingers, trying to assess her reaction. It was obvious she hadn't had any idea that Miss Brindle had planned to have Liora take the job. "I haven't said anything to her yet. So if you'd rather she not work for you, then please say so now, and not after she's gotten her hopes up for a job."

From out in the dining room a raspy voice called. "Where's that coffee?"

Dixie jolted, hefting her skirts as she hurried toward the pot on the stove. She flapped a hand at him over her shoulder. "Liora will be fine. I should have thought of her long ago." She lifted the pot and grabbed a hand towel from the rack near the stove. "Here, Kin. Press this to your eye there." She handed the boy the towel before she scurried to the batwing doors. Tossing a glance over her shoulder, she paused just long enough to shoo him out the back door. "Go on. And tell her she can start right this minute if she's of a mind to."

Joe might have smiled if the other events of the morning hadn't so totally sapped his ability to do so. "Kin, I'll be right back, ya hear? Miss Pottinger is going to get you some breakfast. Can I count on you to stay here till I get back with Miss Fontaine?"

Kin's head barely moved, but Joe did catch the slightest of nods and took that as the kid's agreement.

It wasn't until a cold blast of northern air hit him when he stepped back into the street and headed for McGinty's that he remembered the bashing his head had taken. As though pain came with the remembering, a wave of it started radiating out from the general area of the wound at the back of his head. He reached up to touch it as he pushed into the alehouse, and his fingers came away bloody. He grimaced. But there wasn't anything he could do about that right now.

He took the stairs two at a time, ignoring Ewan's curios stare, and paused in front of Liora's door. He knocked three times.

He heard her moving before the door opened. She pulled it open only slightly at first, but when she saw it was him, she pulled it farther. Her eyes widened in proportion with the width of the space. "Joe! What happened to you?!" She latched on to his arm and pulled him into her room, then plunked a chair in the middle of the floor and motioned him to sit. "Let me look at that!"

To his surprise, she stepped not to the back of his head to look at the wound he'd just been feeling, but right up in front of him, leaning close to peer at his forehead. She was looking at the spot where Davis's elbow had connected with his skull, he realized.

He swallowed at the closeness of her face, allowing himself a moment to let go of all this morning's upheaval and to simply revel in her beauty. A beauty that made him ache with the want it built inside him, and the counter-ache that bloomed when he reminded himself nothing could ever grow between them.

She prodded at his forehead with gentle fingers, making him wish she could be this close for other reasons. But he could never see himself finding a life with a woman who'd been willing to sell herself.

She seemed oblivious to all he was feeling. Her nose wrinkled. "I think this is going to need a stitch."

He watched her rosebud lips say the words, and then perfect white teeth clamp hold of her top lip as she looked down and caught him watching her.

He blinked and leaned back a little, clearing his throat. "I have another one at the back of my head. Might need stitches too. Do you mind taking a look?" He tipped his face to the ground, scrunching his eyes closed tight when he knew she could no longer see the grimace. Every time he thought he had these longings for her whipped into submission, they would lay low till the most inopportune moments—like anytime Liora was in sight—and then spring to life with even more potency than before.

She clucked and hummed over the knock he'd taken to the back of his head, swiping at the area with a damp rag. "Joseph Rodante, I can see the white of your skull! What happened to you?"

He winced as she withdrew a sewing needle and thread from a drawer in her desk. "Let's just say the bars on the cells in the jail are made of good sturdy steel."

She paused before him, pulling her finger along the thread. "Want me to get you a shot of whiskey from the bar?"

He clenched his teeth and shook his head. "Just make it quick."

She gave him a look that said he was crazy, but tipped her head in a *whatever you say* gesture.

Thankfully, this time when she stepped near he was so

concentrated on not making a fool of himself with a gasp or a whimper, that he had his eyes closed and didn't have to be tempted by the allure of wondering what it might feel like to run the backs of his fingers over her cheek.

Her needle must have been sharper than he'd given her credit for, because he barely felt prick of the needle above the other pain he was already feeling.

It only took her a moment to finish at both the front and the back. "There. Four stitches and you are almost as good as new. You really should try to lie down and get some rest, however."

Joe shook his head, realizing that he hadn't given her any of the pertinent news yet. He quickly filled her in about Kin's father, and then told her about Dixie wanting to hire someone and saying she could start right this minute.

Liora's eyes widened and brimmed with tears. "She's offering me a job?"

Joe nodded. "You have Miss Brindle to thank for suggesting you, but Dixie thought it was a splendid idea." She didn't need to know that was a slight exaggeration.

"Oh, Joe!" Liora threw her arms around him, sending a shock wave through him. Instinctively, his arms came up to wrap around her. "The Lord just answered my prayers! I can really start right now?"

She pushed back from him and spun in a circle as though trying to decide if she needed to take anything with her. Her hands flew up and patted at her hair.

Joe chuckled and held the door open for her. "You look fine. Grab your coat and I'll walk you over. She looked like she was having a time keeping up with everyone. Oh, and bring that needle and thread too. Kin's going to need a stitch or two as well, if I don't miss my guess."

"I'm so thrilled! You have no ideal!" She jolted to a stop. "Well not about Kin needing stitches, you understand, but—"

Joe laughed. "I understand."

"Yes. Good." Liora grabbed up her coat and tucked the needle into the front pocket. She then hefted her skirts and trotted down the stairs like a little girl running down to see the tree on Christmas morning.

Joe couldn't help a grin as he followed in her wake.

⁂

Dixie swept into the kitchen and swiped at her forehead with the back of one wrist. She had run so hard and fast this morning that she was sweating. Apparently, the cold wind that had been blowing this week had given every logger in the district a hankering for a hot breakfast. She was down to three eggs left in her bowl with orders for six, and she hadn't even fed Kin yet. She hoped her hens had not let her down today.

She'd been so busy this morning that she'd hardly had a chance to think about the two vials of laudanum in her pockets. And yet, conversely, the thought of those vials hadn't been far from her mind all morning. Flynn had indeed given her another vial of the liquid, along with instructions on its use, just before he'd left for the logging camps. She'd carefully tucked it into the pocket opposite the one with the stolen vial so he wouldn't hear the jars clinking together. And any time she paused or moved and one of them bumped against her leg she found herself considering a new way to get the whole of it down Steven's throat. But she'd been so busy this morning that she'd hadn't been able to get away from the kitchen.

No matter. Her last guests had just been seated. The diner shut down at eight thirty each morning so school could be held, and she'd decided that even though school was out till the first of the year she would keep the diner on the same schedule as always. So she only had to feed them, and then Kin, and then she would be free to go upstairs to the room where Steven lay all alone at this very moment.

She glanced at Kin. Did she dare go out to get the eggs? That would mean leaving him alone for longer than the two or three minutes that it took to run plates to the tables. And what was she going to do with him when she needed to dash upstairs? She certainly couldn't take him with her. The boy had faced enough trauma today without watching her give a lethal dose of laudanum to her lout of a husband.

The dilemma was solved for her when a soft knock sounded at the back door. She opened it to find Liora hunched against the wind. Despite her reservations over hiring a woman of Liora's former profession, she couldn't help but be thankful to have her help. Besides, who was she—a woman planning a murder—to judge?

"Please, come in." Dixie stepped aside and let her in.

Liora stood rubbing her arms, looking a bit uncertain.

Dixie would need to walk her through how things worked, but there was no time for that now. She motioned her to the sink. "You can wash up there. Do you know how to scramble eggs?"

Liora looked uncertainly toward the stove.

"Never mind. I've rolled out some biscuits there on the side board. The cutter is just there. Please cut them out and put them in the iron skillet at the back of the stove. I'm going out to gather more eggs." Dixie slipped on her gloves and lifted one of the hot bricks she kept warming on the rock shelf behind the stove. She paused by the door. "Oh and Liora..." She waited till Liora turned to her, then nodded her head meaningfully toward Kin.

Liora tipped a nod of understanding as she washed her hands at the sink.

Out at the henhouse, Dixie swapped the warm brick for the now cold one that she'd put in last night and covered it with the old bent pie tin again. The pie tin kept the bricks from getting too soiled.

She quickly displaced the hens from their nests and gathered the eggs, thankful to find nine larger and two small ones. A quick scoop of food into their trough and she closed the lid to keep the heat inside. The log walls of the hen house—natural insulation—along with the hot brick, helped keep the interior warm, even through the coldest months.

With the eggs held carefully in her apron, she lifted the cold brick and hurried back inside.

She put the brick into the sink, where she would scrub it later, and gently settled the eggs into a bowl and filled it with warm water.

Liora had all the biscuits cut and in the iron skillet and had busied herself cleaning Kin's forehead. Dixie looked closer. It appeared she was stitching the boy up. Dixie was pleased to see she'd taken that initiative.

With the eggs scrubbed, she nodded her thanks to Liora, who once more washed up at the sink. "Now let me show you how to scramble the eggs. Put the biscuits over the hottest part of the stove there and drop three healthy scoops of butter into the pan."

While the biscuits bubbled in the melted butter, Dixie pointed out the potatoes she'd already grated. "We have three orders for two eggs, potatoes, and biscuits. The potatoes go on the griddle here. Butter into the frying pan here. Then you crack the eggs like so." Dixie demonstrated how she cracked two at a time, one with each hand.

Liora's eyes grew wide. "It might take me some time to master that."

Dixie smiled. "Never fear. We'll work together." *At least until I go to jail, leaving you to run the place on your own.* She flipped the biscuits over, sprinkled some salt over the potatoes, and gave the eggs another stir.

Beside her, Liora's stomach rumbled loudly.

Dixie wondered when Liora had last eaten. Guilt—a feeling that was becoming all too common in her life lately—nudged her. Liora was looking very thin and frail these days. She should have noticed sooner. She always had leftover food that was hardly touched on some plates.

She pulled three plates from the shelf above the stove. "These should be my last orders and then the three of us should be able to eat."

Yet one more delay in getting upstairs, but she couldn't very well just leave without making them a meal.

She scooped the shredded potatoes onto the plates, golden side up. "Let me just take these out to the table. I'll be right back." She slid the eggs on beside the potatoes and added the biscuits too.

With two plates in one hand, and the third in the other, Dixie used her back to push open the doors to the dining room. Kin still had his chin resting on his crossed arms, but at least his face was no longer bloody. He hadn't said a word since Joe dropped him off earlier.

Concern for the boy wouldn't leave her as she set the plates on the table before the patrons. It was good that Kin didn't have to go to school today.

Well she remembered how she'd felt when her mother died. Her father had been a hard man who grew even harder after. And Dixie had fled from home. Straight from the frying pan and into the fire, as it were. A fire she was about to snuff out for the last time.

Back in the kitchen, she squeezed the boy's shoulder. "Are you hungry?"

Kin stirred, sitting up and rubbing his palms down his pants. A frown furrowed his brow as he glanced around the room, as if he might be wondering how to answer that question.

"Never mind. Of course you are hungry. I'll make you something."

Liora was at the sink washing dishes.

Dixie wasn't a bit hungry herself, even though she hadn't had time to eat yet today. Her nervous stomach churned at just the thought of food. She made herself a portion anyhow, because she didn't want to raise questions. It didn't take her long to have three plates filled. She waved Liora over from the sink. "We can finish those dishes later. Come now and eat."

They were halfway through the meal, Kin doing more toying with his food than eating, and Liora eating steadily but with reserve, when the doors to the kitchen pushed open.

Parson Clay poked his head inside.

Dixie felt her eyes widen. He was back already? Wasn't he still supposed to be talking with Zeb about the church building? "You're back early."

He nodded. "Mr. Heath apparently ate something at McGinty's Alehouse last evening that didn't sit well with him."

Liora sniffed. "Ewan's devil hot chili could nearly take the iron off a skillet."

A light of appreciation for the humorous sentiment danced in the parson's eyes, but he didn't smile. He glanced instead at the plate that Dixie had hardly touched. "Mrs. Pottinger, I'm sorry to disturb you, but the doctor said that if Mr. Pottinger needed pain medicine that you were the one to speak to. I believe he requires your attention now."

At the name "Mr. Pottinger" Kin looked a little startled and Dixie realized that with him being in jail he probably hadn't heard the news that had spread like wildfire through the rest of the town after the stagecoach's arrival.

She wiped her mouth with her serviette, hoping that no one noticed the sudden trembling of her hands. "Thank you. I'll be right up." She pushed her plate back, unable to stomach the thought of even one more bite. The time for a decision had come. Was she going to throw her life away on revenge?

She looked at Liora. "If you don't mind finishing the kitchen clean-up, I'll be down as soon as I can to discuss my expectations with you."

Liora nodded. "Of course."

"Thank you."

The resolve she'd felt so certain of only this morning seemed to be slipping from her. Dread weighted her steps as she hefted her skirts and took the stairs to the top floor ahead of Parson Clay. The stolen vial in her pocket felt like it might be glowing bright enough for the minister to see. His quiet tread ascended the stairs behind her.

At the door of room five, she hesitated, trembling. Was this really who she wanted to be?

The minister stepped to one side, looking over at her to see why she hesitated. He cleared his throat softly. "Mrs. Pottinger, I sense a great battle waging within you, ma'am. Is there anything you would like to talk about?"

Dixie jolted and looked at him. Tears came unbidden to her eyes.

He folded his hands in front of himself and simply looked at her, an unfathomable softness in his expression.

The anger she'd felt yesterday morning at the service flared to life. "Let me tell you about the man that you prayed for at your service, Parson Clay." She stabbed a finger against the door to room five. "That man routinely choked me until I couldn't breathe. He relished holding his grip just to the point before I would pass out." She fumbled with the buttons at her cuffs. "That man"—she yanked her sleeve up and exposed her forearm to him—"burned me over and over with his cigar stubs." She jerked the material down again and worked to refasten the buttons, satisfied to see his eyes widen. "That's the kind of man whose survival you were so diligently petitioning the Almighty for."

Parson Clay looked down at the floor for a moment, then cleared his throat. "I'm sorry you went through all that, Mrs. Pottinger. And yet we are responsible for ourselves. We are to be people of compassion and forgiveness. People who offer only good to others, even if they spitefully use us. So..." He hesitated and, if possible, his expression softened even more. "I cannot apologize for my prayers, Mrs. Pottinger."

Perhaps it was the tenderness of his tone, or the kindness in his eyes. She wasn't sure, but now that she'd spilled all of her humiliation she seemed to have lost all her indignation and didn't know what else to say.

"I can assure you that unless such a man repents, come the day of judgment he will find himself facing the harshest ire of the Almighty."

Day of judgment... If she followed through with this she herself would be facing judgment sooner rather than later.

A weariness that could no longer be held at bay fell over her. With a sigh, she took both bottles of laudanum from her pockets. First, the one she'd stolen, and second, the much smaller one that Flynn had given her when he left for the logging camps this morning. She rolled both bottles around in her hand. "Do you think God might consider it self-defense,

Parson, were a woman to put an end to such a man at a time like this?"

The minister cleared his throat, and she heard his feet shuffle, even though her attention was still fixed on the two bottles in her hands. "I think man is ever striving to make gray out of what the good Lord has clearly laid out in black and white, Mrs. Pottinger. Often the Lord asks us to wait for justice. We may not understand it or like it, and it can be wearying, but we are promised that if we wait on the Lord, we will renew our strength."

Dixie's eyes fell closed. The very verse that Flynn had mentioned to her just the other day. "And what happens, sir, when we've given up waiting on the Lord to bring justice a long time ago? Can we ever get back to a place of willingness to wait, and to trusting Him again, do you think?" She lifted her gaze, needing to see his expression as he answered.

His expression held no judgement and there was a world of empathy in his eyes. "Is that what you want, Mrs. Pottinger? To begin trusting once more that His ways are always higher than ours, even when we can't understand why?"

Her hand tightened around the two bottles, and she studied the brass number five on the door. "So you are saying that God would view it as murder."

The man stepped close to her and took her shoulders with the gentlest of touches. "The Good Book promises that in this world we will have tribulation, Mrs. Pottinger. But we are to take heart because our Lord has overcome the world. There is no 'unless' to the command 'Thou shall not kill,' though I do believe that, as you pointed out, a case could be made for self-defense, or the defense of others. However, you and I both know the man lying in that bed inside is in no condition to harm anyone. Sometimes, though we don't understand it, the Lord asks us to remain in our trials for a time."

Dixie's gaze flew to his, eyes narrowing. Was he saying that he thought it would be the Lord's will for her to stay with such a man?

The minister held up his hands, palms out. "I'm not condoning his behavior, mind you, or encouraging you to return to a relationship with him. But I get the impression that you have been somewhat angry with God for some time now? Am I correct?"

"I have." She nodded.

She thought of Kin sitting downstairs having just lost his father because the man couldn't let go of his anger over losing his wife. She thought of Rose, who would truly be left alone in her elder years, if Dixie followed through with her revenge. She thought of herself—caught, tried, pronounced guilty, and sentenced to hang—walking slowly from the jailhouse to face a noose, and looking out over the crowd comprised of people she cared about. Flynn would be standing in the front row because it would be his job to pronounce her death. She pictured the pinched furrows of pain and sorrow crinkling his brow as he watched her. The sadness in the blue of his eyes.

With a blink, she came back to the present. That wasn't the future she wanted. She didn't have a choice in some things. But as the minister had just said, there were other things she could control. Herself. Her actions. Her choice to hope or not to hope in a Savior. A wave of longing to let go of all her anger and vengeance swept over her. She met the minister's gaze. "Would God take me back? If God will take me back, I would like nothing more." She searched his face almost desperately, holding her breath.

He tilted his head and squeezed her shoulders. "Mrs. Pottinger, I assure you He would love nothing more."

A breath puffed from her and she thrust the bottles of laudanum at him. "Please take these, Parson."

The bottles clanked loudly against each other as he gathered them into his hands.

Dixie pressed one palm to her chest, feeling suddenly like a bird just freed from a cage. "If you could give him the dosage he needs? Twenty drops. I've a sudden urge to go pray."

He smiled at her. "It does my heart good to hear you say so, ma'am. I confess that I wondered how the Lord was going to use me in a place such as this, and yet I find that He orchestrated my arrival just in time."

She was once again struck by how much younger he looked when he smiled. And awed by the fact that the Lord may have sent him here at just the right moment to save her from herself. "If you'll excuse me, Parson." She hefted her skirts and hurried into her apartment and fell to her knees next to her bed.

She spent the next half hour weeping in repentance, crying out for forgiveness, and begging God to give her the strength to do what was right. And when she finally rose and washed away her tears, it was with dread but firm resolve settled in the pit of her stomach.

She had to confess to Dr. Griffin what she had done.

Chapter Twenty-three

Joe returned to the boardinghouse for Kin two hours later. He poked his head through the back door.

Liora looked up from where she was blacking the stove and motioned him in.

He stepped into the warmth of the kitchen, wiping his boots on the mat. *Lord, bless Charlotte Brindle for her thoughtfulness.* Working here at the boardinghouse was going to be so much better for Liora than trying to find odd jobs out in the cold this time of year. Already she seemed to have more color in her face. Of course, that could be from working near the hot stove.

Liora offered a sympathetic twist of her lips and a meaningful glance in Kin's direction.

Right. He wasn't here to stare at the beautiful woman. Joe gave himself a little shake.

The boy didn't seem to have moved, for he still sat morosely in the same seat at the little kitchen table.

Joe approached the boy's side. "Kin, we've...uh...we're ready for you to say goodbye to your pa, son."

Kin stirred. He looked up for a moment but a semi-vacant look remained in his eyes. The kid was still in shock. But he did get to his feet and start for the door.

Joe was glad to see that his cuts had been stitched up. He met Liora's gaze across the room, tapped his forehead in the same place Kin had been injured, and then mouthed, "Thank you."

She nodded, her lower lip pooching out to indicate she felt sorry for the boy.

Joe didn't let his gaze linger on the pout. At least not for too long. He hoped. Hurrying after Kin, he dipped his chin in her direction and gave her a little farewell salute.

He felt sorry for the boy too. They all did.

When they stepped outside, he made sure the door latched tightly behind them and directed Kin back to the jailhouse.

Normally a body would need to be buried right away. But he and Reagan had talked it over. With the bitter cold they'd been having, there wasn't any worry about the body decomposing too much so long as it was kept in the cold. And that way the boy could have a few days to adjust before the burying.

In the meantime, they didn't know what to do with Kin so he would need to be returned to the cell until they could figure out where he was going to live. Clearly, he was too young to remain on his own. And there was still the matter of the charges to figure out.

Reagan had hammered together a pine box. They just needed to know if the boy wanted any of his pa's effects.

Kin's footsteps faltered as they stepped into the jailhouse and he saw the coffin.

Joe squeezed his shoulder and directed him to a table where they'd laid out the contents of Luther's pockets. It wasn't much. The makings for cigarettes... A couple pennies... But there was a ring Joe felt certain Kin would want.

"This is what we found in his pockets. We wanted you to have it."

Kin nudged aside the cigarette papers and reached immediately to pick up the gold band. He rolled it between his fingers. "He didn't sell it."

The words hadn't really been spoken to him, so Joe held his silence.

"It was my ma's. I thought he sold it." Kin swallowed and blinked hard. His focus traveled across the room to where the coffin was. "We used to be happy when she was alive."

Joe had no words. What had the kid been through these past few years? He couldn't imagine.

He let the boy stand by the pine box for as long as he seemed to need to. And then, feeling like the lowest man alive, he motioned back toward the cell. "Your pa's burying can wait a few days. I'm sorry but we can't let you go just yet. We need you to stay here until we decide if criminal charges will be pressed and if not, make a decision about who you will stay with.

A bit of fire flashed in the boy's eyes. "I can take care of myself!"

Joe nudged him toward the cell. "I know. I'm sure you can. We can talk about that, you, me, and the sheriff. But for now, you have to stay here."

With a weary sigh, Kin sank onto the cot.

And Joe tried to close the cell door as quietly as he could.

❦

Dixie paced feverishly to the window in the entryway of the boardinghouse, waiting for Flynn to get back from the logging camps. He still wasn't in sight down the street. She dropped the curtain back into place with a frustrated groan. Flicking her fingernails against one another, she spun on her heel and paced across the room to the desk, where she turned to retrace her steps. How was she going to tell him what she'd done? She pictured the look of betrayal that was sure to cross his face.

With another groan of despair, she hefted her skirts and

headed up the stairs. She might as well spend her time doing something useful. She would see if Rose needed anything.

Just this morning, Flynn had determined that Rose no longer needed the benefit of the steam, so he'd removed the tenting sheets.

Rose was propped up against her pillows when Dixie poked her head into her room. Her favorite book of poetry rested on a bolster before her.

Rose put down the book and motioned her over.

Dixie sat on the counterpane next to her. "Can I get you anything?"

Rose shook her head. "Is Steven really here?"

Dixie's throat closed up, just at the mention of him. She nodded. "I've not been in to see him, today. But yes. Though he's hurt very badly." She didn't add that part of the reason for her staying away stemmed from the fact that she'd planned to kill him.

Tears glistened on Rose's lower lids. "He wasn't always as insufferable as he is now. I wish you could have known him when he was a young boy. He would bring me daisies from the garden, and sit and listen to me read for hours. Something changed inside him when his father died. It was as if he chose to be a different person. And I never could reach him after that."

Dixie didn't know what to say so she reached out and squeezed Rose's hand.

"I have to see him," Rose said emphatically.

Dixie felt her eyes widen. "I'm not sure you should be up and about. Flynn has been fighting for days to bring you back from the brink."

Rose leaned her head back, seemingly exhausted just from having this conversation. "It's only across the hall and it's important to me."

Dixie lifted the cup of now-cold tea from Rose's bedside table. "Here. Try to finish your tea. Dr. Griffin should be back from the camps soon, and I'll ask him Will that suffice to keep you abed until then?"

Seemingly too exhausted to fight for more, Rose nodded and took a sip of her tea.

"You should try to rest in the meantime."

Rose's gaze looked troubled. "Do you think he might die before I get a chance to see him?"

Dixie's first thought was that Steven was entirely too mean to ever die, but the truth was, she didn't know. She shook her head. "Flynn says he's hurt bad but he's taking a lot for the pain and seems to be resting. I'll try to get Flynn to let you go over to see him this evening."

A knock sounded on the door just then and Dixie's heart lurched. She knew that knock. Flynn was back from the camps.

Feeling like her feet were made of lead, she made her way to the sitting room door and opened it.

Flynn stood, hat in hand, looking weary. Dark circles beneath his eyes revealed that he was operating on too little sleep.

Dixie motioned him inside. "Come in, please. We were just talking about you."

"Oh?" He brushed past her and headed for Rose's room, tossing a questioning glance over his shoulder to indicate she should explain.

Dixie pushed the door shut and followed on his heels. "Rose is hoping to go across the hall to see her son."

Flynn stopped and spun toward her so quickly that Dixie almost crashed into him. Searching her face, he lifted one broad brown hand to scrub at the back of his neck.

Was he simply surprised that Rose wanted to see Steven? Or was he considering if it was a good idea?

After a long moment, he eased out a breath and his shoulders seemed to sag. "Yes, I suppose she would want to see him. I'll set up a chair for her to sit in. I think she's past the point of danger now, thank the Lord, so a few minutes sitting with him shouldn't hurt her."

"She'll be happy to hear that." Dixie curled her fingers together so tightly that she felt her fingernails biting into the flesh of her opposite hands. There was more that needed to be said. She opened her mouth, but no words emerged. She snapped her jaw closed and pressed her lips together with her teeth.

Flynn tilted his head, studying her. "Was there something more you wanted to say?"

Dixie managed a nod. "But it might take a while, so please"—she tipped a nod to Rose's room—"feel free to check on her first."

The tiniest flicker of a frown touched his brow before he gave a nod and turned for Rose's chamber once more.

Dixie loosed a breath and fairly collapsed onto the settee. How was she ever going to make it through this conversation?

He was back much too quickly for her comfort. Setting his doctor bag and his hat on the table near the door, he smiled over at her. "Her pulse is steady and she's no longer running a fever. I can still hear a little of the infection in her lungs, but with continued treatments of the acetylsalicylic acid, I think she will make a full recovery."

"I'm so relieved to hear it." Dixie wished she could relish the good news. She really was happy about it, but her stomach was in knots because all she could think about was the confession she needed to make.

He rested his hand on the wing-backed chair across from her. "May I sit here?"

Dixie leapt to her feet. "Oh, yes. Of course. Forgive my manners."

Flynn sank into the chair, searching her face even as he offered, "Please don't concern yourself."

Dixie wanted to pace, but she forced herself to return to sitting primly on the settee. Her hands couldn't seem to be still, however. Her fingers fidgeted as though she were sitting before the piano in McGinty's Alehouse.

"Dixie." Flynn's voice was soft and bolstering. "Whatever it is, out with it."

Yes. She'd better do just that before she lost her nerve all together.

"I stole some laudanum from your bag because I wanted to kill Steven with it!" She dropped her eyes closed, not wanting to see the look of disappointment on his face.

"And did you?" There was an underlying note of panic in the question.

She shook her head, finally daring to meet his gaze once more. "I couldn't go through with it. I talked to Parson Clay instead, and he took all the laudanum from me and has been administering it to Steven today."

She was surprised to see a soft look of understanding touch Flynn's expression. "I almost let him die myself, you know."

She held her breath and searched his face.

He nodded. "I know. I've never before been tempted to ignore my Hippocratic Oath. But the temptation was sore upon me. Then I realized that despite all the evil he may have done, he's still God's creation. And that it wasn't my place to take his life. But, I want to assure you again, if he lives I'm going to do my very best to see that he comes to justice for all that he did to you and his mother."

Dixie swallowed and nodded. "Can you forgive me?"

Flynn narrowed his eyes. "Perhaps it is I who should ask you to forgive me. I never should have tasked you with administering such delicate medicines."

Dixie cringed. "You did hear me say that I stole some laudanum?"

He nodded.

"Before you gave me some, I'd already taken some."

"I forgive you. But more importantly, have you asked the Lord to forgive you?"

She nodded. "I already did. I've been running from Him— not hoping in Him—for quite some time now. But those verses you recited to me from Isaiah instilled in me the realization that it wasn't the Lord who had abandoned me, but *I* who had abandoned *Him.*"

Flynn nodded, then stood. "I'm glad to hear it." He picked up his hat and clasped the handle of his black doctor bag. "If that was everything, I probably should get across the hall to check on how Steven is doing."

Dixie held up one hand. "If I may, there's one more thing."

He waited silently, but tipped his head for her to continue.

"I really should go in and see him. But I've been—well, I wondered if you would mind staying with me when I go in to see him later? I need to get dinner going right now, but after?"

Flynn nodded. "Certainly."

"Thank you."

He slipped his hat on and tipped the brim in her direction, then silently left the room.

Dixie collapsed back against the settee. She'd managed it. And she hadn't died in the process. She angled a glance toward the ceiling. "Thank you, Lord."

Chapter Twenty-four

ane Holloway stood in the hotel room in Beaufort where Steven Pottinger had apparently lived for quite some time. He tapped his hat against his leg and turned a slow rotation in the middle of the room. His belief in Dixie's story had just increased one hundred-fold, because three days after Pottinger—whom the hotel staff had known as Abraham Johnson—checked out, the maid had found the dead body of a woman, yet unidentified, beneath the bed. Though there really weren't any clues left to be found, the fact that Pottinger was leaving dead bodies in his wake, proved he had plenty to hide.

The dead woman had already been buried in a pauper's grave since no one knew who she was or where she came from.

Zane would bet he at least knew in which town to start searching for her identity. He lifted the sketch the local officer had commissioned of the woman's face. Though Zane hadn't seen her for himself, the artist looked skilled, and he hoped he'd be able to use the sketch to get good information about Pottinger that might clear Rose's and Dixie's names.

Releasing a breath, he tipped his hat back onto his head and tugged it into place. After another futile glance around the room, he decided it was time to head down to Birch Run and have a chat with the sheriff and townsfolk once again. Seemed he'd come full circle on this investigation.

The train ride took two hours, so he leaned in to the corner of his seat, settled his hat over his eyes, and caught some shuteye.

By the time he arrived in Birch Run he was feeling almost human again, if a bit gritty-eyed.

He started at the post office. Everyone had to gather mail at some point, right? What better place to see if the dead woman was from these parts. He unfolded the sketch from his pocket and smoothed out the creases, but he didn't slide it toward the elderly postmistress yet.

Instead, he leaned into his heels and smiled at her. In all his years of working the law he'd learned that a little flirting with women—even if they *were* twice his age—produced a sight more information than if he just got down to business. And the two years he'd been married to Sarah had taught him a good bit about flirting. He swallowed away the melancholy that always came over him at the thought of Sarah. But this time the thought of her was overlaid by the visage of a spunky seamstress with eyes blue enough to remind a man of summer skies on a cloudless day.

The wrinkled woman before him squirmed and blushed beneath his scrutiny, and Zane realized he was still smiling at her. He cleared his throat and looked down. Turning the sketch so it faced her, he slid it across the counter. "Afternoon, ma'am. I'm US Marshal Zane Holloway, and I wondered if you might recognize this young woman and give me her name?" He dropped his badge onto the counter next to the sketch.

The woman lifted a pair of spectacles from the counter and unfolded them, then settled them on the bridge of her nose with all the speed of a tortoise. But the moment she focused on the image, she gasped and snatched up the page. Tears immediately burgeoned in her eyes. She stroked a finger over the face on the sketch, as though she might be caressing the face of the deceased in her mind's eye. "This is Miss Prissy Singleton. She's been missing for some three weeks now. She used to work here at the post office." She lifted hopeful eyes. "Do you know where she is?"

Zane shuffled his feet, mindful of how quickly gossip could spread in a small town like this. He would hate for word to get to the girl's parents before he could ease the news to them. "Do you know if Miss Singleton had family in the area?" Too late, he realized his use of the past tense might have already given away Miss Singleton's demise.

And the matron's eyes did indeed widen a bit before the tears spilled over. She tugged a handkerchief from her sleeve. "H-her ma and pa run Golden Vittles." She pointed south. "Just next to the bank."

"Thank you. Do you know if Miss Singleton knew Mr. Steven Pottinger?"

The woman's eyes narrowed this time, and she dabbed slowly at her cheeks with the cloth, then shook her head with a frown. "Mr. Pottinger was shot and presumed killed nigh on two years ago now. What does this have to do with him?"

"That's what I'm trying to find out, ma'am." Zane nodded his thanks and folded up the sketch. With a heavy heart, he stepped back onto the boardwalk. That had been surprisingly easy. Now to see if the girl's parents knew if she had a connection with Steven.

It had been ten hours since he had eaten anything, so his stomach rumbled at the tantalizing scents wafting from the kitchen when he stepped into Golden Vittles.

He settled at a table and plunked his Stetson onto one of the spindles of the chair.

A middle-aged woman approached with an apron cinched

about her thick waist. She plopped pudgy hands against ample hips. "We've got batter-fried steak or fried chicken."

"Yes. The fried chicken will do. Thank you. And coffee, strong and black, please."

With a dip of her chin, she hurried away.

Zane felt a little guilty not just spilling his knowledge right away. But he wanted to assess the couple first and see what they were like before he gave them the sad news. Not to mention, these conversations were always difficult for him.

Zane pulled out the sketch of the dead woman and laid it face down on the table.

When she brought his coffee cup and set it on the table with a distracted smile that he supposed was meant to be welcoming, he caught a glimpse of a troubled mother, hurting over the loss of her child. While he waited for his food, he prayed quietly for the couple. Their lives were about to be changed—had already been changed, even though they didn't know it yet.

When the woman brought his plate a few minutes later, he nudged his badge across the table. "Ma'am my name is Zane Holloway, I'm with the US Marshals. Could I have a word with you and your husband, please?"

Her eyes widened as they bounced from him to the badge and back. "Hank! Get out here!" she called toward the kitchen.

Zane pushed the picture across the table and turned it over. Though he already knew the answer, he asked anyway. "Can you tell me if you know this woman?"

With a gasp, she snatched up the sketch, much like the postmistress had done.

Zane's heart constricted as he watched her face. She remained quiet for a long time, simply absorbing the sketch. Finally, she pressed the sketch to her chest and blinked up at the pinewood ceiling.

"So, you know her?" Zane prodded.

"Yes." Her hand trembled visibly when she dropped the sketch back on the table, almost as if she didn't want to be near it anymore. Her face was so pale, Zane feared she might faint.

He stood and hurried around the table to pull out a chair for her. "Here. Please sit."

She collapsed into the chair and covered her mouth with one hand, still staring at the drawing. "How do you know our Prissy?"

Before answering that, Zane wanted more information. "When was the last time you saw her, Mrs. Singleton?"

She didn't even seem fazed that he knew her name without introduction. "She went to Beaufort three weeks ago and hasn't returned. Hank went up to look for her but couldn't find her. Please"—she lifted her eyes to his, tears spilling—"what do you know?"

A man wearing a grease-stained shirt stretched over his ample middle joined them, drying his hands on a piece of toweling. His gaze took in the sketch, the badge, and his wife's tears. His Adam's apple bobbed slowly.

Zane picked up his badge with a heavy heart. "I'm sorry to inform you that your daughter was found..." He hesitated. Why did these conversations never get easier, no matter how many times he had to share them? He looked the father in the eyes, hoping he could see the sincere regret he was feeling. "She was found murdered in a hotel room in Beaufort."

The mother let out a soft mewl and the father yanked out a chair and collapsed into it.

Zane gave them a moment to gather themselves.

Finally, Mr. Singleton lifted his face from his hands. "What can you tell us about her death?"

Zane stalled by taking a slow sip of coffee. If it were his child what would he want to know? He decided on, "It was quick. She likely didn't even see it coming."

The shock must be settling in, because neither parent made a sound.

Zane cleared his throat and eased in to his next question. "Do either of you know Steven Pottinger?"

Both looked up, blinking at him confusedly. The father waved a hand. "Used to be mayor of Birch Run. Rumor was, he was shot and killed by his wife a couple years back."

Zane's disappointment mounted. So he wasn't going to get any answers from them. He'd hoped they might know something useful. Still, he had to try. "Actually, when I left him a few days ago, he was still alive, but I think he may have been the one who shot your daughter."

Mrs. Singleton gasped.

Zane pressed while he had their attention. "Did either of you ever know him to be violent?"

The couple looked at each other. After a long moment, the man stood, wiping his hands on his apron. "If there's nothing else, sir, I think my wife and I would like to be alone for a while."

Interesting... Zane nodded, folding the sketch. He started to put it into his pocket, but stilled when Mrs. Singleton put out her hand.

"Would... I be able to have that sketch, Mr. Holloway?"

He nodded. "I'll bring it back to you when I'm done with my investigation, ma'am."

"Thank you." She followed her husband from the room, both of them keeping their heads held high. But well he knew the grief that would likely take them to their knees once they were out of sight.

He swallowed. At least they had each other.

He took a gulp of coffee that went down hot and hard. He ate mechanically, more because he knew he needed to than for the enjoyment of it. He left double payment on the table and stepped out into the cool evening air. Zane paused on the boardwalk and glanced up and down the street. He supposed it was time to make another visit to the sheriff. What was the man going to say when he learned that Steven Pottinger had been very much alive, at least a few days ago?

Just as he remembered from the last time he was here, the sheriff's office was so cluttered with crates and stacks of newspapers that the door wouldn't even open all the way. Zane had to squeeze through. The paunchy man with flaccid cheeks looked up from behind a haphazard pile of books, so dusty that the title on the top copy was disguised. He was eating a whole pie, straight from the tin.

"Help you?" the sheriff barked, wiping crumbs of crust from his mouth.

Zane's patience was suddenly wearing thin. He tugged his badge from his belt and tossed it down on top of the dusty stack of books. "Afternoon, Sheriff Berkley. You might remember me from about a year and half ago when I came through here because I was assigned the Steven Pottinger murder?"

The sheriff assessed him up and down, then shrugged. He turned to gaze out the window behind his desk as if he had nothing better to do. "What if I do?"

Feeling his eyes narrow, Zane picked up his badge and hooked it back onto his belt. "Steven Pottinger is alive."

The man spun toward him so quickly that his jowls jiggled.

Zane nodded. "He tracked his wife and mother to a town out west. But he arrived under an assumed name. And I backtracked him all the way to Beaufort. In the hotel room up in Beaufort where he was using the alias Abraham Johnson, the body of Prissy Singleton was found. Murdered." Zane folded his arms and leaned in to his heels, letting the information sink in. "Now here's the thing, Sheriff. When I tracked down Mrs. Pottinger she had quite the story to tell. That story involved a certain sheriff that she had sought help from on several occasions. A sheriff who ignored her repeatedly. Even when she showed him the burn marks of cigars left on her arms by her cur of a husband." Zane pulled out a chair, propped his boot atop it, and leaned forward against crossed arms.

The sheriff squirmed uncomfortably in his seat and suddenly couldn't seem to meet Zane's scrutiny.

"How much was he paying you?" Zane let every ounce of anger he was feeling inhabit the question.

The sheriff threw both hands up, palms out. "Now see here!"

The good thing about wearing your pistols strapped down and facing forward was that people generally didn't realize you had laid hold of them till it was too late. Zane's hand was already wrapped around the handle of his pistol. He casually straightened and let the cocking of it make his point. There was something mighty sobering about looking down the barrel of a forty-four caliber Colt at point-blank range. He knew because he'd experienced the feeling more times than he cared to remember.

The sheriff leapt from his chair, eyes darting around the room as he searched for the quickest route of escape. However, he was quite literally boxed in behind his desk, with Zane blocking the only path.

Keeping the gun carefully trained on the man, Zane scratched his prickly jaw, wishing for nothing more than a bath and a good night's sleep before he needed to catch the train back to Wyldhaven. At least now he was getting somewhere. And it was definitely time to put this investigation to pasture. "I have an aversion to being sent on wild goose chases, Sheriff."

The man's face turned so pale that Zane wondered if he was going to be able to remain on his feet. "I only did what I was told to do. He ran this town. And I swear I did not know that he was still alive."

Zane sucked his front teeth thoughtfully. "So, what you mean to say is that you didn't intend to send me on a wild goose chase, but that you did know the Pottinger women were being abused and you didn't have the gumption to do anything about it."

"I knew no such thing!" The man shook his head emphatically.

Zane snorted his disbelief. "I also have an aversion to liars, Sheriff." He lifted his pistol and sited along the barrel, taking careful aim at the man's ear.

"Alright, alright, alright!" The man stumbled back until he bumped into the wall, then cowered behind his hands. "Maybe I did realize what he was doing, but I was in between the proverbial rock and a hard place." His voice rose into a whine. "He threatened my family if I ever so much as checked into any of her stories. Or let anything get around town about it."

That explained why no one seemed to want to talk to him about Pottinger. "And so, being the fine, upstanding, godly man that you are, you let him bully you." With a disgusted release of breath, Zane holstered his pistol. He straightened and dropped his foot to the floor. "Get over here."

The sheriff scuttled around his desk until he stood trembling before him.

"Sit." Zane motioned to the chair his boot had just vacated.

The man did.

Zane pulled out his handcuffs and threaded the man's hands through the slats of the chair, then cuffed his wrists together.

"If there's one thing I've learned over the years, Sheriff, it's that if a man is willing to lie about one thing, he's just as likely to lie about another." Zane sauntered to the area behind the sheriff's desk.

The man's eyes widened. "What are you doing?"

Zane ignored him and opened the top drawer on the right. Several broken handcuffs and a pistol that looked as if it hadn't been cleaned in years were the only items in that drawer. He continued his methodical search to the background music of the sheriff's sputtered complaints until he found a leather-bound notebook at the very back of the bottom left drawer. The notebook contained dated notes about investigations the sheriff had run. And haphazardly jotted though they were, it only took Zane five minutes to find one dated just three weeks previous.

"Followed P.S. to Beaufort. She met S.P. at the Grand Hotel. S.P. left on his own two hours later, and disappeared in the foot traffic near the train station."

Zane's anger surged. For the past year and a half, he'd been hunting the murderers of a man who hadn't been murdered. And this sheriff had known, but said nothing.

With four strides, he was around the desk. He snagged a fistful of Berkley's shirt and leaned down, letting his anger speak for itself.

Berkley cringed and turned his head away. "P-please. I was going to let the Marshals Office know just as soon as he did something worth telling!"

"The fact that he was *alive* was worth telling, considering he'd been reported as *dead* by you earlier. Did you give any thought to the fact that the Marshals Office had the two Pottinger women listed as 'armed and dangerous'?"

Berkley only sputtered. A clear indication that he hadn't been thinking much at all.

Zane didn't release him. "What about Miss Singleton. Did you know prior to her trip to Beaufort that he'd made contact with her?"

More sputtering.

Zane was disgusted. "You did know. And now she's dead!"

Berkley's eyes widened. "You can't pin that on me!"

Zane released him. "How long did you know?"

"I've been following her for a few months. The first time I happened to see them was an accident. They met at a pub where I chanced to be eating while in the city. But she returned home on the same train as I did that night. And she always came home safely from every other meeting, though mostly they met at his hotel where..." Berkley rolled his hand through the air. "I assumed they..." More hand rolling. "So three weeks ago when she met him at the Grand, I thought nothing of it. When she didn't come back home, I just assumed that they'd run off together. I was just happy to have the man out of my life. He made everything miserable."

Zane felt exhausted and yet free. All his work from the past couple years had finally come to fruition. "The investigation into the Pottinger murder is concluded, Sheriff. Rose and Dixie Pottinger's names have been cleared as suspects. But if I were you, I would be expecting a visit from the members of your town council first thing tomorrow morning, because City Hall is my next stop after I return to the Golden Vittles and give the Singletons the final sketch of their murdered daughter."

With that, he pushed out the door and headed back the way he had come, leaving the man hand-cuffed to the chair. The town council could decide what to do with him. He'd meant what he said. This town deserved a better lawman than the one they had. He wouldn't stick around for the aftermath, but he certainly intended to start it rolling. After the courthouse, he would find a hotel room for the night and then catch the train back to Wyldhaven in the morning. Steven Pottinger had some explaining to do if he was still alive when Zane got back.

And dash it all if just the thought of returning to Wyldhaven didn't bring to mind vivid blue eyes and a soft, inviting smile with a bit of standoffishness around the corners. He scrubbed both hands over his face.

He must be more tired than he realized. Either that or his heart had already been lassoed up and cinched down tight.

Chapter Twenty-five

For a week and a half Steven lingered on. He hadn't really come around other than to moan and be given more laudanum since Flynn had tried to extract the bullet.

That first night when Flynn had come with her to sit by Steven's side, she hadn't known if she would be able to remain in the room with him. Her mouth had prickled with metallic fear, and her pulse had thrummed the warning to escape while she still could. She had so many emotions swirling inside her when it came to this man. Dislike. Terror. Anger. Disappointment. Hurt. Futility. Revulsion. Everything in her still cried out with the need for revenge!

And yet, something about the gray pallor of Steven's face, and the moans of pain that he emitted every once in a while, had strangely tugged at her compassion. She couldn't explain her change of heart and yet she'd lost her fear of being near him days ago, for when she looked at the enfeebled shell of the man lying on the bed, she could see no remains of the monster who had tortured her repeatedly. How fleeting life was. Had he looked ahead to the end of his days when he'd been torturing her? Had he pondered that one day he would come to his end and have a Maker to face? Dixie hardly thought so.

Each day when she didn't need to be elsewhere, Dixie, felt compelled to sit by his side. She prayed while she sat. She prayed while she dabbed the feverish sweat from his forehead with a damp rag. And she prayed while she read Isaiah chapter 40 over and over. *Lord, help me to hope in you.* She was determined not to let Steven make her lose her hope ever again.

Parson Clay came by daily, and she found his visits encouraging. Before he left each day he always squeezed her shoulder and quoted John 16:33. "These things I have spoken to you, that in Me you may have peace. In the world you will have tribulation; but be of good cheer, I have overcome the world."

Still, Dixie struggled.

Would God asked her to return to living as Steven's wife? She prayed for strength.

Could she ever forgive him for all he had done to her and to Rose? She prayed for resolve.

This morning she had cooked breakfast for the diners and then left Liora to do the cleaning. As she wiped Steven's brow once more, she considered how thankful she was to have Liora helping her during this trying time. She was efficient and good at finding things that needed to be done without having to be told.

Dixie had also offered Liora a room at a rate that matched Ewan's, even though her boardinghouse rooms were twice the size of his and more comfortable. The girl had jumped at the chance to move out of McGinty's Alehouse.

There was a tap on the door behind her and Dixie turned, expecting to see Parson Clay, but was surprised to see Marshal Holloway instead. "You're back."

He took off his hat as he stepped into the room. "Yes, ma'am." His gaze slipped to Steven. "He's still alive?"

"Yes." Dixie scrambled to her feet, knowing she might be experiencing her last moments of freedom. "Are you back to arrest us?"

He shook his head, and she lost the strength from her legs and sank back into her chair.

"Turns out the sheriff back in Birch Run knew all along what Pottinger was doing to you. He's also known for quite some time that he was alive." He tipped a nod to Steven. "So, I'm here to tell you that all charges against you have been dropped."

Dixie sat in stunned silence for a moment. All charges dropped. Such a relief washed through her! She had to tell Rose!

"Thank you, Marshal.." She jumped back to her feet and lifted a handful of her skirts. "If you'll excuse me?"

He nodded.

She rushed across the hall, great joy surging through her. And to think she could have thrown all this freedom away if she'd followed through on her desire for revenge.

Rose was on her feet when Dixie rushed through the door. She'd been getting out for longer and longer periods each day, but Dixie had urged her to continue resting and going easy at home for a few weeks more.

Now she pulled the startled woman into an exuberant embrace. "All charges against us have been dropped!"

Rose gasped. "Truly?"

"Yes!"

When Dixie released her and pulled back, Rose had tears in her eyes. Dixie waited, hoping Rose could see the question in her scrutiny.

Rose waved a hand. "I just wish he was a different man. I've tried so hard to reach him over the years."

***

When the door opened Kin looked up from his cot in his cell. He wondered how much longer he was going to have to stay there. Who was taking care of his horse? And he needed to make arrangements for Pa's burial. He should have put up more of a fuss last week when they'd put him back in this cell. Joe had said Kin only needed to stay till they figured out what to do with him. But one night had turned into two, then three, then a week and more.

In a typically evasive grown up fashion, the sheriff had said they were "working out some details" and that was why Kin needed to remain in the cell. But Kin knew they were just trying to figure out who to saddle with his care.

Kin had wanted to inform him that he'd basically been on his own since his mother died, but that would have disparaged Pa's name, so he'd refrained.

At least the sheriff had built the fire up good and hot, and then banked it well before he left last night.

Now the sheriff stepped into the room, followed by the minister.

Kin glance down at the rough floorboards between his feet. Here it came. The man was probably here to lecture him about how stupid he'd been. Maybe even flay a section of his hide in repayment for the knock to the head he'd taken when the carriage tipped over.

The sheriff cleared his throat. "Kin, this here is Parson Preston Clay." He swept his hat in the man's direction.

Kin swallowed and nodded a greeting. He hadn't paid much attention to the man the other day. But now he scrutinized him from head to foot, mouth dry. He was a lot younger than Kin figured a man of the cloth should be. And he wasn't soft looking like most ministers Kin had come across. Broad muscular shoulders stretched the material of his black shirt till Kin could see the strain at the seams.

He was surprised to see a kind smile soften the edges of the man's green eyes.

He felt his brow lift. Okay, so maybe the man wasn't here for retribution. Still... An uneasy feeling hung in Kin's stomach. He narrowed his eyes.

The sheriff hooked his hat on the peg by the door. "Turns out the parson needs a place to stay, and you need someone to care for you, so I'm proposing that you allow the parson to stay at your place. At least until you get out of school—"

"I don't need anyone to care for me. And I'm not going back to school." He'd decided all that during the nights when he'd lain awake, staring at the knot in the plank ceiling. "I'm old enough to work for one of Mr. Heath's logging crews."

The sheriff and the parson exchanged a look.

To Kin's surprise, it was the parson who spoke up. "Schooling and work—that's your decision. But you'd surely be doing me a favor if you let me bunk at your place for a bit."

The sheriff, who was just lifting the ring of keys from his desk drawer, gave the parson a surprised look, but didn't contradict the words as he stepped over and unlocked Kin's cell. "After investigation, it has been determined that you didn't have intent to harm anyone on the stage, other than maybe giving them a scare. Though it could be said that you are responsible for the man who was shot, I've talked it over with Joe and with those who were on the stage, and we've decided that you can't be held responsible for what happened. You are free to go."

Kin felt a weight lift from his shoulders. The sheriff could have charged him as if he'd pulled the trigger himself. He knew that very well. He bent and retrieved his hat from the end of the cot. "Thank you, Sheriff." He curled the brim into his palm as he stepped out into the main part of the room.

Reagan hid a grin behind a swipe of one hand as Kin stepped

out from the jail cell. The kid bounced a look from the minister to the floor and then back again, looking like he felt a little stuck. Reagan knew the lean-to that he and his father had lived in wasn't fit for anyone, much less a minister. But he was also counting on the fact that Kin wouldn't feel comfortable turning the minister away. It would be good for the kid to have a male role model to look up to.

Kin shuffled his feet. "My place ain't much to look at. Not sure it's fit for a minister."

Parson Clay's smile was immediate and as large as a moon sliver. He clapped Kin on his shoulder. "If you could see where I grew up—in a tiny tenement apartment in New York City with eleven brothers and sisters and no running water—you'd know that so long as I have a place to lay my head. I'll be just fine."

Kin sighed and his shoulders drooped. He looked like his favorite pony had just died. His gaze lifted to Reagan's. "Can you tell me where my horse is?"

Reagan tipped a nod toward the street. "At the hitching rail out front."

Kin hesitated for a moment, scratching the back of his neck. "What do I owe for his care over the last few days?"

That smile was trying to come out again. Reagan rubbed a hand over his mouth. Looked like the kid might have done some growing up this week. That thought sobered Reagan right up. Well he remembered what it had felt like right after his own pa had passed. "Well now, that's going to be up to old Silas down at the livery. I imagine if you talk to him, he'll let you work it off."

Kin swallowed. "Thanks for taking care of her for me."

Reagan nodded. "Wouldn't have thought to do anything else."

"And my...pa?"

With a tip of his head, Reagan said, "The parson there bought a wagon, and your pa is...in the back. You sure you want to bury him out at your place and not in the new church cemetery?"

Kin nodded. "Next to my ma." With that the boy slipped on his hat. "Pa wouldn't have appreciated being buried so close to a church, no how. He never could stand the sound of an organ."

Reagan watched them walk out the door, Kin's feet scuffing the floor like he was bound for the gallows instead of home. Reagan didn't let himself chuckle until the door clicked shut. That kid was a handful. He didn't envy the parson taking on the shaping of that life. But from everything he had seen, Kin sure could use the parson's influence.

Reagan rose to get himself a cup of coffee.

The door opened even before he filled his cup. Reagan paused pouring and looked up. His brows lifted. "Timothy King! Good to see you." He wondered what the sheriff from Cedar Falls was doing in his town. "I was just pouring some coffee. Can I offer you a cup?"

King shivered exaggeratedly. "You sure can. It's colder than an iceberg out there."

Reagan chuckle. "Yeah, I think we are in for quite a storm in the next day or two." He handed King a cup and filled it from the pot.

Nudging the chair across from his desk, Reagan said, "Please have a seat," then moved around to take his own chair.

There was a moment of silence while King savored his first sip, then he looked up and met Reagan's eyes. "You'll of course remember the outlaw Patrick Waddell."

"Generally hard to forget a man you shot to death."

King nodded. "Yes. As it turns out, Patrick Waddell owned

a piece of property. And, from all the research I've done, he owned it straight up legally."

Reagan shifted in his chair and leaned forward. He rested his forearms on his desk. Immediately, his thoughts went to Liora. It would sure be a financial blessing to her if she stood to inherit. "Where is this property?"

King motioned with his hand to the northwest. "It's only about five miles from here. Smack dab between Camp Sixty-Five and Camp Sixty-Six. Nearly ten acres."

"Well, isn't that something." Reagan leaned back in his chair and propped his boots on the corner of his desk. "You know his daughter lives here in town, right?"

King nodded. "That's why I'm here."

Reagan felt a surge of happiness rise up inside him. These were the kind of days in law that kept him going. It wasn't often that he could do good things for people. But it looked like today he'd be able to do something good twice.

King reached into his jacket pocket and pulled out an envelope, tossing it onto the desk. "If you can get her, all she has to do is sign the papers saying I gave her the deed, and the land is hers. Waddell didn't have any other family, as far as we can tell."

Reagan stood and reached for his jacket. "I'll go get her right now. She just works two doors down at Dixie's boardinghouse."

Liora was scrubbing dishes at the boardinghouse sink when Reagan found her. "Liora, could I bother you to come with me for a moment?"

She lifted her hands from the sudsy water, a frown puckering her brow. "Of course." She said it with ease, but there was an underlying ring of tension in the acquiescence. "I was just finishing up."

"You aren't in trouble or anything like that," Reagan rushed to reassure her.

She rinsed her hands and dried them on a towel and then followed him back to the sheriff's office. He sank into his seat and relished the look on her face that turned from shock to surprise, and then to awe as Sheriff King shared with her about the land her father had owned.

She signed the paperwork with trembling fingers, and King handed over the deed. "Congratulations."

Liora scanned the document, disbelief still wreathing her face. "I really and truly own ten acres? And only a few miles from here?"

King grinned. "You really and truly do."

"I can't believe it." Still staring at the deed, she leaned into the planks next to the door as though she needed the strength of the wall to keep herself upright. She laughed. "Only yesterday I was trying to figure out how I was going to pay this month's rent. Now I have a job and I've found out that I own land."

"I'm happy to be the bearer of such good news, ma'am." Sheriff King stood to his feet. "Well, I better get on over to my son's place before the weather outright freezes these old bones."

Reagan nodded. Sheriff King's son, Ben, was Wyldhaven's postmaster. "Thanks for stopping by, King. Enjoy the holiday. If Miss Brindle continues to have her way and the weather holds out, there will be a celebration for the whole town come this Friday. In fact"—he looked at his pocket watch—"I'm supposed to be to a planning a meeting about that in just a few minutes."

"Oh, that's right. I am too," Liora added.

King fingered his hat as he stepped to the door. "Ben was

telling me about the festival. I think it's one of the best ideas I've heard in a long time. I wish our town did something similar. I'll be looking forward to it. Good evening now." He tipped his hat to Liora and stepped out into the wind that howled over the mountains.

Liora dipped a small curtsy. "Thank you again, Sheriff." She followed King out the door, still wearing a stunned smile.

Reagan leaned in to the back of his seat and propped his feet on the corner of his desk. He really couldn't be happier for her.

Chapter Twenty-six

ixie had left Flynn and Rose by Steven's side about forty-five minutes ago when she'd come downstairs to finish preparing the breakfast she planned for tomorrow morning. She liked to serve canned preserves with her oatmeal, and she always put the fruit in covered colanders to drain overnight. All day long, Steven's breathing had been increasingly labored.

Liora had already completed the dishes and left the kitchen by the time she'd arrived, so Dixie had taken the extra time that had afforded her to straighten the pantry, which had been badly in need of some attention. Once again, she was so thankful for Liora's presence.

Now she stepped into the dining room to join the planning meeting Charlotte had called. Though this was the final meeting before the Christmas festival that was set for three days from now, Dixie knew they'd had several other meetings that she hadn't found the energy to attend. She hoped she would be able to offer some help, even though it would be of the last-minute variety. And she was thankful to be able to think of something other than her worries over Steven. But just as she was about to sit at the table where Joe, Charlotte, Reagan, and Jacinda waited for the meeting to begin and for others to arrive, Rose rushed into the room. She was out of breath. It was the first time she'd been downstairs in weeks.

"Dixie," she panted. "Best you come right now."

Dixie felt her heart leap into her throat. Everyone around the table knew that Steven had been clinging to life by the thinnest of threads these past couple days. She tossed a glance to Charlotte. "I'm so very sorry. I've been no help at all for your festival."

Charlotte's eyes softened. "No. No. Please, have no concerns. We'll be just fine, and we'll be praying."

"Thank you." Dixie squeezed her friend's shoulder as she passed behind her. She felt every eye in the room drilling into her back as she made her way toward the stairs. As she left the dining room, she almost bumped into Marshal Holloway and Liora, who had just come down the stairs, apparently to attend the planning meeting. "I'm sorry. Excuse me." She stepped around them, feeling a bit like she was walking through a thick fog.

Marshal Holloway made a reply, but it didn't register.

Dixie paused at the bottom of the stairs, looking up. Rose had already disappeared back into Steven's room. She'd been sitting with her son for longer and longer periods of time lately, and Dixie knew this had to be rending Rose's mother-heart asunder. Dixie willed her heartbeat to steady. She prayed for God to help her to want the best for Steven. Yet guilt overshadowed the prayer. She couldn't help but feel a measure of relief to think he might be passing.

She took the stairs slowly. The door to room five creaked as though even the hinges knew her heart was weighted with the upheaval of an uncertainty.

Rose started apologizing the moment Dixie stepped through the door. "I'm sorry, Dixie. I didn't know what else to do. He said he would kill him if I brought anyone but you." She wrung her hands before her.

Dixie's focus snapped to the back of the room. Her eyes widened as she took in Steven holding something she couldn't quite make out to Flynn's throat. Flynn's hands were out to his sides, palms facing forward, and his countenance was a bit strained, but otherwise he appeared calm.

Steven, on the other hand, was blinking hard—probably to remove the sting of the sweat glistening on his forehead from his eyes. He swayed slightly. But the moment he noticed Dixie, his lip curled into a sneer. "There you are."

Dixie held out one hand. "Steven, just let him go. Then you and I can talk."

"And have him run downstairs to fetch help? I don't think so."

Dixie swallowed. She dared not look at Flynn. He would have never found himself in this situation if she hadn't been a coward and run into hiding. This was her doing. She had to keep Steven calm. "Okay, so what do you want?"

Steven snorted. "What do I want? I want a mother who wouldn't shoot her own son. A wife who wouldn't betray me in such a heinous manner as to leave me bleeding to death in my own hall!" The muscles at the corner of his eye twitched, a sure sign that he was losing his temper.

Dixie stepped to one side of the door, leaving a clear path for Flynn's exit. "So let him go, and then we can talk about it."

Steven leaned forward, his face turning crimson as he vehemently rasped. "I don't want to talk about it!"

Flynn flinched, and Dixie saw a trickle of blood seep down his throat. She also caught a glint of metal reflecting the light of the lantern on the table.

But the exertion had cost Steven. He swayed on his feet. And it seemed that fact enraged him even more. "I *will* slit his throat, I swear I will. Don't think I didn't notice the way you two looked at each other that first day!"

Dixie's heart was pounding like the pistons of a steam engine now. She refrained from even another glance at Flynn, keeping her gaze fixed solely on Steven, instead. "I tell you true when I say that I have been faithful to you, Steven."

"She has," Flynn asserted, swallowing gingerly.

Steven swayed again and gave his head a little shake. His eyes blinked slow and heavy now. But his scoffed breath held plenty of derision. "Faithful, you say? Do you call it faithful to leave your husband on the brink of death while you ran all the way across the country to hide?!" Once again, his cheeks flushed scarlet.

Dixie knew that bringing up the fact that he'd been beating her nearly to death only moments before that would simply anger him more, so she held her silence.

Steven's nostril's flared. "Got nothing to say to that, do you? I thought not." His focus flashed to his mother, who still stood wringing her hands at the foot of one of the room's cots. "Traitors and betrayers, the both of you."

"Steven, please." Those were the first words Rose had interjected into the situation.

They didn't seem to do anything to soften Steven's heart. "I've been lying here on my bed, gathering my strength until I was strong enough to take you both off the high horses you climbed up onto. Seems you both are rather fond of the good doc here."

Dixie felt the blood drain from her face, but again words failed her. If she said the wrong thing and angered him, he would strike before she could even move. She felt paralyzed.

She was surprised when Flynn spoke almost casually. "You could kill me, Pottinger, to inflict pain on your women, but then what? How are you going to get out of the building?"

Steven blinked and swayed a little further this time before

he regained his center of balance. "They are my women, as you say. I'll simply march them down the stairs and out the front door."

Flynn blew out a breath of dismissal. "There's both a US marshal and a sheriff downstairs in Dixie's dining room. And even if you got past them, it's the middle of December in the mountains of Washington. Where are you going to go to hide in those conditions?"

"Silence!" Steven tightened his grip and another trickle of blood joined the first on Flynn's neck.

Dixie felt every manner of terror clawing at her insides.

Steven widened his stance as though he might need the extra balance.

Think! What might distract him? Jesus, please... And suddenly she knew. "Would you like a glass of scotch, Steven?" She drilled her focus into Flynn's for the first time since she'd come into the room, willing him to read her plan in the message of her eyes.

His brow furrowed slightly.

Good, at least he'd noticed she was trying to communicate something to him. Maybe that would be enough.

Steven licked his lips. "You have scotch?"

Dixie pointed behind Steven. "I do. It's just in the cabinet against the wall back there."

Steven started to turn to see the cabinet she meant. But in doing so, he loosened his grip on Flynn for just a fraction of a second. It was all the space Flynn needed. He thrust his head upward and Dixie heard the loud *crack* of his skull connecting with Steven's chin even as she saw Steven's head snap back. Flynn shoved Steven's arm up and at the same moment he lurched forward and spun around. With that one quick twist he had Steven's arm angled up behind him. He leaned in to him, propelling him forward into the wall next to his bed.

Steven cursed and thrashed. He knocked the lantern on the table and it crashed to the floor. Flames immediately sprung to life along the floorboards, and licked against Steven's pant leg.

He screamed, and Flynn leapt back lest he catch flame too. He yanked for the quilt on the bed. "Lay down!" he yelled to Steven. "Get on the floor!"

Dixie shoved Rose toward the door. "Run!"

She should run herself, but she couldn't just abandon Flynn to deal with Steven!

Steven still screamed as he spun in a confused circle, his terrified gaze fixed on the flames that now consumed his leg up to his knee.

Flynn shoved the man hard, knocking him off balance. He collapsed to the floor, but still tried to scramble away from the flames. His screams grew louder.

"Hold still!" Flynn yelled. He dove on Steven's legs with the thick quilt bundled into a ball in his arms.

In a panic, Steven tried to kick Flynn away, but Flynn threw a punch straight into his face, which knocked him back to the floor. Steven twitched once, but seemed to be out for the moment. Flynn rolled the blanket firmly against Steven's leg.

Dixie stood with one hand pressed to her chest. He wasn't going to be able to get the flames out!

"Dixie!" Flynn yelled. "The mattress!" He tossed his chin toward the flames that still made their way along the floorboards of the room.

Right! Dixie lurched into action. This was her business, her livelihood. She couldn't just stand by and watch it burn to the ground!

She grabbed the pitcher of water from the washstand by the door and dashed it onto the mattress of Steven's bed. The water spilled out and soaked into the material. She wished for more water, but there was none ready to hand. That amount would have to do. Taking one edge of the bedding, she upended the heavy tick onto the floor, wet side down. It flopped onto most of the flames and there was a sharp sizzling sound. Only a small patch of flames was left now, licking weakly at a new board.

Hefting her skirts high, she stomped on those flames with her boots. By the time she'd gotten those out, the room had fallen to silence. She spun in a circle, searching in a panic for more flames. Smoke hazed the room and she coughed, but it looked like she's gotten the fire out before it had done too much damage.

Her gaze darted back to Steven and Flynn.

Flynn sat on his haunches, wrists resting against his knees. Next to him Steven lay so still that for a moment Dixie thought he was gone, but then he coughed and rolled to one side. A scream of pure agony unlike any Dixie had ever heard before slipped from him.

Flynn's eyes filled with compassion. He reached out and touched Steven's shoulder. "Let me get you something for that pain."

At that moment, Rose burst back through the door with Sheriff Callahan and Marshal Holloway fast on her heels.

⌁❦⌁

It had taken hours to restore order after Steven's attack. They'd had to move the infirmary to room six because Sheriff Callahan had deduced that the floorboards in room five were too damaged to bear weight. The floor of that room would need to be redone before she could rent it to anyone.

Steven had been tied to the bedframe, hand and foot, but

with the extra dose of laudanum that Flynn had given him, he'd been mentally incapacitated since Flynn had knocked him out. For his sake that was probably a blessing, because his leg had been very badly burned.

The Christmas planning meeting downstairs had wound to a close practically before it had begun. Everyone had gone their separate way with the plan to meet back in the dining room just after breakfast hours on the morrow.

Dixie had just seen the last of them off, and now she peered around the door of room six.

Rose sat in the chair by Steven's bed, wiping his brow with a damp cloth. Flynn stood behind her, one arm folded across his ribs while the other rested upon it. His hand tugged at the several days' worth of stubble on his chin. The white bandage stood in stark contrast against the sun-browned skin of his neck.

Flynn looked up and met Dixie's gaze across the room.

When she hesitated near the door, he motioned her closer.

"I need you both to know that I did everything I could to try and save him. But despite my efforts I think his time has come. He might have made it if he hadn't exerted himself in such a manner today, and if he hadn't gotten burned so badly. But he tore open his wound and lost a lot of blood. In his already weakened condition...I'm afraid his heart..." His hand dropped to Rose's shoulder. "I know this has been especially hard on you."

Dixie appreciated that he seemed to understand a little of what Rose must be going through. She herself felt only numbness. She glanced down at the lax form on the bed.

His last words had been ones of hatred and derision. He'd been so confident in his own strength. And she'd been so terrified of it. Terrified enough, even before he'd attacked Flynn, that she'd almost taken things into her own hands. She had feared that Rose was going to die, yet she had lived. She had feared that Steven was going to live and yet now, he lay on the bed, his last breaths gurgling in his throat like his soul was exerting every effort to cling to this mortal soil.

It suddenly became even more clear to her why it was so important to hope in the Lord. It was the only One who knew the end from the beginning. He was the only One who held the power to both preserve or take a life. People might plan and boastfully proclaim, yet it was the Lord who decided whether those plans and proclamations came to fruition. And if anyone left this plain before making their peace with God... Dixie shuddered to think what Steven's destiny would be. For a life lived in rejection of God's ways—a lifestyle that essentially shouted for God to stay out—would certainly result in God granting that wish for eternity.

She stepped to Rose's side and took her hand. "How long does he have?"

Flynn swept a gesture of uncertainty. "Minutes. Hours, maybe. Sometimes they linger on far longer than I expect."

In the end, it wasn't hours. Only a few moments later, Steven's last breath rattled past his lips and silence settled in the place of the death rattle.

Rose hitched a little gasp and covered her mouth. Dixie wrapped an arm around her. "I'm so sorry, Rose. I know this must be so hard for you. Come. You've been up far too long today. There's nothing we can do for him now. Let's get you back to your bed."

Rose complied without resisting.

At the door, Dixie tossed a look back at Flynn, feeling bad that she was leaving him to deal with the body alone.

He gave her a nod of reassurance and waved her through the door.

Chapter Twenty-seven

~~~✿~~~

Kin woke to the smell of frying corn fritters. He stretched and squinted at the window. Light barely made the pane a lighter gray than the frame around it. Yet he felt more refreshed than he had in weeks. He'd slept hard.

The first thing the parson had done when they'd arrived at the house two days ago was to start sawing boards from the old dried log that Pa had felled but never done anything with. He'd sent Kin back to town for nails and a hammer when Kin had told him he didn't think Pa had any around. And by the time Kin had arrived back home, the parson had sawn several boards. He'd given two to Kin with instructions to make a cross while he dug Pa's grave.

Ma's grave lay in a nice spot under the tall cedar at the back of the property. They put Pa next to her.

The minister had dug a small hole about a foot in diameter into the frozen ground, then he'd built a fire right in that hole. He'd fed it with pine cones and dried pine branches until it was so hot that Kin had been able to feel the heat all the way across the yard where he'd been working on engraving the cross. After several minutes, the minister had put out the fire, dug out the coals and set to digging the grave again. He'd worked that way off and on for some hours. Warming the ground enough that a shovel could penetrate it until he'd gone at least a man's height deep. Kin had finished the cross and tried to help, but mostly the minister had done the hard work. He'd said some nice words over Pa, and then they had covered him over with the cold dirt. Kin had felt a bit empty as he'd stood there looking down at the grave of his last remaining relative on earth. After a long moment, the minister had clapped him on the shoulder and gone back to cutting boards.

He'd cut until he had enough boards to cover the cracks in two of the cabin walls. Then he'd shown Kin what he wanted him to do. It had been Kin's job to measure them to length, and overlap them on the cracks and nail them into place while the parson cut more boards for the other two walls. The parson said it was only a temporary fix, but that it should get them through the winter okay.

Kin never remembered sleeping warmer during the winter. In fact, the house was so warm at this moment that he didn't even have need of his coat—a first, of a certainty, in December.

Kin was still sitting sleepily on the edge of his cot when the parson brought over a plate and passed it to him. Kin's stomach rumbled loud appreciation. "Thanks," he mumbled. If he was forced to share his cabin with the man, it at least came with some perks. The parson hadn't stopped working since he'd set foot on the property.

Parson Clay nodded. "Figured we should eat a mite early today so we can head into town and help with the final preparations for the Christmas festival."

Kin's appreciation for the meal and the man's work ethic deflated. "Don't see how they need our help."

Parson Clay took his own plate and sat on a log-round upended by the stove. He met Kin's gaze across the room. "If everyone who'd been asked to help said that, where would the world be?"

Kin's shoulders slumped. "At home curled up in their warm beds."

Parson Clay chuckled. "Perhaps I need to aerate the section of wall near your cot again? Make it so cold in here you'll be happy to get out of the place just to get your blood pumping."

Kin wasn't sure if he was serious, so he made no more comment. It had sure felt good to sleep through last night without having to get up to restock the stove. And he didn't want to go back to the way things used to be.

The minister smiled. "I'm just having a little fun with you. How about we say grace and then after we help in town, we take a little break to do some fishing?"

Kin lifted his gaze to search the man's face. "You mean it?"

"Of course I do. I never joke about fishing." He winked.

Kin couldn't help the grin that snuck onto his lips without permission. "I know a good log for grubs, even this late in the year." He felt a little guilty for being so excited about fishing with Pa only in the grave for a day.

"Well, good then. Looks like we'll be all set."

Kin pushed his guilt aside and tucked into the corn fritter and leftover baked beans with renewed zest. Looked like the day wasn't going to be a total bust after all.

Here lies Steven Pottinger. Husband & Son. 1864-1891. Dixie stood at the foot of the first grave dug into the ground of Wyldhaven's new church cemetery and stared at the wooden cross that someone in the town had hastily put together for them. How sad that they'd had nothing kind to say about the man.

The minister had come into town with Kin to attend Charlotte's planning meeting, but when she and Rose had approached him, he'd gladly taken time to do the short service they'd asked of him.

Now as she watched the men laboring to return the frozen soil into the grave, Dixie guiltily considered how she'd really only asked for a service for Rose's benefit. If it had been up to her, she would have been tempted to let the men remove his body from the boardinghouse and never think of him again.

The wind sliced down off the mountain with enough force to bring an ache to her joints. She was thankful that Rose had already returned inside at Dr. Griffin's insistence. But once she'd arrived at the funeral, she'd found that she couldn't bring herself to leave until the deed was fully done. So she stayed watching shovelful after shovelful tumble into the gaping earth to cover the hastily-made coffin that contained Steven's body.

She huddled into herself, rubbing her hands up and down her arms.

Someone stepped up beside her.

She glanced over to see the minister standing next to her. His arms forming an X before him as he stood with his Bible clutched casually in his hands.

He tossed her a sideways glance. "Something seems to be troubling you, ma'am?"

She sighed, her focus wandering back to the half-filled hole. "I prayed about forgiving him, Parson. I'm just not sure I managed it before he passed."

"I see."

He didn't speak for so long afterwards that Dixie was certain that was all he was going to offer about the matter. Her heart sank a little. She had failed at one of the most important tasks a Christian was charged with. To forgive as the Father in heaven had forgiven her.

Just when she'd decided she should probably get inside and

see if she could still be of use to Charlotte, the minister spoke again. "Do you know what the Bible says about how God feels when it comes to sin?"

"He doesn't like it." Dixie braced herself for the minister to tell her that she was right and therefore God could no longer love her.

But he only nodded. "The Bible goes so far as to say God hates sin. There's a lot of emotion behind a word like 'hate.' It can't just be viewed in a glass case all on its own. It comes with baggage. And yet, when we confess our sins, the Bible says that God is faithful to forgive us those sins. I don't believe that means God no longer hates our sin. He still hates our sin, but He chooses to see the sacrifice His son made on our behalf instead of focusing on our sin. It is the same with us. When we choose to forgive someone, we don't lose all the emotions we had when they treated us poorly. We just choose not to hold those evil things over their head any longer. And the interesting thing is that as we choose to walk in that forgiveness, we somehow seem to lose the harsh and angry feelings as time passes as well." He looked over at her and clapped a hand to her shoulder. "Don't sell yourself short, Mrs. Pottinger. I believe you have forgiven the man, but don't expect the feelings of anger and betrayal to dissipate overnight. In fact, it is only good and right that you should feel anger and betrayal, for those are the very evidence that you are indeed made in the image of your Creator. I believe you have proven your heart of forgiveness by the fact that you chose to shelter and care for your husband and treat his wounds despite all that he'd done to you."

Dixie's relief was so great that she literally felt her knees go slack. "Thank you for that. I do want to forgive him. I'm just not sure what to do with all the..." She spiraled her hands around over her heart as though to indicate churned up soil.

"It is never wrong to feel anger about sin. It's how we handle that anger that so often turns into sin of its own." Once more he settled one hand against her shoulder. "How about we let these gentlemen finish filling in this hole and you and I return inside to see if we can help Miss Brindle with her Christmas festival?"

"Yes. I would like that. Thank you." They started back toward the boardinghouse before Dixie remembered to say, "And thank you for taking care of Kin. He's a bit of a mischief-maker, but he's near and dear to all our hearts 'round these parts."

Parson Clay cleared his throat. "Yes. Well... I know a whole lot more about being a big brother than I do about being a father, but I'm happy to try and guide him a little. I lost my own pa when I was just seventeen, so I know something of what he's going through."

"Well, he's blessed to have you." Dixie hefted her skirts, since they were close to the boardinghouse now. "If you'll excuse me. I'm just going to go in the back door and bring coffee in to the dining room for the meeting."

The parson tipped her his hat, and they parted ways.

Dixie had been in the kitchen only long enough to get coffee grounds and water added to the coffee pot and was just setting it on the stove when Flynn stepped in through the dining room door.

He had his hat in his hands and a searching look in his eyes. "You doing okay?"

She took in the rigid planes of his face that were currently softened in concern for her. The gentle hazel-blue of his eyes lured her like a magnet. But then her gaze dipped to the small white bandage against his throat, and her heartrate was suddenly tripping along at a pace much faster than its norm.

"Yes. Thank you. I'm fine." She spun toward the wood bin and took up two pine logs that would burn hot and fast so the coffee would heat quickly. For the first time ever there was nothing preventing her from exploring her feelings about one Doctor Flynn Griffin, and she wasn't sure how she felt about that. It thrilled her. It terrified her. It made her want to sing at the top of her voice so the whole world could hear. And it made her want to run to her room and hide beneath the covers, never to come out again.

A vision of the blood that had trickled down Flynn's throat when Steven had hold of him made her hands tremble.

She tugged open the stove door and shoved the chunks of wood inside.

"Dixie..." His voice was gentle and coaxing. "This is me you're talking to."

The stove door clunked shut, but she used the excuse of arranging cream and sugar and mugs on a tray to keep her back to him. She waved a hand over her shoulder. "The past few days have been...a little trying is all. I'll be fine in a day or two. How was Rose when you got her inside?"

She heard a soft breath puff from him. "I was a little concerned with her inhaling such cold air when she's just getting past this pneumonia, but she seemed to be breathing just fine, even with the stairs. She's up in her chambers, resting."

"Yes. Thank you for insisting she come inside. I was concerned about her as well." She closed her eyes, but all she could see were flames leaping up to consume Steven's leg, and Flynn battling him to be able to put them out. What if Flynn had been severely wounded also?

She spun to face him and gasped to find him standing so

close that her arm had brushed against him as she turned. Her hands moved of their own accord—one to rest against his chest, the other to touch the bandage at Flynn's throat. "I'm so sorry." Unaccountable tears blurred her vision. "All of this was my fault. If I hadn't run—"

"Don't." The word was hard and short.

She lifted her gaze to his. He was so close that she could see the amber flecks in his blue eyes. Feel the rise and fall of his chest beneath her hand. "But—"

He shook his head and tossed his Stetson down on the table next to them. "Not another word. None of this was your fault." He pulled her gently toward him until her head rested against his chest and his chin rested atop her head. "You had every good reason to run from a man such as that."

She closed her eyes and simply relished the feel of his arms, warm around her. His breathing, soft and sibilant beneath her ear. And never in all her days did she remember ever feeling so safe and comforted.

He was here. He was safe. And *she* was safe, truly safe, for the first time in many years.

She released a sigh along with a silent prayer.

Thank you, Jesus.

But she had to know... She hadn't yet had opportunity to find out how Steven had been able to take him captive. "Tell me what happened up there?"

Flynn released a short breath. "I was shocked he had the strength for it. One moment he was lying there all still and quiet. I had just examined his wound and noticed that the infection was spreading. When I turned to reach for the carbolic acid, he leapt from the bed with that pocket knife in his hand and demanded that Rose go and fetch you."

Dixie felt a shudder slip through her. "If something had happened to you..."

"But it didn't. Nothing happened to me other than a little scratch. I'll be good as new in just a day or so."

"I can't believe he's gone. It feels strange not to have the fear of him hanging over me."

Flynn just held her for a long moment more. But after a while he spoke and there was a note of tension in his tone. "And now that he's gone? Is there any hope for us?"

Feeling suddenly shy about standing in the circle of his arms, Dixie eased back. She'd meant to go for the coffee, but managed to pull away only far enough to smooth at a couple wrinkles on his shirt front. "Flynn, I... You are... What I'm trying to say is, I need a little time, but if you'll wait for me..." She felt as though all the happiness of her future hung on his answer.

Flynn touched her chin. "I would wait for you till the end of the world." A sparkle of humor touched his eyes. "But I hope I won't have to wait that long."

She felt her shoulders relax and did step over to the stove this time. "For now, we'd better get this coffee out to the meeting before they revolt and leave Charlotte to do all the work herself."

Flynn chuckled. "Right. We can't have that."

He held the door for her as she passed, and she felt like she was making an escape when she hurried into the dining room. She had just been freed from her ties to one man. Did she so quickly want to tie herself to another? Yet this was Flynn she was thinking of. He wasn't anything like Steven. Still... She'd never suspected Steven to be a monster in disguise either.

Lord, what am I to do?

She wasn't sure what she had expected after the prayer.

She'd never really heard God speak other than through gentle urgings when she read the Bible. But the moment she finished the prayer she quite clearly heard an audible response.

Hope in me.

It startled her so that she nearly dropped the tray. She glanced around. Had Flynn heard the voice? He didn't seem to have.

He stepped up beside her and studied her for a moment. "You're certain you're all right?"

"Yes." Dixie smiled. "I truly believe I am. For the first time in a long while."

Hope in the Lord. That was something she was more than happy to do.

That and deliver coffee.

Chapter Twenty-eight

Liora still felt as though she were walking on clouds as she descended the stairs.

After the sheriff had given her the amazing news about her property, she had run to her room and cried tears of happiness and amazement and thankfulness to God. She'd gone from being unemployed and penniless and hungry, to gainfully employed and well fed. And now she was a bona fide property owner. She'd hardly come out of her room other than to eat and work for the past few days.

She still hadn't fully decided what she would do with the property, but she'd prayed and knew that God would help her figure it out from here. And just that realization made her eyes prick with tears again. She was so thankful to be able to rest in the knowledge that her Savior wanted only good for her and would direct her steps.

And speaking of steps... She picked up her pace. She was late for the meeting about the Christmas festival. She hoped that it was okay for her to join in. She so wanted to help. But she was a bit leery of how other members of the town might view her presence. She hadn't felt any animosity directed her way when she showed up for the last meeting that had been canceled by Steven's death, but Ewan hadn't yet been present at that meeting. He was the one she worried might raise objections to her presence.

She paused at the side of the doorway and peered quietly into the room.

Across the room, Ewan sat in conversation with Marshal Holloway. Her disappointment rose. She couldn't risk a scene that might once again delay Charlotte's meeting. She would just go back to her room and ask Charlotte later if there was any way she could help.

She started to step back from the doorway.

"Liora? Is that you?" Joe's voice rang out from the end of the table. "Come in. There's a seat for you here."

She hesitated. Stuck. She could already hear that Ewan had quit talking mid-sentence. She could almost feel his squinted eyes drilling holes into her back through the doorway.

"Liora, I'm so glad you've come!" Charlotte's voice from just inside the room was all warmth and welcome. "I've just the perfect job for you. Please come right in. And, oh look! Coffee. How thoughtful of you, Dixie."

Thankful that Charlotte had so quickly diverted attention from her, Liora slipped into the room and took the chair between Dr. Griffin and Joe.

Joe gave her a nod and slid the tray of coffee mugs closer to her. He did a double take of her face. "You okay?"

Her eyes must still be showing evidence of her emotions. She gave him a quick nod and a smile that she hoped would alleviate his concerns, but then quickly turned her scrutiny elsewhere. After all the times she'd thrown herself at Joe in her former life, she didn't want him to think she was doing so again.

Liora studied those gathered as Charlotte stepped to the head of the table with a list as long as her forearm in her hands.

Mr. Heath sat closest to the head of the table with a serious furrow in his brow. Perhaps he was feeling the weight of the fact that he'd been the cause of a man's death? And yet... She followed his gaze across the table to Sheriff Callahan, who was watching Miss Brindle with a soft light of yearning in his blue eyes. Liora suppressed a smile. Could it be that the town founder was not happy to discover that his sheriff had feelings for his teacher?

Ewan sat next to Mr. Heath, his condescending gaze fixed on her.

She squirmed in her seat, but refused to let him cow her into retreat. She would just carry on as normal.

Next to Ewan sat Marshal Holloway. She was thankful to see the man joining in to participate in a community event. Maybe he would stay in these parts and take some of the weight of lawing from the sheriff and his deputy. They both put in such long hours, she felt sure they would appreciate the help. She wouldn't allow herself to linger on the reasons she hoped for them to receive it.

Mrs. Callahan sat next to the marshal with Mrs. Kastain and two of her daughters, Belle and Zoe, next to her. Then came Joe, herself, Dr. Griffin, the new minister, Kin Davis, and Reagan.

Charlotte cleared her throat. "Right. Well, first I want to say how thankful I am to have you all here today. I know I'm asking for you to invest time into something that isn't a regular occurrence here in Wyldhaven, and I appreciate your willingness to help."

Those gathered around the table nodded to her.

Charlotte smiled. She set about explaining how she envisioned the festival starting out at the logging camps and then ending here in town once the men had unloaded the last of the logs from their wagons. "I'd like for us to decorate a Christmas tree in the lot by the river." She smiled at the minister. "If all goes according to plan we'll have a warm church building next year. But for this year we'll just have to make do. We can set up brick fire boxes throughout the field for people to warm themselves by. And I'll have a present under the tree for each of the children in town." She held up the long list that Liora had noticed earlier.

Liora felt her appreciation for the woman grow another size. She was making a list so she wouldn't leave any of the children out.

Charlotte had started to go on, but Marshal Zane Holloway leaned back in his chair and spoke. "Actually, I'm sorry to say, but just yesterday I heard that there was a large landslide over the tracks in Montana. Word was that all train shipments will be delayed for quite some time. It will be at least three weeks before they can get enough men in there to get the tracks cleared was the way I heard it."

Charlotte dropped the list of children's names onto the table in front of her and leaned her palms on either side of it. "Say it isn't so!" Her alarm was clearly evident to all.

"I'm afraid it is." The marshal looked like he wished he hadn't needed to tell her.

Charlotte sank back into her chair as though all the strength had just left her legs, and there was such a look of misery on her face that before she could think better of it, Liora offered, "Don't despair. I'm sure we'll come up with something to give the children." Every eye in the room turned in her direction, and she wished that she could sink under the table and disappear. Instead, she took a breath, hoping her voice would remain steady. "When I was a girl I used to carve little animals from pieces of wood. We could make something like that for all the boys. And maybe sew new aprons for all the girls?" In the moment of silence that followed, Liora held her breath. She fully expected everyone in the room to dismiss the idea out of hand.

Mrs. Callahan spoke up. "I think that's a fabulous idea! I've lots of scraps of material that I'd be happy to donate for making the aprons."

Joe leaned forward and peered past her toward Kin. "I know Kin is some handy with his pocket knife. I bet he could carve animals just about as well as any of us, and I'd be happy to help do that too."

Liora didn't dare look at Ewan. He would surely condemn the plan as stupid at any moment.

But Charlotte spoke again before Ewan had voiced any denunciation. She stood to her feet and some of the color seemed to have returned to her face. "Very well. Yes. We can still carry this out. I think those are splendid ideas. Thank you, Liora." She offered a genuine smile, and Liora gave her one in return.

Charlotte glanced at a much shorter list that she pulled from her apron pocket. "Now let's see... Who would like to decorate a Christmas tree for the center of the field?

Mrs. Kastain offered. "The girls and I would be most happy to do that."

Charlotte nodded her thanks and pressed ahead. "And building the fire boxes? I think four should do."

Ewan lifted a hand. "I'll build those. I have extra bricks out back of the alehouse I've been meaning to use to build an ice house."

Charlotte smiled at the man. "Thank you, Mr. McGinty."

Liora almost laughed aloud at the pleased smile on Ewan's face when Charlotte called him 'Mr. McGinty.'

And so the evening went.

By the time Charlotte called her little planning meeting to a close, everyone had a task or two ahead of them and Liora felt certain that this was going to be the best Christmas festival anyone had ever experienced—of course she had to keep in mind that most of the residents of Wyldhaven had never yet been to a Christmas festival. No matter. This one would outshine any future ones they might attend.

Charlotte smiled her thanks to all of those who were leaving the room. Despite her disappointment over the fact that the toys she had ordered would not arrive in time for Christmas, she couldn't help but feel great relief that the Christmas festival was actually going ahead as hoped. With all that had happened in the past few weeks, she'd feared that her plans would get shoved aside.

She gathered up her papers and studied her list once more. People had signed up for every item that she had thought of. She felt a little thrill race through her. The only problem would be if she had forgotten to put something on her list. But she had gone over and over the events, and she felt fairly confident that she had covered every aspect of the evening. As long as she hadn't overlooked anything, the evening should go off without a hitch.

Someone came to stand beside her. She looked up to see Reagan twisting his Stetson through his hands. Her heart thumped just like it did each time he took a moment to speak to her.

He glanced over the emptying room. "Feels to me like the meeting went really well. How are you feeling about it?"

Charlotte gathered up her papers and hugged them to her chest. "Yes, I'm very pleased. I'm hopeful that we'll have a lovely Christmas festival."

Reagan leaned a bit closer and lowered his voice. "Now would be a good time to talk to him, don't you think?"

Charlotte felt her eyes widen. She glanced up to see Mr. Heath watching them with a great deal of interest. She swallowed and started toward the door, whispering to Reagan. "I'm still not certain. What if we both lose our jobs?"

Reagan followed her. "That's a risk I'm willing to take, are you?"

She hurried her steps. If they could just escape Mr. Heath's scrutiny, maybe they could have a moment of solitude to make this decision.

But escape was not to be. Behind them, Mr. Heath cleared his throat rather loudly. "Miss Brindle, Sheriff Callahan, if I might have a word with you please?"

Charlotte's eyes fell closed for just a moment before she turned slowly toward Mr. Heath. She tried her very best not to look guilty, but probably managed about as well as Washington Nolan did whenever she caught him gawking at Zoe.

Still...she and Reagan had done no wrong. So what could Mr. Heath want with them? Had she done something wrong in the meeting? Yet Reagan had hardly spoken during the meeting, so why would he want to speak with Reagan also?

She lifted her brows and pressed her lips together, waiting for the man to speak. She willed down the trembling deep inside. She loved her job here. And it would make her most discouraged, indeed, should he require her to step down.

As the silence stretched, she considered the evening past. Perhaps Mr. Heath, who had also been very quiet during the proceedings, did not approve of her trying to entice the town into enjoying a Christmas festival?

Beside her, Reagan leaned into his heels and waited silently for Mr. Heath to state the reasons he'd asked to speak with them.

Mr. Heath seemed to be waiting for the room to empty, for as soon as the last person had exited, he folded his arms and bounced an assessing glance between them. "You two have anything you would like to tell me?"

Charlotte looked to Reagan, feeling all her dread and befuddlement rising like cream on fresh milk. There was no skirting the conversation now.

"Sir?" Reagan asked, obviously stalling for time. He tossed her a glance, and she appreciated that he hadn't just barreled into the conversation without gaining her permission to do so.

Mr. Heath blew out a breath of disgust. "Don't go and give me that innocence and ignorance blather. I see the way you two are looking at each other."

This was it then. After all their care to avoid each other since learning of Mr. Heath's rules, they were still going to be in trouble. "Mr. Heath, I promise you we haven't…" She felt at a loss for how to go on and simply let the sentence die.

Reagan shot out a hand and settled it against the small of her back. It was a gesture that calmed her and filled her with courage.

He raised one brow, seeking her permission.

There was nothing for it now. She gave him a small nod.

Reagan returned his attention to Mr. Heath. "Sir, we are attracted to each other, true. But I assure you that ever since we received your rules by telegram and post we have both put loyalty to you and duty to our jobs ahead of our feelings."

Mr. Heath pursed his lips. "So the damage was already done before you received my rules? Well…I suppose that is my fault then." A twinkle sparked to life in his rheumy eyes. "Young people these days seem to move mighty fast."

Charlotte didn't know how to respond to that. It was true that she and Reagan had fallen into an attraction rather quickly after her arrival.

Beside her, Reagan shuffled his feet, obviously at a loss for a response also.

Mr. Heath leaned onto his cane and scratched his chin through his long white beard. "So I don't have to worry about losing my sheriff or my teacher, then?"

Reagan removed his hand from her back, glanced at the ground, shuffled his feet, and then returned his gaze to Mr. Heath's. "Not unless you are going to fire us for being attracted to each other."

Charlotte felt like her heart might just beat right out of her chest. She watched Mr. Heath intently, searching his face for any hint of how he might respond.

Mr. Heath waved a hand and started walking out of the room before he replied, "As long as both of you are abiding by my rules I don't see as there's anything I need to do about it."

Charlotte felt all at once elated and deflated. They hadn't been dismissed, but neither had they gained permission to court. She waited until the sound of Mr. Heath's boots had shuffled away into the distance. Then she widened her eyes at Reagan. "Well at least we haven't been discharged."

One side of Reagan's mouth lifted in a sardonic grin. "I figured that as long as we were abiding by his rules he wouldn't make a fuss about it. But you sure are making it mighty hard to abide by those rules right now. You are a fearsome attractive woman when you've just narrowly escaped dismissal, Miss Brindle. All pale and needy looking." His grin grew to maddening proportions. "Ah, but there comes your color returning now."

Charlotte gave him a huff of disgust and, lifting her skirts, spun away from him. "At the very least Mr. Heath has spared me from having to spurn you myself."

His laughter floated from behind. "Do have a care, or you'll find yourself walking home alone in the dark."

She wrinkled her nose at him over her shoulder, knowing he was too much of a gentleman to actually mean the threat.

His twinkling gaze never left her face as he leaned past her to open the door to the street. "But then again... Perhaps a gent can sneak a quick kiss in the dark as he escorts a lady home?"

It was all Charlotte could do to maintain the stern schoolmarm look she leveled on him. "Not if he wants to keep his job."

Reagan pressed his hat to his chest as he pulled the door closed behind them. He gave her a mock bow and a bold wink. "Yes, ma'am."

And as she stepped out before him, she was left to wonder whether he'd been agreeing to not kissing her, or to the fact that he might lose his job if he did so.

Her face blazed warm enough to heat the street.

Heaven's mercy! The man was going to cost her Wyldhaven's teaching position of a certainty. And she was likely to enjoy every moment of the process.

Chapter Twenty-nine

ixie bent to pull another sheet of cookies from the oven. She tried to push her concern for Rose to one side. For the past few days, Dixie had hardly been able to coax any food down her, and Rose had wanted only to keep to her rooms. Just as a precaution, Dixie had finally called Flynn, and he was upstairs seeing Rose now.

She pushed aside her worry by thinking through the final plans for the Christmas festival.

It had been two days since Charlotte's planning meeting. Two days in which the town had kept very busy putting all the plans into place. Excitement was running high, so high that one could almost reach out and touch it like snowflakes in the air.

The stiff brown grass in the field near the river had been cut down with a scythe, and raked up and hauled away.

Ewan McGinty had built four brick fireboxes, one at each corner of the field, where people would be able to gather and warm themselves.

Parson Clay and Kin had hammered together a wooden dance floor that now sat in the center of the field. The parson had said the boards could later be used for the flooring in the new church, and that he would be pleased to utilize boards that were first christened in joyous celebration of the Lord's birth. Kin had rolled his eyes at that sentiment, and it had been all Dixie could do not to laugh at his expression. She was thankful to see that though the boy had lost his father, he didn't seem to be withdrawing from the world, and she knew that the parson had a good deal of impact on that. She sent up a little prayer of thanks to the Lord for sending the man at just the right moment in Kin's life.

As she quickly lifted the warm ginger cookies from the tray, she pondered the other preparations that were in various stages of completion for tomorrow's celebrations.

The Kastains had outdone themselves with the beautiful decorations that hung on the tree that the sheriff and Deputy Joe had cut and set up in the field. The girls had strung together dried holly berries and small pine cones to form long sweeps of red and brown garland. Mrs. Kastain had been busy crocheting small white doilies, which looked like lacy snowflakes and would be added to the tree tomorrow. Red apples, polished to a sheen, sat ready on Dixie's counter to be added to the tree just before the festivities. People would be able to eat them before they froze, that way. And Mr. Hines from the mercantile had donated fifty cents worth of red and white penny-candy peppermint sticks, which would also be added to the tree in the afternoon. Dixie smiled in anticipation of seeing the children of the town enjoying the minty hard sugar. The last decorative touch to the tree were the candles that had been tied to the ends of many of the branches. They would be lit just before the party started.

Dixie grinned in excitement. She couldn't wait to see how the tree glistened in the frosty air tomorrow.

"Someone looks happy."

She spun around to see Flynn standing by the door from the dining room. "I am happy." The truth was she hadn't felt this happy in a very long time, except for her concerns over Rose.

Yet guilt nagged at her for her happiness. Rose had hardly

stopped crying since Steven's death, though Dixie couldn't seem to bring herself to feel anything but relief. And she really was concerned about Rose's wellbeing. She probably shouldn't feel so happy in light of that. "How is she?"

He spoke low and stepped further into the room, setting his coat and hat and doctor bag on the table by the outer door. "I'm happy to report that her lungs are still clear and she's doing really well. I think her desire for solitude these past few days simply has to do with her grief over her son."

Dixie nodded with a breath of relief. "Thank you for checking on her. I've been worried, but I think you are right."

He took a step closer to her. "It's good to see you happy, Dixie. Really good." His blue eyes captured hers, and there was a soft light of pleasure about them that made her catch her breath.

She'd told him she needed time. But did she really? She'd known this man for a year and a half. He had been one of the first to greet Rose and her when they had come to town. And though she'd guarded her heart because of her circumstances, she'd admired him from almost the first day.

Her desire for time stemmed from a lack of trust in her own judgement. After all, Steven had fooled her in totality. And yet with her newfound determination to hope in the Lord, she'd been doing a lot of praying over the past several days. And each time she'd prayed about the future, the visage of a certain handsome doctor had come to mind.

It would be easy, so easy, to loose her feelings to travel where they willed. And she had a strong idea of just where they would take her. But she had Rose to consider now. She couldn't grant Flynn permission to come calling only a few days after the death of her first husband and Rose's only son! It would crush Rose. And Dixie loved her too much to do that.

Flynn's brown hair was in need of a trim. It curled just slightly on the collar of his shirt, and her fingers itched to reach out and touch it.

Her face heated, and she fisted her hand and spun away. She quickly set to scooping more dough onto the empty cookie sheet. "There are warm cookies on the rack there." She tipped her head toward the sideboard where she'd just laid out the last batch.

"Mmmm. Ginger. Not as good as your cinnamon ones, but a good close second."

"I didn't know you preferred cinnamon. I can make a batch of those next."

"Perfect." He spoke around a bite of cookie. "I'll stay and help you."

She spun toward him, a spoonful of cookie dough in one hand. "You will?"

He stuffed the last bite of his cookie into his mouth with a nod. "If you'll let me."

"D-don't you have patients to attend?"

He shook his head. "I've done my rounds for today. So unless there's an emergency, I'm free."

Elation and apprehension vied for preeminence. "Oh, all right."

"Dixie, I'll only stay if you want me to," Flynn said. His face shone with sincerity.

Dixie's heart warmed to him seven times over, and she rushed to reassure him. "No, no. I—I want you to stay."

"Perfect." He grinned. "Where do we begin then?"

Dixie motioned to the bowl that was almost empty. "Just let me finish scooping these ginger cookies and then we can mix the next batch while these bake. There is an apron hanging just inside the pantry if you would like to put one on."

Flynn scrunched his nose and waved a hand. "Let it never be said that I was caught wearing an apron." He winked.

Dixie laughed. "Men! Well, don't blame me when your suit ends up with flour all over it."

Flynn gave her a bold look. "Unless you are planning to start a food fight with me, I don't think I'll have any problem."

Dixie cocked an eyebrow at him. "Obviously you haven't spent much time in a kitchen, Dr. Griffin."

Flynn gave her a mock bow of concession, but still did not go for the apron.

Dixie smothered a chuckle and only offered a shrug. "All right. It's your suit." She spooned the last scoop of cookie dough onto the cookie sheet. "If you'll just grab the gunnysack of flour from the pantry while I wash this dish, then we can get started." She bit back a grin, knowing what the result of that mission would be.

And she was right. By the time Flynn returned with the twenty-five-pound bag from the pantry, the front of his suit was covered with flour. He glanced the length of himself and dusted at the white powder with his jaw cocked over to one side.

Dixie could no longer withhold her chuckle, and stepped into the pantry. She returned a moment later with her largest apron and pressed it against his chest.

A twinkle of acceptance lit his expressive eyes.

She used a rag to clean the mixing bowl in the sink. "I promise not to tell anyone that you wore an apron, Dr. Griffin."

He laughed and gave another bow—a deeper one this time. "I concede to your obvious prowess in the kitchen, oh wise one."

Dixie dried the bowl and tried not to think about how much she was enjoying herself with him here in her kitchen. "The canister of sugar is also in the pantry. Top shelf on the left. If you can fetch it, I will fetch the eggs."

When they had both returned to the counter, Dixie reached for her measuring cup. "Now, cinnamon cookies, you said? We may as well make a double batch."

Flynn put his back to the edge of the counter, folded his arms, and looked into her face. "Yes. Cinnamon. It reminds me of the eyes of a certain beautiful woman I have an affinity for."

Dixie's face immediately blazed as hot as the stove. "Do go on with you." She set to scooping flour into the bowl.

He leaned closer to her. "Go on you say? Very well." He winked. "This woman not only has the most beautiful cinnamon eyes a man could ever encounter, but she has skin as flawless as a pitcher of cream, and a blush as comely as a sunrise."

If Dixie had thought her face warm before, it certainly was more so now, and yet for an entirely different reason. He spoke of flawless skin, but...

The whole time Flynn spoke he never took his eyes from her face. "Indeed. She truly is the most exquisite woman a man could ever hope to lay eyes on." He reached out and stroked the backs of his fingers along her forearm.

Dixie set her measuring cup down with a clatter. "Oh, you've gone and done it now, Dr. Griffin." She should tell him. Make him understand.

His brow furrowed in concern.

It pained her to see him hurt. And the words she needed to say would only bring more pain. Maybe even make him walk away. So instead she forced a laugh. "I can't remember how much flour I have scooped into the bowl."

Hope in me.

Flynn's frown softened into a smile. "Then my job here is just begun. Would that I could make you forget your very name."

She wanted to leave it there. To let him think that was the only thing bothering her. But it just wouldn't do. *Lord, don't let him be too hurt, please.*

Dixie pushed the bowl of flour away and pressed her hands into the counter, feeling the weight of her next words as though they might be punches she were about to throw. "Flynn, please. You must stop." She looked over at him, and the questioning hurt in his eyes nearly made her keep silent again. She forced herself to go on before she lost her courage. "You speak of flawless skin and comeliness, yet..." A tremble threatened to steal the strength from her legs. "I—I have s-scars, Flynn. Scars on my skin, though it's easy enough to keep most of those hidden. But there are others... Scars so deep inside that I don't know if they will ever be healed." She searched his face, willing him to understand that she might never be whole enough for him.

He would walk away now. *Should* walk away. She had nothing left to offer him.

Instead, he stepped closer and took her hand.

Dixie blinked back tears and held her breath.

He hooked their thumbs together and drew her hand near and pressed her knuckles to his cheek. Holding her close, he reached up with his other hand to tuck a stray curl behind her ear. "There is something interesting about scar tissue. Do you know what that is?"

She huffed a little laugh and blinked hard, willing her tears not to fall. "That it's ugly?"

He shook his head solemnly. "Oh no, dear Dixie. That's not it at all. When a wound heals over and forms a scar, that area is much tougher—much stronger—than it ever was beforehand." He turned his head slightly and placed a kiss on the back of her hand. "You may have scars inside, Dix, but they are only proof of what strength resides in you now. Do you know what else is interesting about scars? Over time they soften, become malleable, sometimes even become such a part of us that they seem to disappear altogether." He took both her hands in his. "Steven stole so much from you. I know he did. But don't let him steal your future too. Don't let him steal your happiness. Don't let him steal *us*."

Dixie felt the tears spill over and course down her cheeks. "I will try, Flynn. I'm just not certain—"

"Dixie?" Ma's voice came from just beyond the kitchen door.

Dixie scrambled to put some space between herself and Flynn, but not in time. Ma had already stepped into the room. Her focus flitted between the two of them. "Oh. I'm sorry. I didn't mean to interrupt. I'll just—" She started to retreat from the room.

"No!" Dixie rushed to reassure her. "You aren't interrupting. Flynn was just leaving." She gave him a pointed look. "Is there something I can get for you?"

Ma paused and turned back to face her.

Flynn tugged the apron off over his head and set it on the sideboard. He squeezed her shoulder, lifted his things, and left silently through the outer door to the street.

Ma watched him go and then her gaze fixed in sharp focus on Dixie. "He's a good man."

Dixie swallowed. "Yes. He is." She prayed Ma wouldn't be hurt by what she'd seen.

Ma shuffled toward her and cupped her face in both hands. She squeezed just slightly. "It would give me no greater pleasure than to see you happily settled with another man, dear daughter."

"Truly?" Dixie searched her face for sincerity.

Ma swung her head in a little gesture of reassurance. "Most truly. From the bottom of my heart."

Dixie smiled, blinking back tears of relief. "You are the last person in the world I would ever want to hurt."

Ma smiled and patted her cheeks. "The only thing that would hurt me would be for you to give up your own happiness because you thought it was what I might want." She dipped her chin, and Dixie almost chuckled at the mock stern look leveled upon her. "You would be a fool not to accept that man."

Lower lip tucked between her teeth, Dixie felt a smile play around her lips. "I really would be, wouldn't I?"

Ma nodded. "You would, indeed."

Without another moment's hesitation, Dixie pulled the woman into her arms and hugged her tight. "Thank you. I love you just as much as I did my own mother."

Ma eased back and once more cupped her face between both hands. "The good Lord sent you to me, certain as the sun will rise in the morning. I have not the words to tell you what a blessing you are to me."

Dixie smiled and blinked away tears of happiness. "I think you just did."

Ma grinned. "Well, words are a poor reflection of the actual feelings. But they'll have to do." She nodded. "They'll have to do." She stepped back and glanced around the room. "Now, I don't suppose I could get a cup of tea?"

Dixie's elation lifted another notch. Ma wanted to eat! "Absolutely. And how about a biscuit with honey to go with it?"

Ma nodded. "Yes. That sounds lovely. Thank you."

As Dixie prepared the tea tray, it hardly even felt like her feet were on the ground.

She had to find Flynn. Maybe they could make this work, after all.

Flynn slipped on his coat as he stepped out onto the street. He tugged the collar up around his neck and hunched his shoulders. The clear blue skies they'd been experiencing for the past few days had dropped the temperatures by at least ten degrees.

And his heart felt just about as cold.

He released a sigh and glanced toward the sky. *All I want is her happiness. And I truly feel that I'm the one to give that to her. Haven't I been patient enough?*

Dixie had sparked his interest from almost the first moment she and Rose had arrived in town, and he'd been pursuing and biding his time ever since. He'd felt like he was thrashed sixty ways from Sunday when Dixie had told him she was married. And then when Steven had showed up in town as his patient, and he'd, Lord forgive him, been tempted to take matters into his own hands, he'd felt like his heart was shattering into a million pieces. But he'd trusted God and promised himself he would be happy with the outcome, no matter what. Then when Steven died, he'd felt hope springing to life like the first rays of sun peeking over a dark horizon in mid-winter.

And now to find that perhaps that man was reaching out from the grave to continue to steal Dixie's happiness... Flynn felt the sorrow of that as deeply—maybe even more so—as he felt the biting cold here on the street.

He had hoped that maybe during this season—a season that of all seasons ever celebrated ought to be one that offered hope—he might be able to convince her to give them a chance. Yet he had failed.

His heart was heavy with the truth of it.

He pushed into McGinty's and trudged up the stairs to his room. He dropped his bag onto the table by the bed and flopped back onto his mattress, arms spread wide. He stared for a long moment at the slats of the pine-board ceiling, and then with a huff of resignation sat back up again.

There was likely still work to be done. He'd better go down and see if Reagan or the parson needed his help with anything. There was no point in pouting like a schoolboy on his bed.

They would all be heading out to the logging camps first thing in the morning. The men would probably be preparing the wagons in the livery stables. He would head there first.

Once he arrived back on the street, he paused to tug his gloves into place. Was the sunlight dimmer than it had been only a couple hours ago? Or was that his morose mindset painting the skies gray? Likely the latter, for thick frost covered every surface that wasn't already covered with snow, and the sun shimmered off every facet as though diamonds had been sprinkled liberally over the town.

He started to turn toward the stables, but a glint of cerulean to his left caught his attention. His heart scrambled up into his throat even before he turned.

Dixie stood before the boardinghouse, a bright blue shawl tugged around her shoulders. Her gaze was soft and inviting as she studied him.

He swallowed and checked the street behind himself to make sure he was still the only one standing here, for her gaze said something entirely different than her voice had said but fifteen minutes ago.

Behind him, a door opened then closed. But he couldn't tear his focus from her.

She started towards him.

"Doc! There you are." Sheriff Callahan spoke from behind him. "I was just heading to the stables. Can you join me?

We've only one more wagon to fill and then we'll be all ready for tomorrow."

Dixie paused, and Flynn would have liked nothing better than to give Sheriff Callahan a good thrashing in that moment. He tossed a glance over his shoulder. "Give me just a moment?"

The sheriff glanced between him and Dixie, and his mouth lifted in understanding. "Sure." He clapped Flynn on the shoulder. "I'll meet you down there."

When he turned back, Dixie was already retreating. She waved him on. "Go ahead and help. It's not important. We can talk later."

"Dixie, are you sure? Please—"

But she had already disappeared back into the boardinghouse.

He hurried forward and yanked open the boardinghouse door, but the lobby was empty. He stilled. She must have hit the interior running. He debated about going inside to hunt her down, but maybe giving her some more time would be a good thing. Or maybe it wouldn't.

He growled and let the door swing shut. His frustrated breath fogged the air before him.

Grumbling about some things he'd like to do to Sheriff Callahan, Flynn turned reluctantly for the livery, but deep in his heart that stubborn hope thrust its rays of light over the horizon again.

Chapter Thirty

With the pale morning light streaming through her window, Dixie stood before the long cheval mirror in the corner of her room. Her hands fluttered over her black skirt and adjusted the golden silk of her blouse.

She laughed at her nerves. She hadn't been this anxious about an outing since, well, she couldn't remember when.

Yesterday afternoon, she had gotten Rose's tea and biscuit as quickly as she could. And once she'd carried the tray upstairs, she had grabbed her shawl and headed outside, determined to find Flynn and tell him she'd changed her mind. But when she'd stepped out onto the street and seen him standing there, all her hesitation had rushed to the fore. And when Reagan had come out of the office, she'd taken the excuse for escape and run with it, quite literally.

But an evening of prayerful pacing in her bedroom, and another talk with Rose had convinced her that if she didn't at least try to see if these feelings between her and Flynn could go anywhere, she would regret it for the rest of her life.

She was choosing to keep her hope in God. And His word said that He had good plans for her. Plans to prosper her and not to harm her. Plans to give her a hope and a future. She didn't know if Flynn would be part of that future—only time would tell that—but she knew that she *wanted* him to be part of her future. At the very least, she wanted the opportunity to get to know him better now that she didn't have Steven to worry about.

She gave herself one last assessing look and decided she would have to do. She didn't have anything very colorful or Christmassy to wear. She would probably look like a dull weed next to Charlotte and the other women at today's party.

She turned from the mirror and lifted the blue hat that matched her shawl from the bed.

Rose stepped into her doorway, still wearing her long flannel night dress and cap. "Oh my, you look lovely." Tears brimmed in her eyes as she smiled.

Dixie glanced at the clock on her bedside table and lifted her shawl. "Thank you. Are you sure you are going to be fine here all on your own today?"

Rose waved a hand. "Go on with you. You've brought me a pot of tea and more snacks than I'll be able to eat in a month of Sundays. Please, take time to enjoy yourself. I certainly plan to enjoy myself, snuggled all warm and comfortable beneath my covers with my book." She leaned forward and whispered. "I might not even get dressed today."

Dixie smiled. "What are you reading?"

"*Pride and Prejudice.*" Rose hummed a delighted sigh.

One of Dixie's eyebrows lifted. "How many times have you read that one now?"

Rose batted the question away with the swipe of one hand. "'Tis of no matter. It's a book that can never be read too many times."

Leaning close, Dixie pressed a gentle kiss to a crepey cheek. "I'd best be off. The wagon might leave without me and I'll be left to walk to the logging camps, alone in the cold snow."

Rose squeezed her shoulders and returned the kiss on Dixie's cheek. "The good doctor won't let them leave without you."

Just the mention of the man returned Dixie's nerves to full roil.

Obviously having read her expression, Rose dipped her chin and gave her a firm look. "You just remember that any man would be lucky to have a wonderful woman such as yourself. And you also remember that Dr. Griffin claims a relationship with the good Lord that my poor mean son never did."

Just the reminder of that seemed to calm Dixie's tumultuous emotions somewhat. "He does, doesn't he?"

Rose nodded affirmatively. "He does, indeed."

"You're sure you are going to be fine on your own?"

"Get on with you before I lose my patience and boot you out."

"All right. All right." But Dixie couldn't resist one last squeeze of the woman's shoulders. "Happy Christmas Eve, Rose." She started for the door before the woman could chastise her more. "Tomorrow I'll bake some quail that Kin Davis came around selling yesterday afternoon. And we'll sit by the fire and you can read me the best parts of your book." She didn't mention the lace shawl that she'd spent a good part of the last few months crocheting in her room during the evenings where Rose wouldn't see it.

Rose headed across the main room of their chambers toward her own bedroom door. "I'll look forward to it."

"Rose?" Dixie paused with the door partially open, waiting for the woman to look at her. When she turned, Dixie offered her a smile. "I really am glad to see you doing so much better."

Rose nodded. "And I'm glad to be so, as well. Have a good day, now."

"You too. I'll pop in to check on you when we get back to town this afternoon."

And with that, Dixie left her in their apartment. As she practically skipped down the stairs, she felt as light as the flakes of snow that had started to fall outside.

Kin Davis huddled near one of the fireboxes and watched the proceedings going on around him. All across the field citizens of Wyldhaven laughed and chatted and mingled in a swirl of colors that made him want to smile.

Kin had thought he would be bored by the day's proceedings, but found instead that he'd quite enjoyed the experience, despite the fact that he'd just sat back and mostly kept quiet.

Earlier, they'd all met at the livery where the men had loaded four wagons with hay and people had piled onto the wagons and Sheriff Callahan and Marshal Holloway had played Christmas carols on their guitars, one seated on the front wagon and one on the rear. Everyone had sung their hearts out—well, except for him because he couldn't carry a tune even if he had a new galvanized bucket. He'd taken it all in from his place on the bench near Parson Clay, who was driving the first wagon. He'd been thankful not to have to sit in the hay. He'd done his fair share of sleeping in haymows, and it always left him itchy the next day. He'd enjoyed the music as he'd studied the snowflakes that drifted down from the blue-gray sky above.

Parson Clay had a strong mellow tenor voice that Kin honestly could have listened to all day. But they'd arrived at the logging camps before the sun had even reached its zenith.

The contests out at the logging camps had been fun to watch. Butch Nolan, Wash's pa, and his team had won all of the races, and people were still spilling into town from down near the river where the last leg of the last race had ended just a bit ago.

There were tables and tables of food. And as soon as the parson had said the prayer, Kin had gotten in line to fill his plate.

Several had brought hams. And old Mrs. Carver had brought two of her largest turkeys, baked to golden brown perfection. There were mashed potatoes, baked potatoes, sweet potatoes, and potato pies. There was enough bread to probably feed an army, and so many preserves Kin's mouth watered just looking at them. Pickles, and salads, and creamed corn, and green beans cooked with bacon and onions and slathered in butter had filled every available surface of his plate. He'd lamented the lack of room on his plate as he'd passed the dessert table. Mrs. Callahan had brought several apple pies with thick cinnamon scented juices bubbling over the lattice tops. And Mrs. Pottinger—or was she back to "Miss" again now that her husband had died?—had brought plates and plates of fresh baked cookies. There was a chocolate cake, three tiers high and covered with thick chocolate frosting. And another pie that looked like it had strawberries in it. Merengues, and puddings, and plates of fudge had all called his name. But he'd had to pass them by with the hope that there would still be some available when he got done eating.

His hopes were not dashed, for it seemed that everyone else had also filled their own plates as full as he had. And, though he barely had room for dessert by the time he'd polished off the last roll smothered in blackberry jam, he'd heaped his plate almost as full of sweets as he had food. The last bit of Mrs. Callahan's apple pie mocked him. Would he explode if he ate it? He grinned and scooped it into his mouth. If he did, he would die happy.

He felt like an overstuffed scarecrow as he waddled across the field to deposit his plate into the bin meant for them. Several ladies bustled back and forth from Dixie's Boardinghouse kitchen to collect the dirty plates, or to bring out more food to replace dishes that had been emptied. Kin had carried a bin full of dirty dishes to the back door of the kitchen where it was whisked out of his hand, and then he had parked himself back by the firebox and simply enjoyed watching the bustle.

But now things were starting to wind down. The women must have decided the kitchen was under control, because most of them had returned to the festivities taking place in the field.

Miss Pottinger cranked the handle on a gramophone set on a table near the dance floor and couples swept onto the platform, their shoes clanking on the hollow boards in time to the rhythm. Doctor Griffin, who had hardly left Miss Pottinger's side all evening, was laughing with her about something or other. Kin smiled. Mrs. or Miss, it didn't matter, she was probably the prettiest lady here.

Well, maybe with the exception of Miss Liora, who stood off to one side of the gathering by herself. With her blond curls splaying like a golden halo around her head, and her Christmas red dress that was accented with lace at collar, cuffs, and hem, she could have been on a holiday postcard. Kin felt a bit sorry for her standing there all by herself, but then Deputy Rodante stepped up to her side and nodded a greeting to her. Hands clasped behind her back, she rose up on her tiptoes and the skirt of her dress swung a little. She looked relieved to have someone to talk to. And he'd bet it was no hardship on the deputy's part to be the one to rescue her.

Kin grinned and turned his focus back to the dancers.

The doctor took Miss Pottinger's hand and led her onto the dancefloor, and Kin felt a bit of pride in the fact that he and PC had built that floor. PC was what he'd settled on calling Parson Clay in his head. It worked two ways, because the man's name was Preston, so whether Preston Clay or Parson Clay, PC worked just fine.

Remembering the package that was still in his pocket, Kin glanced around the clearing, wondering where the man had gotten to. And then he spotted him near one of the other fireboxes. Much like Kin was doing, he stood with his arms folded over his chest, seeming to simply enjoy his observation of those around him. Their eyes met across the clearing, and Kin nodded at the man. He supposed if he had to live with someone now that Pa had passed on, it wasn't so bad being saddled with the minister. Kin still wrestled with the fact that if he hadn't done what he'd done to try and get Pa's attention, Pa might still be alive. And yet, Dr. Griffin had been the one to say that Pa's heart had been so severely damaged from the drinking that it was likely that anything could have caused the attack that took him.

Truth was, Kin wasn't yet sure what to do with the muddle of emotions that overtook him when he pondered it, so he kept shoving the thoughts to one side. The minister said time was a gift from God that healed all wounds. Kin supposed that was true. He still thought of Ma now and then, but he didn't miss her so fierce as he'd done right after her passing.

Someone stepped up beside him.

He turned to find Wash holding his hands out to the warmth of the fire. Bits of hay still clung to Wash's clothes.

Kin grinned. "Did you enjoy your hay ride with Zoe?"

Wash shushed him, looking around to see if the comment had been overheard.

Kin only laughed. He knew no one had heard him because he'd been watching the crowd and no one had been close enough to hear his lowered words.

When Wash was assured of the same, he grinned. "I might

have at that." Wash searched those gathered, and Kin knew exactly who he was looking for.

He thrust his chin in Zoe's direction. She was chatting with a group of girls who were admiring the decorated Christmas tree and the piles of presents beneath it. "Might as well go ask her to dance."

Wash's face turned so red it rivaled the polished apples hanging from the branches of the candlelit tree. "Nah, I couldn't."

"Why not," Kin prodded.

Wash kicked at the snow beneath their feet. "Don't know how to dance."

Kin shrugged. "Me either."

They both turned to study the couples swooping around the dance floor. Though it was still afternoon gray clouds had swept in to obscure the sun and someone had lit several lanterns that sat on tables around the dance floor and gave the area a festive look.

Several adults stood around the edges of the dance floor looking as though they might *like* to dance, but they weren't. Marshal Holloway stood talking to Sheriff Callahan, but his gaze kept drifting to Mrs. Callahan, who was in conversation with Miss Brindle catty-corner from the two men. And every time he returned his focus to the sheriff, Mrs. Callahan looked over at him as moony-eyed as a newborn calf.

The sheriff and Miss Brindle, on the other hand seemed to be doing their level best to focus their attention anywhere but on each other.

But old Mr. Heath was sitting in a rocking chair that had been placed by one of the fireboxes, and his gaze kept traveling first from Sheriff Callahan to Miss Brindle and back again.

Kin gave a little shake of his head. It was clear the sheriff and Miss Brindle had an interest in each other, but hanged if he could tell what Mr. Heath's business was in it all.

Beside him, Wash shuffled his feet. "You got a new coat, I see."

Kin looked down and smoothed his hands over the fine brown leather of the wool-lined duster. He still could hardly believe how warm it was. "Yeah. The minister said I did good work helping him put together the dance floor for today, so he bought me this from the mercantile. It was machine sewn and came all the way from San Francisco!" He swiped at his mouth. He hadn't meant to sound so excited about a silly coat. He covered the slip with a shrug. "It was partially a Christmas present too because I really didn't work enough to earn all of it, but the minister said the rest of it could be my Christmas present. Whadya get?"

Wash shook his head. "Nothin' yet. Pa always makes us wait till Christmas morning to open our presents." Wash's gaze moved to the minister. "Hear he's staying at your place?"

Kin shrugged. "He don't take up much room. And he's some easier to live with than Pa ever was."

Wash nodded. "Still right nice of you to give him a bed."

Wash's younger brother Jackson bounded up to them just then. He tugged on his brother's arm. "Wash, come on, I need your help. You have to ask Belle to dance so's I can ask Marsha Belgrade."

Wash snatched his elbow from Jackson's grasp. "I'm *not* asking Belle Kastain to dance for anything in the world."

But Jackson was not to be put off. "Well then ask Zoe for all I care. I just need you to come over there with me. And you don't need to worry about the fact that you can't dance. All you have to do is move your feet in time to the music just like Pa was showing you last night."

"Jackson!" Wash leaned close and tried to whisper the next words, but Kin heard them plain as day. "You aren't supposed to tell that Pa was giving us lessons."

Jackson didn't even seem fazed by his brother's chastisement. "Come on, it's *Christmas*!"

Kin grinned at the two brothers. It was times like these that he could be thankful he was an only child. The thought sobered him. He was an only *only* now. He didn't have any family left at all.

Wash reluctantly said his goodbyes and Kin's grin returned as he watched the brothers argue all the way across the field, only to cease speaking abruptly when the girls by the tree took note of them.

Footsteps approached again, and PC spoke from by his side, his attention on the Nolan brothers who looked as though they were stuttering to beat the band as they attempted to ask the girls to dance. "You got any special young lady you'd like to ask to dance?"

Kin's gaze darted to Belle Kastain, who was even in that moment being escorted onto the dance floor by Wash. He chuckled to himself that Jackson had somehow talked Wash into dancing with her. And the truth was, it didn't bother him even a little bit to see them together, which surprised him somewhat. He lifted a hand to the back of his neck and replied to the parson's question. "Nah. Not really."

PC clapped him on the shoulder. "Well, never fear. Your time will come. Some pretty lady will knock you off your feet one of these days."

Kin angled a glance up at the man. "What about you? You got a lady pining for you somewhere?"

The man pursed his lips and shook his head. "Only my ma."

They both laughed at that.

PC jostled Kin's shoulder. "I guess we're just a couple of old bachelors, huh?"

Kin studied the snowy ground near his feet. "Yeah, I guess so." And surprisingly, he was perfectly content with that.

He tugged the small, paper-wrapped package from the pocket of his new coat. He'd been meaning to give PC the gift all day, but had felt awkward each time he'd tried to do it, so he'd better get it done or it would be New Years and he'd still be packing it around in his pocket. He tapped the package against one hand and looked up at PC. "So...I caught a few quail and sold them, and—" He didn't know how to finish, so he just thrust the package at the man. "I got you this."

His insides squirmed around worse than a canful of fresh-caught fishing worms.

PC just looked at him for a long moment, a glimmer of appreciation shining in his eyes.

Kin shifted and thrust his hands into his coat pockets. "It's not much."

PC turned to face him more fully. "A gift is everything when it comes from a friend." Slowly, he untied the ribbon and peeled back the brown paper. The small Bible with the hand-tooled russet leather cover slipped into his hands.

Kin scrubbed at the back of his neck, unable to tell by the minister's expression if he'd made a good choice or not. Maybe the man already had a pocket Bible. Kin figured he probably wasn't very apt at this gift giving thing. Truth was he hadn't given anyone a Christmas gift since Ma had passed.

The silence stretched as PC rubbed his hand over the cover, and then carefully flipped through the pages. He paused on the inscription page where Kin had carefully penned "To Parson Preston Clay from Kincaid Davis, December 24, 1891."

Kin pointed. "It's smaller than the big one you carry around and I thought it might come in handy to have a small one that could just fit in your pocket, you know for traveling and such but if you already—"

PC reached out and gripped Kin's arm with one hand.

Kin looked up.

"It's a perfect gift. Thank you. This means more to me than you will ever know."

The tension inside Kin released as though a trigger had been pulled. He grinned. "You like it?"

PC nodded and immediately reached inside his coat and deposited the Bible in his breast pocket.

"Good." Kin nodded. "I'm glad you like it." He hesitated for only a moment before offering. "I like my coat too."

PC gave Kin's shoulder another squeeze, and then they both returned their attention to watching the milling crowd.

Soft snowflakes drifted from the sky. Laughter and music floated on the gentle breeze. And the crackling fires shot sparks of orange into the afternoon air like tiny firecrackers.

Kin couldn't remember a time when he'd felt more content in his entire life.

Chapter Thirty-one

ixie laughed and clapped with all the others as the current song came to an end. She allowed Flynn to lead her from the dance floor.

She'd worried that she wouldn't be warm enough today, but she needn't have concerned herself. She'd hardly stopped moving for even an instant. And from the moment she'd sank onto the blanket that Flynn had thoughtfully covered the hay with in their corner of the wagon, she had felt as comfortable with the man as she ever had with anyone. They had talked through almost every moment, quietly sharing how they'd both grown up, where they'd attended school, and how they'd come to be here in Wyldhaven.

Dixie hadn't known that Flynn had studied medicine in San Francisco. Nor that when he was young he'd had a brother who had died of an infection from a cut in his foot, which was what had spurred him into the field of medicine.

As the hayride had rumbled through the dim light of the snow-weighted forest, he'd told her about his and his brother's first pet, a scraggly cat that they'd rescued from a gunnysack that had bobbed up onto a riverbank one day while his family had been picnicking on the shore. They'd named the cat Survivor, and he'd affectionately been known as Sur.

Flynn laughed. "That cat never really was right in the head. He must have had quite a trip down that river."

"Oh, that's very sad," Dixie lamented.

She felt more than saw Flynn shrug. "Yes, I suppose it is. But my brother loved that cat and it laid with him for weeks while he was so sick there at the end. I always had the poignant thought that God might have sent Sur to us just for Foster. He disappeared not long after Foster passed, and we never saw him again."

Dixie reached out and squeezed his hand in the dim gloam. "I'm sorry. I've gone and pried out a sad story on a day that should be joyous and fun."

When she would have pulled away, Flynn kept hold of her hand. "No. No. It's always a joy to remember Foster. We had such good times together. So, what about you? Any siblings?"

Doing her best not to let the wonderful feel of his fingers laced with her own make her babble, Dixie had shaken her head and told him she was an only child. She'd told him about her mother's passing and how her father had become hard and insufferable afterwards. She'd glossed over her relationship with Steven, mostly because she'd told him that story already.

One story had led to another and somehow, even with her break away from him to help with the kitchen duties, the hours had flown by, and here they were standing breathlessly beside the dancefloor. And still she hadn't gotten up her courage to tell him that she would be pleased to have him call.

Flynn smiled down at her. "I do believe you are going to have the heels of my shoes worn right down to nothing by the time the day is over."

Dixie laughed. "I'm quite parched. And I think it's almost time to hand out all the presents to the children. Shall we get some punch and a cookie?"

He leaned down and whispered conspiratorially, "Maybe even two cookies!"

Dixie mirrored his conspiration. "Or three!"

Flynn tapped her nose with a soft chuckle. "I like where your thoughts are taking you, Dix."

The words caused a hitch in her breath. It suddenly seemed like they were the only two for miles around. He stood frozen before her, and she couldn't seem to pull her gaze from his. The late afternoon light touched a bluish halo around his dark curls, and the sounds of chatter and music all around them faded away.

"Flynn, I've been wanting to talk with you all day."

His lips quirked. "We *have* been talking all day."

"No. I mean—"

He gave her a nod. "I know. And I've been *wanting* you to talk to me all day." He winked.

Dixie glanced around, suddenly wishing for nothing more than to just be alone with him for a few minutes. "Can we..." She gestured to the street. They would still be in sight of many people so it wouldn't be against propriety, but they would also have a bit more privacy. "Maybe—"

"Can I have everyone's attention please?" Charlotte clapped her hands from the center of the field.

Dixie's shoulder's sagged.

Flynn snickered and leaned close to Dixie's ear. "Everyone is against us."

She smirked at him. "Later?"

He nodded. "Of a certainty. I'm going to hold you to it."

Feeling both relieved and anticipatory, Dixie returned her attention to Charlotte.

"There will be more dancing, and visiting and eating in a moment, but before the day grows too late, I wanted to just say a few words. We'll then have our students do a presentation of the nativity. And then we have *presents*!" She flung her arms in a grand gesture toward the mound of packages beneath the Christmas tree near her.

Children whooped and leapt and cheered.

Charlotte held up her hands. "All right, all right, all right. First a few words of thanks." She sought out Tom Harris, the foreman of Mr. Heath's logging operation. "Mr. Harris, thank you so much for agreeing to give the men this afternoon off. I know that providing for their families is important to them, but I hope we all can agree that times like these—times of joy and frivolity—are also important for families and for communities."

Reagan was the first to start the clapping, and Dixie hurried to join in as other's followed suit.

Charlotte once more held up her hands until the gathering quieted. "So many—so, so many—of you have helped to bring this day together. And I truly couldn't have done this without your help. So Ewan, thank you for building the fireboxes. And Parson Clay and Kin, thank you for putting the dance floor together. We've already made such good use of that today, haven't we folks?"

More cheering and clapping followed.

Charlotte continued her list of thanks, until Dixie was nearly certain there wasn't a soul left in town who hadn't been thanked.

"And lastly"—Charlotte seemed to be searching the crowd for a specific face—"I'd like to thank Mr. Heath for even making it possible for us to be here in the first place."

Everyone went wild. Whistles and whoops and warbles joined in with the calls of thanks and appreciation directed Mr. Heath's way.

Mr. Heath looked pleased as punch with the recognition. He tottered to his feet in a manner that made Dixie realize he'd aged quite a bit in the year and a half that she'd known him. He grinned so big that she could see he was missing two teeth in the back of his mouth. And when he waved one hand above his head in thanks for the recognition, he almost lost his balance—likely *would have* were it not for Ben King's quick grab of his arm. Mr. Heath didn't even pause in his waving.

The children performed a beautiful rendition of the Christmas story, complete with a goat who kept nibbling on Joseph's— Grant Nolan's—tunic, much to the amusement of the town. When the Christ-child was born and the angel-choir had sung their last song, everyone broke into more loud applause.

Charlotte let the applause go on until it died down of its own accord, and then she motioned to Kin Davis, and Washington and Jackson Nolan. "Could I have you young men help me hand out these gifts? There's one with every child's name on it."

The boys each stepped forward and gathered several presents.

Dixie released a sigh of pleasure at the squeals of delight that came from several of the girls and the whoops of excitement that emanated from the little boys.

Liora, Kin, and Joe Rodante had sawn, carved and sanded little forest animals for all the boys. Dixie had looked them over before they'd been wrapped, and she'd seen a porcupine, several deer, elk, frogs, bears, and wolves. And Mrs. Callahan and Belle Kastain had sewn brand new aprons and pot-holders for every girl in matching sets.

"Look, Mama!" one little girl called, holding up her set. "Now I can help you in the kitchen!"

"Isn't that lovely," her mother replied.

Aidan Kastain and David Hines were already playing with their animals together in a pile of snow by the road.

"And then my wolf eats your rabbit!" Aidan proclaimed, pouncing his wolf on top of David's toy.

Dixie smiled. She must have missed seeing the rabbit.

"No, no," David chided. "This wolf and rabbit are friends. The wolf would never eat his friend!"

Beside her, Flynn leaned close enough to speak in her ear, though his attention remained fixed on the celebrations all around them. "This is one of the best things we could have done for the town. Miss Brindle is brilliant."

Dixie's attention had been drawn to Mr. Heath, tottering his way across the field in Charlotte's direction, with Sheriff Callahan in tow. She couldn't hear exactly what Mr. Heath said, but he gestured between the sheriff and Miss Brindle, and then motioned to the town and then to the dance floor. Charlotte's face bloomed into a smile so large it threatened to split her face, and Reagan scooped her up into his arms with a whoop that drew most everyone's attention as he spun her in a circle. Charlotte banged on Reagan's shoulders, insisting that he put her down. Her cheeks were as rosy as the wildflowers that bloomed just outside of town each summer.

Dixie smiled. "Yes. I believe she is."

Flynn leaned close and took her hand. "How about we take that walk now?"

Dixie's heart lurched as his fingers slipped between hers. "Yes. I would like that very much."

As they walked past the dancefloor, Marshal Holloway was bowing before Mrs. Callahan, and by the smile on his face, it appeared the woman had just agreed to a dance with him.

Dixie and Flynn strolled down the street quite a ways without saying a word. Finally, when the racket from the gathering had died down to a dull roar in the distance, Flynn tugged her to a stop and turned to face her.

His gaze swept the length of her. "You look absolutely

beautiful today." He adjusted her shawl at her shoulders. "Are you warm enough?"

Dixie's heart was hammering so fast that she didn't think she could cool down if a veritable blizzard blew in. "Yes. I'm fine. And thank you."

Flynn lifted one of her hands and toyed with her fingers. "Yesterday after our talk, you came outside. Were you looking for me?" He lifted his golden and blue gaze to hers.

Moistening her mouth, Dixie nodded, but she couldn't seem to find any words to speak.

He stroked his thumb along her first finger. "And is that what you wanted to talk to me about today?" There was a light of hope in his eyes.

"Yes," she managed to whisper.

"Well then. I would very much like to hear what you wanted to say." He tilted his head, his attention fixed steadily on her face.

There was nothing for it but to just plunge ahead. She wanted this. Wanted it with every fiber of her being. So why was it so hard to find the words?

Because it was *risk,* she suddenly realized. What if he rejected her?

And yet didn't the lessons she'd been learning recently far surpass that concern? Yes, this was taking a chance that she might be rejected, but she gained her peace from so much more than the acceptance of one person. She could step out in faith with the belief that God really did want good things for her, even if this one thing didn't turn out to be it. She could let go of self and apply herself instead to *hoping in the Lord.* Like an eagle soaring on stretched wings trusted in the currents of air that held him aloft.

She took in a steadying breath. She could do this. "Flynn, if you'll still have me, I'd—I'd like to give us a chance."

"If I'll still have you?" He threw back his head on a laugh, and then his hands settled around her waist and he swung her high and in a complete circle right there in the middle of the street. Not once. Not twice. But three times, until Dixie really did feel rather like an eagle soaring—if a very dizzy one.

When he settled her onto her feet, she clutched his shoulders for balance. "Well..." she chuckled. "I can truly say I wasn't expecting that response."

He bent forward until his forehead nestled flush against hers. "You make my heart sing in ways I never knew it could, Dixie Pottinger."

Dixie rubbed one finger over the middle button of his shirt. "And I never knew you to be such a poet, Dr. Griffin."

He grinned. "You've never given me a chance to show you."

She laughed. "True enough. I've been busy trying to keep you at arm's length ever since we arrived in town."

Flynn's face turned serious, and he lifted both hands to cup either side of her face. "I know you've been through so much, Dix. And the last thing I ever want to do is hurt you. Is it okay with you if I pray for us a moment?"

The man couldn't have said anything that would have made her love him more. "I would like that very much."

And standing there in the middle of Wyldhaven's only street with their foreheads still pressed together, pray he did. He asked the Lord to help them build their relationship on the foundation of His Truths. The prayer was short, but Dixie knew it had been heartfelt, and he'd affected her in a way no other man ever had.

She remained where she was, eyes closed, and just breathed him in for a moment. And when she opened her eyes a little later, he was watching her with contentment in his expression.

Dixie sighed out her own contentment and stepped closer to him. "Flynn?"

"Hmmm?" He wound his fingers into the curls of hair by her ears.

"Kiss me?"

His lips parted into a satisfied smile. "That is a request I think I can consent to. But I beg of you to be kind in your future requests, for I fear that my weakness for you will have me giving in to your every whim."

She smiled and lifted up on her toes, tilting her mouth toward his in anticipation. She whispered, "I will take it as a personal affront if you don't, dear doctor."

A low rumble of humor escaped his throat. "Then by all means I shall do my best not to let you down."

His mouth captured hers then, and Dixie forgot all about the cold, and about the crowd of people gathered just down the street. She lifted her arms around his neck, and barely even noticed when her shawl fell to the ground at their feet. Flynn's hair-that-was-still-in-need-of-a-trim slipped through her fingers like silken strands.

With one of his hands at the small of her back, he drew her closer. The other hand he settled against her chignon.

And as Dixie relished the softness of his hair, the hard planes of his chest, the smell of his cologne, and the taste of his kiss, she couldn't help but feel like God had fulfilled his promise to renew her strength. She'd been through years of battle, and yet she'd come out the other side to this wonderful man waiting for her.

She might *just be* soaring on eagles' wings.

Dear Reader,

I hope you enjoyed this second foray into the town of Wyldhaven.

When I was writing book one, *Not a Sparrow Falls*, and bumped into Dixie, I knew that I wanted to explore her story more. Forgiveness is one of those tough concepts that I seem to keep exploring in my books, perhaps because it is a concept that I have struggled to understand over the years. I hope the message in these pages will help others who have pondered this Biblical command, like Dixie did.

As for Flynn, Doctors of the late nineteenth century frontier towns were a singularly devoted class of people. They often didn't have offices. Instead they visited patients in their homes, which many times were long distances from town, sometimes in areas so uninhabited that there were no roads. They crossed raging rivers, climbed mountains, and traversed miles of barren wilderness, not only in good weather, but also in raging rainstorms and winter freezes, putting their own lives in danger to reach their patients. They answered the call day and night, and often went for days on little sleep because they were often the only medical help available.

Because of these conditions, they could only take with them a limited number of supplies. The quintessential doctor's bag had to be well stocked, but obviously couldn't hold every medicine they might need, so they often were restricted in the way they could help their patients.

Despite all these hardships there are many stories of doctors giving their all to help their communities to the very end. They birthed people into this world, and sat by the bedsides of those leaving it for the next. And in between they did their best to keep the ones in their charge, healthy and happy. It was this spirit of self-sacrifice that I wanted to capture in Dr. Flynn Griffin from Wyldhaven. Did he touch your heart like he did mine?

Keep reading to find some discussion questions for book clubs. There's also an opportunity to get one of my stories for free if you'd like to join my newsletter.

Until we meet again in the pages of another story, may the God of all ages protect and keep you as you walk along your way.

Wishing you God's greatest blessings,

Lynnette Bonner

Please Review!

If you enjoyed this story, would you take a few minutes to leave your thoughts in a review on your favorite retailer's website? It would mean so much to me, and helps spread the word about the series.

You can quickly link through from my website here: http://www.lynnettebonner.com/books/historical-fiction/the-wyldhaven-series/

Want a FREE Story?

If you enjoyed this book...

...You might also like *My Blue Havyn*, a story set in the country where I was born and raised, Malawi, Africa. To start reading in just a few minutes, sign up for my newsletter on my website and the free book will be sent to you!

(My newsletter is only sent out when I have a new release to announce, so you won't be getting a lot of spam messages, and I never share your email with anyone else.)

Here's a little about *My Blue Havyn*...

 When Havyn Jessup agreed to join her church's building trip, she had no idea the man who broke her heart was coming as well. The last thing she wants is to spend time with the now internationally famous actor, Levi Carter. Even if it is in Africa, where he might, if God had any sense of justice, be eaten, one tiny bite at a time, by a pride of hungry lions. Two whole weeks. She'd never survive that long.

Levi is elated to learn that Havyn will be joining the building team. He had planned to look her up just as soon as he got home to tell her what a fool he'd been. But there is no time like the present. And what better place to ensure she would hear him than when she was strapped in at thirty thousand feet above sea level? Two short weeks. Could he convince her he was a changed man in that amount of time?

Once you sign up, you will receive an automated reply with a link where you can download your free story. Enjoy!

Book Club Questions

1. At the beginning of the book we learn that Rose isn't really Dixie's mother. These two women in a sense "stuck closer than a brother." Have you ever had a friend you felt that way about? What do you think forged that tight bond of friendship?

2. Rose saw the truth of who her son was and defended her daughter-in-law, yet continued to love her son. Can a mother's love ever be severed?

3. Do you think Rose did the right thing by shooting her son?

4. At the beginning of the book we discover that Reagan and Charlotte are struggling with their feelings for one another because of a new rule that's come to light that prohibits the teacher from courting. This rule was quite common back in the 1800s and early 1900s. Do you think this rule was fair? Why or why not?

5. Jacinda Callahan is a woman of great compassion who wears her emotions on her sleeve. She's worried about her son getting into a relationship because she fears he could be hurt or killed on the job and she doesn't want another woman to go through what she's been through. Do you think her worry is justified?

6. Marshal Holloway makes a statement about the fact that if there is a concern about death then women shouldn't marry a man of most any profession. Death comes for us all, and generally in an unexpected manner. Do you think he's correct in his assessment?

7. Kin Davis is a boy trying to break through to a stubborn and ensnared father. He obviously didn't go about it the

right way. Do you think he is responsible for his father's death? Why or why not?

8. Do you think Kin was responsible for Steven Pottinger's death? Why or why not?

9. Guns and the use of them, especially in the wild west, were an undeniable part of American history and our freedom as a people. But with freedom comes risk. When a government steps in and tries to remove all risk, they invariable have to remove some freedom. Do you agree with that statement?

10. Do you think Mr. Heath is responsible for Steven's death? Explain.

11. Dixie almost made a tragic mistake in the name of self-defense that might well have cost her freedom or even her life. Given that an individual's perception of danger can be subjective and therefore faulty, discuss the pros and cons of relying on such a motivation to take a life.

12. What part did factors like isolation, past betrayal by law enforcement, and feelings of helplessness play in her decision making? Make comparisons to some of today's domestic violence headlines. How much has changed or not changed over the centuries. Why and why not?

13. How might Dixie's level of spiritual maturity and understanding of God's character have impacted her thinking and the outcome— for better or for worse?

14. What is forgiveness? What isn't forgiveness? Do our feelings determine whether we've actually forgiven or not?

15. At the end of the book, Dixie came to the realization that sometimes a fear of moving ahead or taking a risk is actually a lack of trust or hope in God. Do you agree with this conclusion? Why or why not?

ABOUT THE AUTHOR

Born and raised in Malawi, Africa. Lynnette Bonner spent the first years of her life reveling in warm equatorial sunshine and the late evening duets of cicadas and hyenas. The year she turned eight she was off to Rift Valley Academy, a boarding school in Kenya where she spent many joy-filled years, and graduated in 1990.

That fall, she traded to a new duet—one of traffic and rain—when she moved to Kirkland, Washington to attend Northwest University. It was there that she met her husband and a few years later they moved to the small town of Pierce, Idaho.

During the time they lived in Idaho, while studying the history of their little town, Lynnette was inspired to begin the Shepherd's Heart Series with Rocky Mountain Oasis.

Marty and Lynnette have four children, and currently live in Washington where Marty pastors a church.

CPSIA information can be obtained
at www.ICGtesting.com
Printed in the USA
LVHW091604061120
670968LV00002B/166